A NOBLE
DESTINY

BOOK ONE

The Quest to Preserve Austria

Elizabeth Sunflower

A Noble Destiny : The Quest to Preserve Austria
Copyright © 2023 by Elizabeth Sunflower.

This book is a work of fiction. Names, characters, businesses, organiza- tions, places, events and incidents either are the product of the author's imagination or are used fictitiously. Any resemblance to actual persons, living or dead, events, or locales is entirely coincidental.

For information contact :
www.elizabeth-sunflower.com
Book and Cover design by: Miblart
Editor: Paul Blane

Ebook ISBN : 979-8-9886053-0-0
Paperback ISBN : 979-8-9886053-1-7
Hardback ISBN : 979-8-9886053-2-4

Revised November 2023

First Edition: July 2023
10 9 8 7 6 5 4 3 2 1

ELIZABETH SUNFLOWER

CHAPTER 1

Pitch black; why was it so dark? The left side of my head was killing me. My hand instinctively reached for the left side of my face, but everything seemed fine. Had I done something to myself? My hand was holding something. I think it was a handle.

There was a little light coming through. Maybe I had been knocked out?

No, no, I was standing. More light seeped in, but hardly enough to break through the gloom. Things began to come into focus. A shovel, I was holding the handle of a shovel in my hand. Beyond the shovel was quite a deep hole in the ground, and a body. The vision strikes me like a bolt of lightning. Pictorial fragments crash together in my mind. Abruptly, the movie of memory plays out before me, and I understand. I was in a cemetery, and the body below me in a hastily dug hole was an enemy. An enemy who had discovered our purpose and forfeited his life thereof. Compassion, remorse, and regret flooded over me, but I pushed them back. I will deal with that later. The body had to be buried quickly, and I needed to return to the Chancellory without further delays.

Other than a small lantern beside the grave, the night was moonless, which explained the near impenetrable darkness. As I shoveled the dirt over my victim, my mind played through the latest moon cycles. If my calculations were correct, we had just entered the new moon. How fortuitous for me, if not for my friend in the tan shirt. My psyche grappled with the daze I had just been in; was it tied to that horrible pain in the left side of my head? No pain now. Physically, I felt great, and mentally, everything seemed fine.

What was that paper out of Harvard? Cannon & Bayliss, I believe, yes, that seems accurate. They had put forth that trauma would cause an increase in the permeability of capillaries, causing what was referred to as shock. Perhaps that was what had struck me, shock. Yes, that seems reasonable. Stamping down dirt before the last round of shoveling, I realized how much of it I was covered in. Questions would undoubtedly arise if I appeared in public. Perhaps a trip to the apartments was in order before returning to the Chancellory.

I scattered detritus over the makeshift resting place. There was a prayer for the occupant and a prayer for forgiveness. The latter I had not expected, but my soul needed some penance. Prayer would suffice to discharge the debt for the moment.

Now, where did the lantern and shovel come from? Oh yes, the caretaker's shed behind the chapel. For all my lack of clarity now, clear thinking had prevailed earlier. There were some rags in the workshop. These were hastily used to wipe off as much dirt as possible. Brushes sufficiently cleaned the shoes that had been carefully beaten outside to leave little trace of my passing. The rags were stuffed in my coat pocket. Everything was placed back as closely as possible to the position I remembered finding them in. With the lantern out, the blackness permeated everything, and the disconnected feeling from earlier crept in. Pushing it back, I closed my eyes and let my senses take complete control. Slowly, with small, deliberate steps, I returned to the yard.

Once out on the street, there was more than sufficient light, too much. I stepped back through the gate to the cemetery, leaning into the shadows. The walk back to the apartment would take at least an hour. I had not brought my now lifeless companion along on an hour's walk through the streets of Vienna. So how? I leaned back against the cool wall and closed my eyes momentarily.

If only the automobile were here. Alas, the memory was clear. My brand new Gräf & Stift C12 was at the apartments. There was no help for it. I would have to make my way back through the alleys. I hoped to pass unnoticed. Quickly, I walked back out and took the path around to Seippgasse. Seippgasse is a short residential street with minimal light that ended at the wall of the cemetery. I stepped around the corner, and recognition struck.

There, just a little further down Seippgasse, was a linen truck, parked discreetly on the street. Behind the wheel was one of my oldest friends and co-conspirator, Karl Stecher. An audible sigh of relief escaped my lips as I opened the door and climbed in.

He said nothing but shot me a questioning glance as he started the engine. I motioned to my watch, and he pulled onto the street with a knowing look. It could and would wait until we were somewhere safe. There was no need to risk another overheard conversation resulting in another unnecessary death.

As Karl drove through the quiet city streets, my mind wandered. Like rats, I thought. You see one, but there are a hundred just behind the woodwork, silent, listening, waiting for you to turn out the light when you exit the room. Then they scurry out to do their busy work. Indeed, Nazis were exactly like vermin. This train of thought continued for the duration of the drive. The buildings passed by in a haze. Arriving at the apartments, I was startled, having been lost in my spiraling thoughts. We had pulled in beside the building; Karl cleared his throat as the truck idled. It was just enough to rouse me from my contemplation. Nodding my head in understanding, I opened the door and stepped out. The truck dropped quietly into gear and slid away. No one was around, all was quiet, and most of the lights were out in the windows above.

Opening the rear entrance door, I surveyed the hallway. Lights dim, no movement. I stepped in, focusing on keeping my average, leisurely pace. At the lift, there was no one, but I chose the stairs. The stairs were routine, and routines were effective for blending in.

We had procured our apartment in the saddle of two buildings. Carriages and autos arrived through the passage below us into the central courtyard of the conjoined buildings. The top floor allowed access to the roof. Elevated above the surrounding buildings. The roof provided a small private courtyard with a container garden surrounding the outer perimeter. The foliage was already strategically placed, allowing unfettered observation from within, but making it difficult to see anyone from the exterior.

The interior of the apartment was similarly beneficial; the rear rooms offered a sufficient view of the courtyard for both buildings. The front view allowed for surveillance of the front of the Chancellory facing the street. With the fascia recessed, it naturally obscured detection while we peered from behind sheer curtains. The roof courtyard allowed nearly a 360° overlook. We had spent months locating a property that fit our purpose; it was time well spent and would save at least one life.

Franz was lingering close to the door as I padded out of the hallway into the foyer of our rooms.

"I'll grab your robe; stay put." Just like that, he was gone.

Opening the pocket wardrobe, I removed the soiled rags from my coat, gave it a quick brush, and placed it on a hanger. Grabbing a laundering sack from a drawer, I quickly undressed, dropping all the items in. Franz handed the robe over, grabbed the sack from the floor, and disappeared. I swept the small pile of debris from the polished floor onto a newspaper. Folding it carefully, I went through the sitting room into the study and deposited the newspaper in the cozy fire.

Hard to say how much time had passed before I noticed the change in the room when someone else enters, creating a subtle nudge of energy that bumped up against mine. The faint hint of another's breath mingling in the air. There was no need to look; it seemed we had been friends since birth. Franz was staring at the back of my head; he strode over, poured a cognac, and made his way to one of the wing chairs beside the fireplace. I turned and took the chair behind me.

Glancing at Franz, I said, in a low voice, "Remind me why a group of aspiring scholars is engaging in clandestine operations for the Fatherland?" I sighed a long heavy sigh, "No, disregard the blathering of a guilty conscience."

"Let me answer you anyway," Franz encouraged, "A group of drunk brothers lost in Munich were on holiday; they stumbled into a beer hall full of desperate people and heard a ridiculous little man spouting inhumane speech. Then ten years later, that ridiculous little man took control of Germany." Franz spoke the words slowly and quietly, while he looked at me with fire in his eyes. He swirled the cognac slowly, shifting his gaze to the liquid in the glass.

The fire pulled me into it again. My thoughts were adrift, just as the embers crackling up the flue. We were wary of speaking anywhere, but now it was at the forefront of everyone's thoughts. My mind turned again to my dirt-covered friend who had been discovered on the other side of the door in the Chancellory. A place we thought secure, yet there he was, eavesdropping on the other side of the door, Nazi armband plainly in sight, even though they were forbidden to be worn. Thankfully, his boot had scuffed the door, or none of us would have known. The poor fellow pleaded innocence. He had become lost in the maze of the Chancellory, heard voices, and was about to seek help to find his way. I let him in without a single thought and broke his neck. Instinctually, every fiber of my being knew his real purpose and what had to be done. No one would claim or look for him. He was supposed to be a ghost, his clandestine activities kept covert, unseen.

A glance up at the clock on the mantle brought slight concern. Karl should have deposited the truck back where it had been borrowed from by now. Leaving the comfort of my chair, I turned to leave the room and, nodding at Franz, said, "I'll go get cleaned up. Karl should be back anytime." Making my way up to the second floor, I stepped into the lavatory. The slight shadow on my chin would wait for morning. Just this moment, I wanted to get the dirt off. 10 minutes later, I was in my room dressing when I heard a tap on the ceiling below me. Karl had returned.

Downstairs, our little group was together again. Arrangements were already agreed upon. I would slip over to the Chancellory to confirm clean up. Franz would contact all parties making new arrangements in a secure location. Karl would pack and then get some rest before boarding the train. Circumstances here needed to be relayed back to what we regarded as our headquarters. Communication channels would need to be reassessed, monitored, and adjusted. We would follow once we completed our original mission. We wished Karl well and departed for our tasks.

The Chancellory itself had not been safe since the assassination of then Chancellor Engelbert Dollfuss on July 25, 1934. Truthfully, though, it was doubtful it had been secure since the Nazi fascists started gaining steam in 1929. Prince Starhemberg was Vice-Chancellor at the time of Dollfuss's demise, making him next in line. Instead, Kurt Von Schuschnigg would be appointed Chancellor of Austria on July 29, 1934. The bullseye placed on Schuschnigg at that moment was enormous. The fascists needed Austria under German control. They would use any means necessary, and they drove that message home with the Dollfuss assassination.

The Chancellor and I were both from Innsbruck, cousins, in fact, although we had had little contact with each other until these last seven years or so.

I found the Chancellor sitting at his desk, head down, focused on the document before him, lines of worry etched across his forehead. Finding a Nazi listening at your door mere hours ago will do that. Indeed, watching your cousin dispatch him, then scrambling to get rid of the body is sure to induce worry in even the most Stoic character. When he looked up at me entering the office, his entire body seemed to relax, and I swear I heard a small sigh. "Were you able to find the restaurant I recommended?" he tried to say casually, but there was a definite edge. How nice it would be to speak plainly. Yes, I did find the cemetery. Burying our Nazi friend went well. Alas, innuendo, and code would be the language now.

"Yes, indeed, it exceeded expectations," I replied, sitting in an overstuffed chair facing the desk.

"May I offer you some refreshment?" he countered.

"You are too kind, Chancellor. Perhaps a small nightcap," I replied.

He rose from his desk, stretching a little, and crossed to a masterfully crafted credenza I admired. He poured some of what looked to be schnapps into two glasses and replaced the top. Handing me my drink, he motioned at the chair opposite, and I nodded. He seemed to drop into his chair heavily. We were all tired. It had been an exceedingly long night.

Reaching over, he gently tapped his glass to mine and said, "zum wohl!"

I replied in kind, "zum wohl," and we both swallowed the burning liquid in one gulp. I placed the glass on the table between us and initiated our next coded message. "Mayrhofen is celebrating Maria Hilf next week; the trip may be worth it. Perhaps you could send a representative to the celebration?"

"Yes, my assistant scheduled something if I'm not mistaken. I will make a point of checking the calendar and have a confirmation sent," the Chancellor replied.

We sat in silence, listening, but all was still and quiet. The Chancellor's exhausted assistant awaited his patron's retirement for the night in the antechamber. We smiled at each other, one with gratitude, one with sympathy, and reached over to grasp each other's hands in an odd but reassuring handshake. Like two champions on an Olympic platform honoring the other's achievements in front of a roaring crowd. Victorious for one more day!

The anxiety of the last few hours began to melt away. Sitting in the comfortable stillness. Finally, we rose from the dangerously comfortable chairs, patted each other on the back, and stared at each other momentarily. Everyone in our little conspiracy understood too well the cost of failure. Keeping our beloved Austria free and independent meant everything. She had been suffering brutally under the Treaty of Saint-Germain and was finally coming to terms with losing her people, lands, finances, and strength. The foolish pride of the monarchy had killed millions and decimated Austria. Exchanging parting pleasantries, I made my way back toward the apartments. The Chancellor was a lone man standing against an all-consuming tempest, and I prayed that God would grant him strength.

A few minutes later, I entered our building. The deep allure of sleep drove me up the stairs to the apartment. After a hasty toilette, I settled into my room, stoked the fire, and undressed for bed. Sleeping nude was a habit everyone in my life had tried to break me of. The war should have done it, but it may have made it worse. Being in the same clothes for days without the luxuries of bathing or changing regularly is abhorrent. Climbing between the chilly sheets, I laid the robe across the middle of the bed in preparation for Frieda's inevitable morning arrival with coffee. My eyes closed. It felt so good to relax.

Only seconds after closing my eyes, I felt a dull pain in the left side of my head. My eyes opened to light streaming between tiny gaps in the curtains. It could not be morning! But Frieda's footsteps confirmed it. It felt as though my eyes had just shut. Three taps on the door, and she burst into the room without waiting for permission.

"Guten morgan, Mein Herr, up up up, you must not sleep the entire day away! It is nine, and Herr Karl has already left for the train station. He asked me to tell you auf wiedersehen and not to forget his appointment."

Frieda continued chattering while she opened curtains, masterfully pulled me from my bed with my robe thrown over my front, fluffed pillows, replaced me in bed, set the breakfast tray on my lap, poured coffee, unfolded the newspaper, buttered my toast, and laid the napkin on my chest. Then she patted my head, as was her morning custom, picked up the clothes that were draped over the chair, and breezed out of the room in the same fashion as she had entered, her voice trailing behind her.

In a way, Frieda was born into my family. Her mother was my mother's lady's maid. Her father was my father's valet. Although it was highly unusual for her to choose to be in my service, she had. Everyone tried to explain to her that she needed to seek service with a mistress, and she had received many offers of employment with prominent families. But Frieda refused! She insisted it was neither my fault nor hers I had been born a male and refused to hear of service to anyone else. Lines were drawn, which Frieda crossed like a general in the heat of battle. Over the years, we had come to a few agreements, but overall, she ran the household, and we were the better at it. "We" means our motley crew of brothers in the war, academia, conspiracy, and life. We were unsure how long we could keep her safe, though. Her parents were both of Jewish descent, and although she did not bear the strong characteristics of her father, she did bear a few traits we worried about.

When our group formed our association, we took up residence at the family's small estate in Munich. Frieda moved in before we did, not, I might add, at anyone's request. At length, we convinced her to dress as a widow in all black, complete with a hat and veil. Vehemently, we insisted she speak with no one that did not require the interaction. Putting her to the test, we all took turns following her. True to her word, she did her errands, kept her veil down, eyes averted, voice demure, and played the role of a melancholy widow with grace and ease. As soon as she entered the house, though, the captain was back at the helm. Any property hummed with order and efficiency when she was present. In Munich, she carried the burden of the whole property on her own. With five in residence, including her, I put my foot down and insisted on a laundry service and chef. Holy Mary, Mother of God. A mutiny was narrowly avoided. We spent an entire week in covert psychiatric influence to maneuver her into acquiescence. Ultimately, it was much like the widow ruse we had insisted on. Compliance came out of necessity, not willingness.

Vienna posed a significant danger for her too. After the previous night's impromptu discovery of the Nazi spy, leaving Frieda without anyone to protect her was out of the question.

Throwing on a pair of trousers under my robe, I grabbed a quick cup of coffee and stepped across the hall. I had just lifted my fist to rap on the door when I heard, "Came for coffee, did you?" from Franz through the door. Pushing in, I took a chair by the window. There was a marvelous view of the Chancellory. Field glasses were sitting on the little table adjacent to the chair. Franz sat propped up in bed, polishing off the better part of a pig and what looked to be a half dozen eggs.

"Planning on a marathon later?" I teased.

"The way things are going, you never know; good to be prepared,"

Franz replied.

Picking up the field glasses, I watched the coming and going of those with business at the Chancellory. The usual types you would expect on any weekday morning. Hopefully, Schuschnigg had managed to get a few hours of sleep.

In our typical ability to read each other's minds, Franz said, "I'm genuinely concerned about Frieda's presence in Vienna. I was planning to discuss it with you once we laid things out today."

"I anticipate it taking us both, but let's put her on the train for home. What do you think?" I asked. Franz pushed the tray away, leaned back with a contented sigh, and sipped his coffee. Stepping back to the window, I allowed time for consideration. After a few minutes, he climbed out of bed, coffee in hand, and stood looking out the window next to me. He had that conspirator's look.

"We'll lie," Franz offered, "Her mother has taken ill. She is needed both to tend to her mother and replace her duties with the Mistress. Of course, we will need the whole court to participate in the feint. Otherwise, this will play out very badly."

"The plan is better than kidnapping her; she'll be livid but safe. I will phone Father when she goes to the market," I said.

In unison, we both started the following sentence, "Papers will need to be..." and laughed. We would indeed need papers showing her. To prevent questions, one of us would typically travel with her as our wife. But on the trip to Innsbruck, she would be alone. We agreed that it would be better to be cautious now than suffer the hindsight of regret.

CHAPTER 2

Without involving my cousin, obtaining official documents could be tricky. The covert process meant using disreputable sources who would be happy to collect added fees for reporting to those who paid well for information. I would procure my identification documents legitimately. Claiming the loss of my current one would do the trick. Officials also played the information game, dealing in documents for money. They rarely wanted to risk their position within the government though. My father took more convincing. He was every bit as concerned for Frieda as we were. However, lying meant asking him to violate his honor. The call ended with a promise to get back to me later that night.

Set up in the study, we spent the day planning, fine-tuning, and reciting plans. The day sped by, and in the late afternoon, a telegram arrived. Wilhelm Dorn, the senior member of our group, if you could call thirty-eight senior, wired with information from Munich. Wilhelm's message used an old code, one we had invented in school. Karl would not arrive in Munich until later that night, though, so we were confident the change was not due to the current situation at our end. It took Franz and me both working on it to decipher the message. We were more than rusty. Even more disturbing was that he needed to change codes with no warning. A reason which was hinted at in the message.

CONFIRMED GERMAN DINNER IN AUSTRIA STOP ANTICIPATE MANDATORY ATTENDANCE STOP HOST PLANS LATE WINTER OR EARLY SPRING STOP MAY NEED EXTERMINATOR HERE WILL CONFIRM STOP

Was our translation correct? Did we have the dreaded date, confirmation of a late winter or early spring putsch? They had been able to spend the last four years planning and learning from their previous failed attempt, and failure was not an option this time. I sat staring at Franz, thinking about the "may need exterminator" in the telegram. A source or someone similarly resolved to stop the Nazi party is compromised. Franz volunteered, "I'll be packed and on the evening train."

"No, if Wilhelm needed us, the message would have at least implied it. Stay the course, we will get word to the Chancellor," I said.

Franz was already up and headed for the door, saying, "Allow me, please extend my regards to your father," and exited towards the Chancellory.

Father, yes, he should be ringing any time. What time was it? 7:00 pm. Already? So much had to be taken care of. I finished the last items and began to gather everything up. I thought I may as well get everything packed while I had time. Experience dictated that once the plan was implemented, it would gain momentum quickly.

As if on cue, the phone rang. Gräf Von Rieser, aka Father, inquired about Frieda leaving at once for Innsbruck. He also asked if I might come when convenient. I assured him I would prioritize the trip. As soon as my new identification documents were in order. I went over to the cupboard, brought out the Marillenschnaps, poured a heavy splash into a glass, and swallowed it. Taking an aperitif glass from the cupboard, I filled it halfway and set it on the drum table between the two wing chairs in front of the fireplace. Strategically, I placed the bottle beside it, rang the bell for Frieda, stoked the fire, and sat down.

Minutes later, Frieda swept into the room, prepared to cater to whatever need prompted the bell and presenting options. "Mein Herr, do you wish supper? There is a lovely roast just moments away from finishing. Something a bit lighter?"

I gathered myself, Thespian trained concern flushing my face and began my rehearsed drama.

"Please, Frieda, come sit with me." She looked at me with dismay. Before she could launch into an extensive list of questions, I continued, "Frieda, take a sip of the marillenschnaps, yes, just a bit, there we go. Frieda, Gräf Von Rieser has rung from Innsbruck. It seems your dear mother has taken ill." Instantly, her eyes began to water, her free hand clutching her throat. "There, there, Frieda, we must be strong. I believe she will recover, but you are requested to care for her and take on her duties until she can resume them."

Frieda gulped the schnapps and covered her mouth momentarily. The bottle was already in my hand, pouring a more generous portion. While she was still speechless, I added the rest of the details.

"Of course, we will have you on the first train home in the morning. It still runs at half of 8. You'll need to pack for an indefinite trip, so gather all your belongings now." She shook her head in agreement, cataloging what she needed to pack. Sipping from the glass at every finished thought.

Suddenly she set the glass down, stood up, and headed for the door. Turning as an afterthought, she came across the room and grasped my hands.

"Thank you, Mein Herr, you are so kind and generous to release me from my obligations; thank you. I will need to go and pack now." She released my hands, with moist eyes, turned, and left, saying, "I will bring your coffee in the morning before leaving."

I am a complete villain. If it saves her life, though, am I truly?

Franz arrived around nine o'clock, and I had just set out a plate of crackers, cheese, and canned oysters. A treat I had developed a taste for only the previous year. He gratefully devoured my supper and left me wondering what else I could scrape up. Of course, there was the roast. I chuckled to myself. Frieda had forgotten it in her grief. While packing up the study, I caught the whiff of overdone something; going to check, I remembered at once. Too late for the poor chunk of what used to be meat. Well, honestly, I do not know what it was. It was too far gone to tell at this point. I set the pan out back for the strays to pick through.

Although shrouded in code and innuendo, his meeting with the Chancellor had seemed to go about as well as it could. Indeed, the news held no surprise, only a timeline. As winter was almost upon us, decisions would need to be made. We were only acting as support staff in that arena, though. The choices rested on his shoulders. However, other areas required execution, and there was where our focus fell. I relayed the story of how our deception with Frieda had gone and the plans for early in the morning. I had a departure date for the day after tomorrow for our trip, pending my credentials. The temptation to leave on the train tomorrow crept in, but Franz, being the voice of reason, assured me Frieda would be fine, and we were better for having our means of transportation. Part of me thought he just wanted his chance behind the wheel again. He was correct, though. We were at a disadvantage relying on the train.

Sleep found me early, and I awoke long before anyone else. Time for a bath; it was heaven laying in hot water. The tub on the second floor was nearly 6' long, allowing you to stretch out and relax. A meditative state slowly began to creep in. Sliding down in the tub, I let my mind drift. Slipping away, floating, I saw a face in my mind's eye before me, blond hair, blue eyes, laughing, menacing. Startled, I sat up; my head must have slid under the water. The vision went faster than it had come. I shook it off, washed my hair, and reluctantly got out.

I wiped the mirror with my towel looking at my reflection. Overall, I seemed a handsome fellow, I thought. The thick black hair was my father's, but the ice-blue eyes were my mother's. I was tall, 6'2" last time I was measured, with a strong jawline, which I was in the middle of scraping a razor across as I heard Frieda stirring upstairs. My skin was dark, but not Mediterranean dark, just dark enough. Black Dutch, my mother had told me, true Germanic tribesman. Mother had pale blond hair and skin like fine porcelain. She was not petite; her height must be close to 5'8", but she was lithe. No, my skin was my father's, like my head full of hair.

Frieda was moving things around. I dressed and made my way upstairs. We had everything down to the auto in 10 minutes. Frieda was pouring coffee as Franz made his way into the kitchen.

"Thanks for leaving me a bit of hot water," Franz joked. He approached Frieda, took her hand, and bowed, "At your service, my dear

Frieda." She burst into tears and ran to the lavatory. Franz looked at me in horror and said, "Exactly what did you say again?" I waved him off, got up, and went to speak to the lavatory door.

"Frieda, I told you Father says she will be just fine, please wash your face, and we'll get you to the train station." Water turned on, a nose was blown, and a properly straightened Frieda appeared.

Franz went over everything again on the way to the station.

"You will have Gräf Alexanders credentials. Should anyone inquire, he is your husband, and you are headed home to see your mother." Frieda nodded acknowledgment while Franz continued, "Do not volunteer anything. You were married Yule 1934. I know we go over this every time, dear Frieda, but we want to be sure you are safe."

Frieda sat up straight and tall, saying, "Thank you both for your kindness. I will be careful and do everything you have said."

We bought her tickets, brought her luggage, and placed her on the train. I made a big show of her being my beloved wife. She could not help but giggle and blush. Once she was seated, I found the ticket inspector and tipped him generously to ensure my wife had everything she wished. With a flourish of adoration, I left her seated comfortably in her private compartment. On his word of honor, the ticket inspector said no one would be allowed to occupy it with her. Then we posted up with me waving from the platform until the train was out of sight.

When we returned to the automobile, the teasing began at once. Franz was on a roll.

"No, I think Frieda would make you a wonderful wife, Alexsander. On the return to the apartments, I propose we stop and choose a suitable engagement present. I will be your best man; it can be a whirlwind wedding. Of course, I will still expect breakfast and coffee after you are married. However, it will be fine if you need to serve it while she refreshes herself."

The teasing continued off and on most of the day, of course. My credentials arrived by messenger not long after we arrived at the apartments. With everything in order, we spent the afternoon loading up and then going through and checking for strange trivial things, like no notepads left around for someone to scribble the hidden messages out of.

We had been invited to dine at the prince's that evening. However, we declined the invitation. We needed to keep him in play, but neither of us had the energy for that cat-and-mouse game tonight. We sent our regrets, truthfully telling of our need to arrive at another engagement in Tyrol the following evening. If we were being watched, they would already know of the invitation to the Chancellor for the celebration in Mayrhofen. There was no need to be covert regarding the destination. Of course, I obliged Franz or myself to the prince, stating his person as our utmost priority upon return to Vienna. Frieda had left us a meal in the ice box with a note of thanks. A message we also burned in the fireplace before leaving. We retired early for a good night's sleep, arose early, broke our fast, and set off home to Tyrol.

"Would you just call me Jim?" I asked Franz, although it was more of a statement than a question.

He shot me a stabbing look, replying with the standard answer, "Yes, just as soon as you stop calling me Fritzy, Sandy." Parting shot received and logged.

It was hopeless, we were on our way to Mayrhofen in the automobile, and I had not drawn the straw to drive this half. Settling back in my seat, I let my mind wander where it wanted. The scenery zipped by while Fritzy hummed some unrecognizable tune.

Jim is much easier when your proper Austrian name is Gräf

Alexsander Jakob Wallner Von Rieser. Fritzy was less than a fan of the nickname, but it worked well, especially in our current game of intrigue. If strict formality is adhered to, the entire thing becomes unnecessary, as only titles and surnames would be significant.

The story of the nickname is a brilliant anecdote, boring dinner parties spring to mind. Our tale begins with a year abroad at Cambridge University. My initial entrance to the procured student accommodations brought me into a large hall. A group of fellow students seemed engaged in a somewhat lively debate. Upon seeing me in full formal dress, they turned like a wave in the ocean. The Earl, as I would come to call him, inquired, "Just who might you be, sir?"

"Gräf Alexsander Jakob Wallner Von Rieser of Tyrol, Austria, at your service," I stated formally with a click of the heels and a grand bow. I approached the situation as a gentleman would and a soldier should, with a full appreciation for the implications of being here with the war just over. I expected a certain amount of agitation, if not outright hostility.

However, all I heard was, "Jim," he said it with authority, and everyone laughed. It was certainly not the welcome I had expected. To this day, I feel the gratitude of those first moments when The Earl made a point of accepting me as one of their own by naming me in a very English way. Everyone came by to shake my hand, laughing and clapping me on the back, saying "Jim" with their greetings. From that day forward, it was "Jim." When I later inquired of The Earl why he had chosen "Jim," he explained that in English, the German name Jakob translated to James, hence Jim. It was also close to the total of German he had remembered. He also recalled a few colorful expressions, which he generously vocalized, along with some numbers. Sechs, if memory serves, was a particular favorite. The name grew on me throughout my time there but met neither my parents' nor Franz's approval. Adding to my parents' displeasure, my educational experience became less about academia and more about philosophy. Let us just say different countries' educational establishments focus on various aspects of learning. Each has merits and minuses. My knowledge broadened from the time spent there, end of subject.

I looked at Franz, perfectly at peace, zipping down the road toward home. We may as well have been twins. Our mothers are sisters and remarkably close in age, also best friends. It would be the same for us. Gräf Franz Joseph Stephen Von Grünne, or Fritzy, as I preferred to call him, called me Sandy. Alexander is a mouthful when you are learning to form words. Sander was the best he could do and slowly became Sandy. My elder brother Otto died of a fever a year before preparatory school. After we lost Otto, Fritzy and I made a pact that we would never leave each other. Although the reality of that statement changed, we strived to be there no matter the circumstances. War, school, love, and service interfered, but we always made it work.

Preparatory school[1] meant Stella Matutina in Feldkirch, Austria, for me. His father, a second cousin to both his mother and mine, enrolled him in Kalksburg College, Vienna. Gräf Von Grünne was the most recent to attend of an extensive line of Grünnes. Naturally, he expected his heir to follow their ancestors in the same glorious manner.

At the risk of both our fathers' wrath, we began planning a grand mutiny, complete with a voyage to the markets of Morocco. There we would buy camels, making our way to Aladdin's cave. Once we had acquired enough treasure, we would travel the world. We were coming back to our parents only after they displayed significant remorse and offered profuse apologies for trying to break our bond of brotherhood.

To my knowledge, our planned mutiny remains a secret to this day.

---

[1]. Gymnasium or preparatory school covers middle and high school levels in preparation for college. Often the schools are residence schools, where adolescents reside while attending.

Before we could act upon a single plan, it was announced we would be attending Stella Matutina together. We both suspected intervention from our mothers. However, there was no proof. Looking back from that passenger seat, I felt a longing for those glorious days. In Stella Matutina, we would establish a group of friends to carry us through things we could not have fathomed then.

"Hey, Fritzy, remember the winter Leopold talked you into borrowing all the robes from the laundry and hiding them in the hothouses? Brother Joseph was not feeling the compassion of Christ that week." Laughter filled the car.

"Poor Leo, we were certain he was going to break. No matter what Brother Joseph tried, he wouldn't give me up." Fritzy fell silent.

I added, "No, he never broke."

Our thoughts fell to the war. Leopold was captured and kept confined in a prisoner-of-war camp. They found him in his cage one morning, all his blankets and clothes stripped away and piled in a corner, frozen. He never broke.

"He was the lankiest guy, not a scrap of meat on him. No one could touch him playing football. I have never seen anything like it before or since," Fritzy said.

"Catching you wasn't exactly a stroll down the lane. That is why you both were consistently in opposition. The two toughest players pitted against each other," I said. Fritzy nodded in agreement.

We faded back into our thoughts as the miles rolled by. The best of us were lost to the war. At least, it seems like that is the way of it. A few were married with families. Others, like the four of us, devoted themselves to other things. I looked over at Fritzy. He should be married with a pack of children running around. "Let's stop and stretch," I said. He gave me a strange look. A few more miles down the road, he pulled into an area with a trail next to a field. The sky was beautiful, the temperature a little too chilly without a coat and hat. I set a good pace down the trail and felt ready for another round as a passenger within 10 minutes.

CHAPTER 3

"Sandy, quit thinking so loudly," Franz said as he looked over at me with a half-knowing smile. "The outcome of the world is not completely determined by you."

"Says the guy who hasn't spoken in an hour," I said, giving him the same smile. Franz shifted in his seat and looked over, there was a question coming.

"Are you certain the Chancellor knows to send the aide and her family if she has one? The conversation was pretty vague."

In answer to his concerns, I replied, "Yes, I'm certain, she is the only Jewish staff member as far as we are aware. The other options would not make sense. When his wife Herma was still alive; she was every bit as involved behind the scenes as he is. Sending her aide for a small ceremony makes a lot of sense with the current climate in Vienna."

Franz nodded in agreement, "Any preference on a stop?" he inquired.

"Leoben? Not quite halfway," I replied.

"The way she handles, Sandy, I would happily make the whole drive," he looked at me hopefully as he said it, but he already knew. We both loved to drive, that is why we decided on drawing straws right at the beginning to prevent squabbles.

"No way, Fritzy, if you are volunteering to chauffeur, you'll have to wait for appropriate circumstances. I am not letting you put all the miles on this lady," I said. We both chuckled and fell back into our comfortable silence.

At Leoben, we stopped for dinner, then I took over driving. Fritzy was asleep about 2 minutes after the wheels hit the road, an ability we did not share, although I wish we did. The air was beginning to change. Tyrol had a certain scent in the air. It is impossible to explain, and many may dispute the statement. For myself, though, it was unmistakable, home. Thoughts now turned to Miss Eigner and her family. We were unable to have a complete and thorough conversation regarding her details. The primary mission was to get her or them out of the country. The best option was Britain or America. Once more, The Earl would honor me with his benevolence by providing passage to Britain before it was too late. Who were we kidding, for many it was already too late. Every day, Jewish people, supposedly moving onto greener pastures, ended up dead in work camps or worse, slaughtered. Although perhaps it was the other way around. Just a matter of perspective. No question remained about the bottom line though. The master race was enacting treacherous plots to clean the chaff from the wheat.

The landscape took on dramatic changes. Valleys of farmland surrounded by mountains began to turn to high peaks. The valleys became narrower although still fertile and lush in the warmer months. Signs of the change to alpine climates were everywhere. Lofts were stuffed full of grass to carry livestock through the winter. The last stores would have been put up. Cellars and larders packed with the summer bounty. Smokehouses are full of meat. In the towns, things were still a struggle. Since the Treaty of St. Germain and financial restructuring, conditions had improved significantly over the previous nine years, but it was a long hard road.

Our families, although technically no longer nobility after 1919, had lost little. Investments and holdings were handled through Switzerland primarily. Finances had always kept to the gold standard, as indeed they still were, partially due to Swiss lineage through my father. Mother's side too had dealings with Switzerland before it was Switzerland, to hear the stories. It went back to the salt and silver mines throughout old Tyrol, also held to the gold standard, without significant investment in other currencies. Land, of course, came with the lineage on both sides, but little of it was still attached to titles. Many had been sold into the families' holdings. Truly, we were grateful every day for our blessings.

Through our faith and affiliations, we strove to assist those who suffered. Even with something as simple as milk and bread. The caretaker of the property we were headed to a perfect example. Released from a camp after the war, destitute with a wife and baby, they had gone to the parish priest at Dom zu St. Jakob 2 to beg him to take the child. My mother was there performing a service, helping those in need. Her heart broke for the couple willing to sacrifice their child so it would not starve. The next day, my father sat with the man to assess his abilities. Finding him an honest, capable man, he drew up a contract that very day. They were clothed, provisioned, and moved to their new home the following day.

Dusk was coming on, I flipped on the radio to see if I could tune in at the local station, doubtful, however, that we would be close enough. News was coming through on a station that was not there before. We only had one station here and this was not it. I knew that voice, I gave Franz a hard nudge. He came awake immediately, looking for the reason he was awakened. He rubbed his face vigorously for a moment, then stopped dead. Looking over at me, we listened, stunned.

"It is obvious that the Austrian and the Czech problems have to be

---

[2]. **Innsbruck Cathedral**, also known as the **Cathedral of St. James** (German: *Dom zu St. Jakob*), is an eighteenth-century Baroque cathedral of the Roman Catholic Diocese of Innsbruck in the city of Innsbruck, Austria, dedicated to the apostle Saint James, son of Zebedee.

solved to further strengthen Germany's political and, in particular, her strategic position. To start with, I am unsure whether both problems can be solved simultaneously, or whether one should deal first with the question of Czechoslovakia, or with the Austrian questions. There is no doubt that these questions have to be solved, and so all decisions are long-made plans which I am determined to realize the moment the circumstances are favorable."

"Did he just announce his invasion?" I asked, staring at Franz. Franz looked as stunned as I must have.

"He truly is a madman, Sandy. We have known that since '23, but you forget until you hear him again." Franz finished his statement and looked straight ahead. The station started broadcasting its adoration of the Führer's messages. I made a mental note of the number on the dial and shut it off.

"We had better ensure our cousin has this information. Put something together, the station was 670 on the dial," I said.

"We'll need to make a last stop for petrol up here, we can send a telegram, Sandy. I'll run over while you fill up." With his plan voiced, he went to work in his little notebook, putting the message together.

I was instantly so grateful I had sent Frieda away. Even knowing they were not moving to Austria yet, there would not have been a moment's peace had we left her there, or worse, sent her back to Munich. The sheer brass of that little fanatic. Yet they follow him like sheep to a slaughter. Throughout Austria, there were small groups of Nazis and Nazi sympathizers. They believe Hitler is the answer, the savior risen again. Why do we see him so clearly, while others walk straight off the cliff?

In town, I pulled into the little station. The gentleman filled the tank, checked the oil, and cleaned the windshield.

"Beautiful, the C12 isn't it?" he asked.

"Yes, just acquired it about a month ago," I replied.

"She is lovely, I wish to have an auto just like this one day," he stated.

He had the local paper, slightly used, but I had him add it to the gas. We settled the bill just as Franz made his appearance. The automobile had a full tank. Franz had brought some sausage, cheese, bread, and a small jar of something.

"Where did you get that?" I said as I pulled away from the station.

"The gentleman in the telegraph office lives in the back. They had just finished supper, and he took pity on me. Something about me looking longingly at their kitchen." He shrugged as he finished the statement and shoved a hunk of bread in his mouth. Laughter escaped me but I was grateful too. We still had another hour or so to go.

Fritzy took pity on his driver and shared a portion of his supper. Generous would be an exaggeration though. The stars were out and shining brightly with the lack of moon. A shiver ran up my spine as the memory of a pitch-black night with a body in front of me. It seemed ages ago, not just a few nights. So much had happened since then. Once the avalanche breaks loose, it does not stop until it hits the bottom. Our snow was barely slipping from the peak, it would only become more treacherous from here. The trick was to stay on top riding it down and it would be a trick.

CHAPTER 4

There truly is no place like home. Mayrhofen, my actual birthplace, is in the shadow of the Alps. One of many hamlets in the Zillertal. The original family estate is situated in the Southeast, a reasonable distance from the little chapel. The property is overseen by the same wonderful family my mother overheard that night in the church. Last count, I believe the children now number 5. An agricultural bounty flows from Die Wiesen, or The Meadows, as the estate is named, and allows it to be self-sustaining and then some. Word was sent ahead, and the main house had been prepared. When I was little, the house seemed like a castle to me. Complete with a looming tower. Now of course, the looming tower was no more than a small parapet made into a hobby room. Father had it built specifically for my mother. It afforded her a lovely view of the valley for her painting. The walls nearly three feet thick, in that respect, you might classify it as a miniature castle. A fortification is the better description.

The chimneys were putting out little sparks that shone in the night sky. Klaus opened the front door to greet us.

"Gräf Von Rieser, Gräf Von Grünne, Welcommen Heim!" Klaus said as we stamped our feet. Hugs were exchanged, and Klaus inquired about our health, driving, and the roads.

"No snow to speak of until we passed Lend. Even then, just dusting the rest of the way. And there is no need to be so formal, no need to use the Gräf or Von anymore, Klaus," I answered.

We were swapping our shoes for a type of fur-lined boot we wore in the house. I never understood why we had to wear these when we were small, but whenever we complained, my mother would calmly offer to give the staff the day off and let us boys take over the upkeep of the floors. To which we would reply respectfully with our gratitude for the clean floors and disappear.

"Nonsense, respect must be maintained, or what will our society come to?" Klaus spoke with a fierce stubbornness that left no room for argument. "Gräf Von Rieser, there will be fresh meats and cheeses in the ice box, along with buttermilk from this afternoon. Misses just churned it for you today. There are loaves of bread, crackers, and dried fruit in the larder with the preserved goods. If you need anything at all, just ring." A bell system ran from the main house to the farmhouse. "Oh yes, I almost forgot, there is a telegram for you on the desk in the study. It just came this evening, they brought it up from town, and the fire should be built up by now."

Shaking his hand gingerly, I thanked him profusely and assured him we had everything we needed for the night. Fritzy had already headed to his room. The automobile would be put in the small barn just down from the house. A telegram had arrived, hopefully it would be from The Earl. I went up to my room and found some pajamas in a drawer and a robe. Fuzzy boot slippers donned. I went down to the study. Well, perhaps a stop for buttermilk before Franz found it. By the time I made it to the study, I was loaded up with a full plate and a glass of buttermilk. Klaus had understated the amount of food they had put out for us. I had a delicious sandwich with a homemade relish of some sort. Thickly sliced, smoked roast, and thick Swiss cheese on freshly baked bread. I swear the bread was still warm when I sliced it. A few pickled beets and carrots and a large glass of buttermilk rounded it off. The entire room was at the perfect temperature. I threw a piece of wood on the fire just to keep it built up nicely and settled in for my large supper.

Twenty minutes later, the plate was pushed away in defeat. My eyes had gotten the better of me. I never had the ability to eat like Franz. Then I remembered the reason I was in the study in the first place. Retrieving the telegram, I went over to relax on the chesterfield close to the fire.

Dear Jim, the Proxy is due to arrive for the ceremony tomorrow STOP At your full disposal STOP Please advise upon his departure STOP Send a case STOP

I wonder whom The Earl chose to send. Well, we will find out soon enough. Cheap price, a case of Alpine beer. Setting the telegram down on the end table, I crossed over to the fire, threw another large log on, and returned to the Chesterfield, where they would find me napping all the time as a child. There was something comforting about watching my father scribbling away at the desk. Fire is a year-round occurrence in this room. The smell of warm leather, and ink. I drifted off to the comfort and warmth of childhood.

Something large but soft slammed into my head.

"You going to lay there all day? Thanks for inviting me to supper! For such a strapping lad you sure eat like a girl," Franz teased, the pillow he threw at my head rolling off onto the floor.

"If we were younger," I threatened.

"You'd what?" he countered. "Come on Sandy, let's go for a run, we're home."

I had slept brilliantly, and the excitement of being home was contagious. Franz was already dressed and ready to go. "Be ready in 2 shakes of a lamb's tail" I said heading toward the stairs. It was more like ten minutes or so, but soon we were out on the trail. It was invigorating, the smell was intoxicating. The air was brisk on the skin, with the warm blood pumping. Memories surrounded us everywhere here. When we were young, Fritzy lived just a mile down the road. Our families summered here almost every year. At Advent, we would return and stay through St. Stephen's Day or just after the new year.

Fritzy kept running ahead and then pulling back. He was trying to bait me into a race, but after 35 years, I was aware of who would win. A mile or so later he resorted to begging.

"Come on Sandy, you could win this time." I gave, in bolting like a deer, he had the good grace to wait until we were back to the property to overtake me.

"Waited all that time, did you?" I panted out of breath. We were back to the slow jog now coming around the yard.

"It seemed only fair to give you the feeling you would win this one," he said grinning ear to ear. I punched him hard in the arm, "Ow!" he said, rubbing his arm. Running, he was impossible to beat, but in boxing, I had him.

The door opened to the most wonderful smells of smoked sausage.

"I'm first to wash up," Franz stated, bolting up the stairs.

Klaus appeared before me, "Breakfast is warm in the oven, Mein Herr. The run was good?" he asked.

"Wonderful Klaus, please extend our gratitude to your wife for feeding us."

"It is her pleasure, Mein Herr. My oldest daughter will be over this evening to take care of the guests. Are you certain you would not like me to send for the cook and perhaps a proper maid?"

I doubted the extra work was appreciated but with children leaving the nest, as they say.

"No, Klaus, it is essential everything is kept in the strictest confidence. Of course, we do not want to burden you or your family either," I said, trying to show my genuine concern.

"Mein Herr, I assure you; it is quite the opposite. Winter days are coming, there is little outside work for us this time of year. Everyone is happy to be busy."

Shaking his hand I said, "We are lucky to have such a wonderful family as yours caring for us." Klaus choked up at the statement. He mumbled something about breakfast again, bowed, and hurried off.

I decided to forget being a gentleman in lieu of possibly losing out on breakfast. In the kitchen, I washed my hands and face, grabbed a plate, and opened the oven door. My fears were immediately put to rest. Even Fritzy could not eat that much. There was a dozen Semmel (buns), sausage, ham, and some type of pastry. On the table were jams, jellies, buttermilk, butter, and boiled eggs. "Good luck eating all that my friend," I said in a faint voice. Halfway through my breakfast, Franz came in, well-groomed and ready to feast. A moment later, he sat down, filled his plate, said "Glory to God," and went all in. At one point he came up for air just long enough to ask for buttermilk and call me a heathen. Truthfully, I became one upon smelling the sausage. Speaking of smelling, I excused myself and went off to clean up and dress.

After breakfast, Franz retrieved the small lock box and brought it into the study. I handed him the telegram and pulled out the maps and documents we needed. We spent the bulk of the morning sorting through what was necessary for the following few days. Everything else was put away and the lock box secured.

Leisure encompassed the afternoon. Playing the waiting game, we both took advantage of the lull to read, lounge, and engage in a fierce round of chess.

"You've bested me again Sandy. In every other endeavor I can almost feel what you are thinking, just not in chess and espionage," Franz stated, sliding back in his chair. Just then, Klaus entered the library with a striking young lady of around seventeen. She was dressed as a house attendant, her blond braids threading around her head. Eyes the color of an alpine lake stared out from under thin sandy brows, her lips were full but not thick, perfectly pink. A little shame crept into my cheeks as I had to wrestle with my baser urges for a moment.

"Gräf Alexsander Von Rieser, Gräf Franz Von Grünne, may I present my daughter, Elsa Bauer. Elsa and I will be attending to your guests this week. With the help of my family of course."

Klaus pushed Elsa forward just a bit as he introduced her. She curtsied and declined her head.

"Gräf Alexsander Von Rieser, Gräf Franz Von Grünne, it is my sincere pleasure to meet you. I will strive to consider all your needs," Elsa said in a clear feminine voice.

My mind got the better of me, wishing she could take care of my needs. Hardly a gentlemanly thing to think! With that, I reined myself in, strode over to her, bowed, and stated the standard "at your service, Elsa."

Standing, I concluded the formality by saying, "Please do refrain from using our titles though. It will be a dreadfully long affair if we must be formal every time we speak. Herr Rieser or Mein Herr will be fine, Elsa."

I had said her name twice and introduced myself in the fashion of meeting a lady, not a servant. Franz watched the whole thing, cataloging it. Franz inclined his head and leaned slightly forward.

"It is my pleasure to make your acquaintance. Thank you for your assistance this week."

Elsa made a small curtsy and stepped back toward her father.

"Supper will be ready at half of 7, Mein Herr," Klaus said, and shooed Elsa from the room.

Franz turned and stared at me, then walked over, and closed the library door, whereupon he turned back on me.

"At your service? Sandy, we have clothes older than that GIRL!" He emphasized the word girl heavily.

"You needn't admonish me, I have quite taken care of it myself, I assure you," I replied.

He looked at me seriously, cracked a wide grin, and said, "She is striking, it took me aback slightly too." We had a good laugh about it. "Let's go grab a bite, supper is still 2 hours away," Franz said.

"Yes, I see you have withered away, alright but if we see Elsa, I'm running in the other direction." Laughing as I said it, Fritzy slapped me on the back.

"Blonds aren't your type anyway, it would never last!" Now we were both laughing as we headed for the kitchen.

I was just stepping across the foyer when the knock came. Upon opening the door, in front of me stood an old classmate from Cambridge, Henry Fletcher.

"Henry, so glad to see you, come in, please come in. You will have to forgive our lack of staff. The main house is closed in the winter and under the circumstances, we did not want any additional eyes and ears. Let me take your coat," I said.

"Great to see you, Jim! No apologies, the scenery is stunning, and the estate is just grand. Did you say you do not live here full-time? What a shame, it is a grand place, just grand," Henry replied.

We shook hands several times, patting each other on the back over and over. I procured fuzzy boots, complete with the story for him, which he loved. Klaus and Elsa came into the Foyer, introductions were made.

Henry tried to perform better than I had upon Elsa's introduction, but the results were much the same. They took his bags upstairs to his room.

"Did you drive? There was no noise from a car," I asked.

"No, no I took the train in, The Earl had arranged for transportation for me. He wanted certain chatter to be kept to a minimum. My driver let me off down the road a bit with instructions. The Earl has all the transportation arranged, but we can go over that later. Any chance of a drink and possibly some food, in that order, if you do not mind, Jim?" Henry said.

"Of course, terrible host I'm afraid," I replied and ushered him into the sitting room. "Have a seat, I'll get you a Bourbon," I offered, moving to the cupboard.

"God bless you, Jim!" Henry laughed. I poured a generous Bourbon neat and brought it over.

"Franz Grünne, at your service," Franz said as he entered the room. He came over to Henry, bowed, and then offered his hand. Henry stood and shook Franz's hand.

"So, you are the infamous cousin Franz, we've heard a lot about you, old boy. Henry Fletcher, it is my honor to meet you. There can certainly be no doubt about the relation to Jim with those eyes, identical."

Henry looked a little stunned just for a moment as he glanced between us. Niceties done, Franz went to the cupboard and poured a small schnapps for both of us. He handed me the glass and we all sat down for the traditional polite conversation before supper.

Henry was back with the government expanding on his position in the war. Covert operations of some kind, nothing he could share now. More to the point, The Earl had chosen him specifically for those skills and our previous friendship. He intended to help in any way possible. Additionally, it brought him to an area that Britain desperately wanted inside information on. Hitler's antics were gaining worldwide attention and

Britain was particularly concerned. Although not nearly concerned enough to rally round the country it left crippled. Of course, none of that was Henry's fault. Taking a deep breath, I let it go. Klaus came in to announce dinner in 20 minutes.

"Well, if you gentlemen don't mind, I would like to freshen up just a bit before we dine," Henry stated. Klaus showed Henry to his room.

"Everyone hated it when you left for Cambridge. Lucky you did though, seems a good man, Henry," Franz admitted, looking into his glass.

"Well, the idea and the act fall squarely on my parents, but yes, it has been fortuitous with the present circumstances," I said.

We chatted a bit about where Henry fell into my life at the university, then made our way out to the Foyer to await his return down the stairs.

"Jim the craftsmanship is just stunning," Henry stated as he descended the stairs.

Walking into the dining room, I replied, "Yes, my father built it for my mother, it was a wedding present I believe. Many of the craftsmen were local to the area. Father believes in keeping the local economy strong. There were some special materials imported, generally speaking, the materials all come from within a few hundred miles. Every stone on the walls came from a local stonemason."

The meal was superb, there was a pheasant, klöße dumplings with sauerkraut, tafelspitz, shoestring carrots, whipped turnips with a thick gravy, and the same heavenly bread from last night. Henry was giving Franz a run for his money in how much food fit in his frame. I requested a coffee, which Klaus produced like magic only minutes later.

"Well, Klaus do you think they will finish it all?" I asked.

Klaus laughed and said, "It is like watching my sons eat, but they are young." Henry and Franz barely acknowledged our comments.

"If you will excuse me, gentlemen, I will meet you in the study when you have completed your mission." With that, I winked at Klaus and took my coffee to the study.

Klaus popped his head in a few moments later. "Mein Herr, would you care for some kuchen with your coffee?"

"That is most kind of you, Klaus, however, there is just no room left in me. (I laughed) Perhaps later if you will just leave me a slice in the larder. Where Herr Franz will not find it, of course. Oh, Klaus! Wait just a moment, we have a lot of food, and we will certainly eat quite a bit of it, but would you be sure nothing goes to waste?" I said.

"Of course, Mein Herr, nothing will be wasted, I assure you," Klaus said as he came into the room to build the fire up.

"Thank you, Klaus." What a gift god gave my family when they brought them into our lives.

A full hour later, Franz came strolling into the study with Henry by his side. They had won each other's respect.

"Jim, I was just telling Franz you must invite me more often. What an amazing meal, and the dessert, what did you call that?" Henry inquired, looking at Franz.

"Kuchen," he replied with a wide smile.

"Yes, kuchen, I must try that again, Franz says there are all different flavors," Henry beamed.

"Nothing could bring me more happiness than knowing we have surpassed the expectations of a world traveler. If the two of you are certain you have completed your culinary rapture, we can get a little work done, if you do not mind, of course?" I said it with humor in my voice. I rang for Klaus, and Elsa appeared. Maintaining my composure, I asked for coffee all around and she disappeared as quickly as she came with a "Yes, Mein Herr." Sheesh, calm down big boy, I said to myself. Perhaps when I returned to Innsbruck, a trip to Madame's was in order. Enough of those thoughts.

We all gathered around the desk plotting out the best course of action.

With Mussolini below us, and Hitler above us, relations with France shaky, and with no one particularly wanting a stream of Jewish immigrants, we needed to be tactful in getting the aide to England. The trip itself should be straightforward. Innsbruck to Zürich then Zürich to Paris and Paris to LeHarve. At LeHarve, The Earl would have a yacht waiting, with smooth seas it should be the easiest part of the trip. Over the next hour, contingencies were planned for and picked. Once everyone had addressed every concern, they thought possible, we finished and spread out to relax.

"Schnapps, anyone?" I asked. Both Henry and Franz happily accepted the offer. Pouring a few fingers in each glass, I passed them around and took my spot by the fire.

"Certainly, there is something unforeseen, Jim, but I believe the highest probability of complications have been addressed," opined Henry.

"Without the information of whom, or if she is arriving with others, I concur, Henry. In our experience to date, people want their children, sick or elderly safe first," Franz stated. All the questions we have will be answered tomorrow, I thought to myself.

Everyone sipped their Schnapps, working through thoughts and winding down for a little while. The feeling was quite comfortable. Henry turned out to be a perfect choice. The Earl had a true gift for understanding people and combining them in the most advantageous ways. Henry spoke, bringing us back to the moment.

"Jim, what is it about this room? I am unable to put my finger on it. The whole thing is stone, and yet it radiates the ideal level of warmth. I must say, it is the most comfortable room I have ever been in." I laughed a little when he noticed and gave him the explanation he was looking for.

"It is quite astute of you to notice, actually. My father worked with the stonemasons during construction to provide the features for the entire house. The Chestnut trim you see runs throughout the house. The trim is not only for aesthetics but acts as a false front for the piping running through the walls. Each fireplace within the house is part of the system. Water tanks were specially made for each hearth. As the water heats, the steam it creates travels through the pipes. Rarely will every fireplace have a fire in it, so the system is designed to self-regulate for the most part. However, there are pressure release valves in strategic places and an entire control system in the basement. The system allows for warm water at any faucet you access, both inside and some places outside. Overall, it regulates the temperature of the entire house. This room always seems especially cozy due to the largest tanks being placed in this section of the house. The obvious downside is keeping a fire going all the time."

"Ingenious, it should be mandatory in every castle. We have radiator heat, but the use of the stone in conjunction with the piping!" Henry laughed.

"If you would like some light reading, I would be happy to bring you a handwritten volume to peruse on the basics? My father felt it insufficient to publish, but I assure you it is worth the read," I offered.

"That would be delightful, thank you, Jim," he replied.

"With that, gentlemen, I believe I will retire for the evening. Henry, it has been a delight, sleep well, you are invited to take a stroll with us in the morning if you like," Franz announced as he rose.

"Sleep well Franz, truly a pleasure," Henry said as he rose to shake Franz's hand.

"I'll be ready in the morning!" I winked at Fritzy, admiring his understatement of the morning run. With that, Franz departed the study.

"I realize how forward this is, Jim, but your eyes are almost identical. Are you certain Franz is not more closely related than a cousin? It is uncanny, obviously, there is the different hair color and so forth, but it is striking," Henry inquired.

"Henry, you are certainly not the first to be taken aback by it. Our mothers are sisters, we both inherited their eyes. It is also part of the reason we always joke about being twins," I replied.

Henry shook his head, "I feel quite secure here, Jim, so let us have a chat about the real payment The Earl would like. Honestly, it is the payment I would like." Henry looked at me quite seriously readjusting in his seat as he continued. "You have developed a small, tight-knit group here, Jim. The intelligence all of you gather is invaluable."

Interrupting, I said, "Well, Henry, you may be overestimating the amount of information we are coming into."

Henry plowed forward, "No, Jim, we don't believe we are. In the kind of fight that is about to happen, everything is important. You were in the game back in the war. I know you understand."

"Indeed, I do, Henry, if you are asking for us to share information, you know I will agree. The problem will be the transmission of that information."

Henry smiled, rose, and headed for the schnapps with a "do you mind" gesture. I waved him on, and he poured himself another finger or two, I declined, and he replaced the lid and headed closer to sit back down.

"We have a machine, it is experimental, but we have had good results. Would you be willing to try it out, and send us information?" Henry asked.

"Of course, I will, even if it wasn't a common enemy, it is the right thing to do. Like you, your country is in every bit as much danger as mine. Moreover, I believe they will do everything possible to keep mine intact. England will not be so fortunate I fear."

It felt like prophecy as I said these words to Henry. He went on to explain the general workings of the machine. He had one with him, and having procured my consent, he would show me the workings, but it was a bit complicated and required time. We agreed to find a way and work it out in the coming weeks or months. In the meantime, we would stick to the methods we were already using.

Our discussion turned lighter, catching me up with the stories of others from school. Too soon it was 11 o'clock and we said our good nights. I found myself in my room staring at my bed like an enemy. I changed into the dreaded nightclothes, grabbed my robe, and headed down for the kuchen I knew Klaus had set aside.

There it was in the larder, significantly larger than I would have sliced, but I blessed him, nonetheless. Buttermilk had been left in the ice box too, perfect. Taking the late-night snack off to the study, I paused, deposited it on the end table, and ventured off to the library. My father's volumes were kept in a specific area making what I was looking for easy to find. I laid the volume on the vestibule table lest I forget in the morning and returned to my sugary feast. What a treat! I must stop eating like this soon or start running morning and night. The mere thought of it made me laugh. The obvious plan was to stoke the fire, pile on some logs, and sleep on the chesterfield. The plan was undertaken at once. My last thoughts were lost to the gods of sleep.

CHAPTER 5

I lay still for a moment; the pain was there on the left side of my head. Like a lost thought, it was gone as soon as I tried to focus on it. My eyes opened, and I stretched feeling great. Klaus, ever attentive, arrived with coffee, still long before anyone else was awake. "Klaus you are like my guardian angel, thank you for the coffee. No one has risen yet?" I asked.

"No Mein Herr, you are the first. I knew you would want an early start this morning." Klaus stoked the fire and then brought in a large bundle of wood to restock the supply.

I sipped my coffee as I made my way upstairs. After a light toilette, I changed into my running clothes and headed down to the kitchen. By the time Fritzy and Henry appeared I was well into my third coffee. Frankly, I was getting a little restless. "Good morning, obviously you both needed to sleep off your eating competition!" I said laughing.

We all joked around a bit and headed out for the run. I was just trying to warn Henry when Franz began to subtly speed up.

"20 pounds says I beat you to the red gate," he challenged.

"But where is the red gate?" Henry asked with a bewildered look as Franz took off.

"Just go!" I yelled at Henry, and continued my normal pace, watching the show.

From my vantage point, Henry might have had a chance. He was about 6' and lanky, and once he got his pace, he was fast. I could see

Fritzy taking it a bit easy on him, not realizing Henry's gain. I picked up my pace a bit, not wanting to miss this. Suddenly, he saw Henry overtaking him and poured it on. They were both stretching it out, but Henry was just so fast. Thinking back to school, I could not recall a time when we had ever run against each other. Henry's ability to run had not been something of which I was aware.

When I arrived, they were both laid out across the light layer of snow on the ground, panting like a struggling freight train.

"Who won?" I quarried as I approached, trotting around their heads, fully expecting them not to answer. I circled around heading back to the estate at a steady pace. About a third of the way back down the lane, two madmen sped past me.

Fritzy yelled something unintelligible as he sped by. My guess was someone had offered double or nothing. I laughed to myself and hoped none of Klaus's family was in the way when they got near the house. I was uncertain about Henry, but I had been hit by Franz more than once and it was a painful experience that took a week or two to recover from.

Arriving to find everything looking normal, I noticed Mrs. Bauer, Greta, crossing the yard. She was shaking her head. Her direction put her in line for their house. All was clear when I entered the vestibule, I changed shoes and headed to my parents' room. Another amenity my father planned out for the house was a full lavatory for my mother just off their main bedroom. In their lavatory, he had designed and built a shower, something my father had experienced on his travels. Having three or four lavatories in one home was extravagant, to say the least. Indoor plumbing had become commonplace here in the early 'thirties but when the house was built it was still a luxury to have a full lavatory upstairs. The shower was a work of art, heaven! The entire bathroom had the same tile, floors, and walls. The shower had benches with overhead streams that came down in multiple places. Reluctantly I left the luxury of a well-placed stream of hot water. My back muscles completely relaxed. Returning to my room to dress I noticed the time. Getting caught up in the luxury of the shower was easy to do.

Warm, clean, and freshly shaven, I joined the others for breakfast. The dining room table had been under attack for some time it seemed. As I sat down, I began laughing, if this is what Klaus dealt with feeding his boys, small wonder he had any food at all. Grabbing one of the last Semmel and a sausage, I made my way toward the butter bowl. The butter had been under barrage for some time, but there was enough to butter the roll. Having poured myself a coffee, I sat back and watched the carnage. They had both looked up and smiled as I came into the room but continued chewing and shoving the next bite in.

Franz remained the reigning champion of the feast when it was said and done. Henry, admitting defeat, pushed his plate away, poured a fresh cup of tea, and leaned back. A look of utter satisfaction rested on his face.

"Klaus, sir, please extend Frau Bauer my compliments. You are indeed a lucky man to have a chef in your home." Henry said looking over at Klaus.

Klaus chuckled a bit replying, "Mein Greta will be most pleased with your compliment, Herr Fletcher, danke." With that Elsa appeared asking to begin clearing.

"Elsa, just do not put your hands too near Herr Franz." I broke into laughter with Klaus and Henry following. Fritzy shot me a smirk and surrendered from battle. He too poured coffee and leaned back.

"Glad we thought to leave you something, Sandy, try to be on time would you!" Franz said, laughter circled again.

"Well, gentlemen, shall we move to the sitting room? I do believe our guests will be arriving anytime. The invitation time was set for eleven o'clock," I suggested.

We retired to the sitting room, bringing coffee along. As we passed, I noticed the volume on the vestibule table.

"Oh, Henry, yes, here is the volume I spoke to you about. If you would just be good enough to leave it on your night table when you leave," I said, handing Henry my father's handwritten journal on steam heating and plumbing.

"Wonderful, Jim, thank you, I'll just sit down and have a go now if you two gentlemen don't mind." Henry took the book eagerly, sought out a comfortable lounge, and was engrossed in moments.

I looked at Fritzy and said, "Library for a round of chess?"

"Wonderful idea!" he replied, and we strolled out leaving Henry in peace to read.

The coffee appeared shortly after being carried by Elsa. I began to apologize for our thoughtlessness, feeling an elbow in my back, I turned to see Franz casting the disapproving father look.

"Thank you, Elsa," Franz said, she curtsied and left the room.

We were several moves in when the conversation returned. "There is no reason not to be polite to the girl," I said.

Franz countered, "You absolutely should be polite, in the same way you would be to Klaus or Frieda."

Grabbing a pawn, I looked up and said, "that is exactly what I was doing."

As I was taking one of Franz's pawns, he said, "Strange, I do not recall you trying to profusely apologize for anything to either of them. Perhaps to your parents' house servants, let me see..." He was tapping his chin for effect. "No, I can definitively say at no time do I remember that happening after the age of 13." He had stopped playing, fully engaged in the discussion now. Stopping myself, I rubbed my face with both hands for a moment.

"I don't know what keeps coming over me. It isn't love, I know what that feels like." We both looked down, I hesitated then continued, "There is some measure of lust in it though, which makes me feel a letch. Just keep being my conscious, I'll try to rein it in until I can get to Madame's for a night." The game resumed. Neither of our hearts was in it though. The talk of love had opened doors we both preferred to keep closed.

Mercifully, an hour later our much-anticipated guest arrived. Klaus retrieved us while Elsa showed them to the sitting room. When we entered, Henry was introducing himself to the trio. He was then kind enough to continue the introductions.

"Miss Golda Eigner, Mrs. Schuschniggs' aide, her brother, Mr. Gideon Eigner, and sister, Miss Geula Eigner, may I present Gräf Alexsander Von Rieser, your host, and Gräf Franz Von Grünne, his cousin." Bows were made, hands were perfunctorily kissed, shaken, and so forth.

"Miss Eigner, if I may, would you care to be shown to your rooms to freshen up?" I offered.

"We would be most grateful Gräf Von Rieser," Golda replied.

"Not at all, if you would do us the kindness of dropping the formality though." I said, turning to escort them upstairs, however, Klaus appeared out of nowhere and brought the procession upstairs to their rooms, relieving me of the duty.

"Fortunately, they are our last guests, I do believe that will finish off the available accommodations. Although, I suppose I could move into Father and mother's room," I joked.

"I will be only too happy to suffer that duty for you," offered Fritzy, knowing full well about the lavatory.

"Straws if it comes to it?" I proposed, and we both broke out laughing. Henry looked lost, so we shared the story of straws for anything we both wanted.

"Are you blokes certain you are not brothers? If they ever devise a test, I think you two should be first in line, not to defame your dear mothers by any means," Henry said laughing.

Elsa brought word a few minutes later that the Eigners would be taking a short rest; asking to be awoken in time for the afternoon dinner. We all understood how frightening this must be for the three of them. Some time to relax, adjust and decompress from the journey would not hurt. I rang Klaus to inform him of early supper, and that we would skip dinner all together. Franz looked grief stricken, Klaus assured him he would deliver a snack shortly.

The three of us moved to the study to go over everything, girded with the knowledge we would have one grown woman and two adolescents.

"This should work out quite well. Golda will easily be able to pose as my wife bringing her siblings home for holiday," Henry said.

It made sense, Golda indeed was sufficiently old enough to be Henry's wife. Ten years was not an unusual span between husband and wife. The easiest way to successfully traverse the trap of thorough questioning is the truth. The closer you can stay to the truth, the better your chances. We ironed out a few added details, and once satisfied, we resumed our earlier positions in the library. Henry had joined us in the library continuing to read. We rejoined our game, with better luck. Mid-morning slowly moved into late afternoon. The smells of cooking made their way through the house. Franz's stomach growled, and I found myself rolling with laughter.

Upon regaining my composure, I accused him verbally "There is no possible way your stomach can be empty! When we get to Innsbruck, you are going to the doctor to be checked for parasites!" Henry burst out laughing, Franz assumed a crushed look, and as if to counter my threat, his stomach growled again.

All three of us broke into raucous laughter.

Golda, with her siblings in tow, came down to the sitting room. Staying in a small group, all three appeared a bit wide-eyed and out of their element. Elsa's voice came through as our laughter died down.

"The Eigners await you in the sitting room at your convenience, Mein Herr." With that, she returned to attending to the guests. As it turned out, one guest, judging from the electricity in the room. Gideon Eigner's eyes followed every move Elsa made, no matter how subtle. His sisters seemed completely unaware of the attraction. Elsa, however, was keenly aware as evidenced by her need to linger closer to him, swish a little more when crossing the room, and repeatedly ask everyone if they needed anything. After a few minutes, it seemed necessary to remove the distraction.

"Elsa, would please show Gideon and Geula around the house, thank you." Gideon was up like lightning, and Geula joined him at a much more lady-like pace.

There seemed to be a slight hiatus once the four of us were left alone in the room, which Henry seemed anxious to resolve.

"With your permission, Jim?" Henry looked at me and continued, "Miss Eigner, just how much do you understand about why you are here?"

Nice opening, I admired Henry giving her control of the conversation. Allowing her to stretch herself and test the waters.

"Well, Herr Fletcher…"

"Henry, please," he interrupted.

"Well, Herr Henry," Franz and I stifled a giggle. A well-bred young lady would not easily drop proper etiquette. "Only what the Chancellor disclosed to my parents and me, the belief that Germany will indeed invade Austria. At that time, the antisemitic practices of the Nazis will be instituted immediately. Every person of Hebrew descent will then be systematically rooted out, killed, or sent to concentration camps. Therefore, for the safety of myself and my siblings, they have told us Gräf Von Rieser will secret us away before it is too late." Her eyes bore just a bit too much moisture. Like a lady though, she held her head up high and did not allow tears to form.

"Miss Eigner, it must be very difficult to leave your parents behind," I said, she nodded a yes. "The entire business is and will be difficult. You see, certain areas are already checking papers. Removing the three of you as soon as possible is essential. I am certain you are all capable of the bravery you will need to show in the coming few days. If I may ask you to accompany us to the study, Henry will lay out the plan, and you may ask whatever questions necessary."

Golda stood, "Of course, Gräf Von Rieser."

I turned and looked at her, "Golda, this truly will require you to adjust, you would honor us if you began by addressing us by our first names." She nodded with an unsure look in her eyes.

Resuming our walk, Franz moved ahead and offered his arm. Golda took it, hesitantly, and they strolled on, touring through the house on the way to the study. We patiently followed and paused whenever he would stop to explain something to her. In the few minutes it took to get to the study, she had become completely at ease.

"There is no one more capable of breaking down female Austrian etiquette than Franz the suave," I said in an extremely low tone to Henry.

Henry chuckled and inquired, "With that hidden charm, you would think him married by now."

Henry must have seen the look of sadness and remorse cross my face for he hurriedly said, "Oh, I see, yes well, another time."

The plan was laid out, weak areas were pointed out to Golda. Henry and Golda meticulously worked through the flaws until they had them ironed out and memorized. Elsa was asked to show the younger Eigners to supper.

"Let us take a break with our brains full, shall we? We may resume with full bellies after supper." I shot Franz a look and continued, "Well some of us will have full bellies." The three of us laughed while Golda looked perplexed. Henry offered his arm, and this time Golda accepted it without hesitation. Dinner, like the previous night, was excessive, extravagant, and extensive. Klaus expressed to our guests that all items on the menu going forward were Kosher. Something none of us had considered. The Eigners were profoundly grateful, thanking Klaus profusely. Golda had insisted on thanking the entire family personally. After dinner, the entire clan received sincere thanks from each of the guests, including myself.

Both Henry and Franz managed to control themselves. Dining like perfect gentlemen throughout the entire meal. I made a mental note to come to the kitchen after the Eigners were in bed to see how long they would be able to abstain. I laughed a little at the thought and received inquiring looks.

"Just thinking of the foot race this morning, by the way, who won?" I quarried.

"Henry soundly beat me both times. I don't understand it, you are so fast for someone your size." Franz said it as if Henry was small.

"Track and Field in school, Franz, I competed in all events. You should see my long jump, if you care to wager, I would be happy to demonstrate," was Henry's explanation.

"I believe 40 pounds is quite enough for this visit, perhaps when you visit again, we'll set up a proper course and have a competition." There was light laughter. Franz and Henry took turns regaling the Eigners with details of the morning's race. Both embellished their prowess equally.

After Dinner, we retired to the study depositing the adolescents in the library where they joined several of the Bauer children of similar ages.

Pulling Klaus aside, I thanked him privately. He assured me it was not an inconvenience as our neighbor is Jewish. They had been friends for years, so asking him to provide the necessary processes and procedures for the animals and food was as simple as asking. Nonetheless, my gratitude was immense.

"On board the trains, will I be expected to join you in, well privately?" Golda asked, her cheeks crimson.

"No, not at all," Henry continued, "With your family traveling with us, the men shall sleep in one berth and the ladies in the other."

"Thank you!" A sigh of relief inadvertently escaping as she replied.

"Please do keep in mind, Golda, you will be known to be married. Although you want to be careful not to do anything inappropriate, you also want to display a respectable level of affection in public," I said.

"Think of how your parents act when they are together in public. Allow that to be your guide," Franz finished for me.

Golda blushed slightly nodding her understanding.

"Will you require any assistance explaining the roles to your brother and sister?" I inquired.

"I believe we will do fine, if there are questions, we may address them in the morning. If there is nothing else for the evening, I would like to retire. Tomorrow will be the beginning of many busy days," Golda said.

We each took turns wishing her goodnight, Henry escorted her to the library to retrieve her siblings, then escorted everyone to the stairs with best wishes for the night's sleep.

Franz already had three glasses of schnapps poured before Henry returned. As he reentered the study, he swung by and grabbed his as Franz set mine in my outstretched hand.

"Well gentlemen, here is to a smooth, safe, and swift journey." We all stood, clinking glasses.

Franz and I both added, "Amen."

"Are you certain the driver will meet you in the morning? We are headed home to our respective parents' houses in Innsbruck tomorrow. There is plenty of room for the four of you in the car," I offered.

"The driver is set, I asked Klaus to have a telegram sent for confirmation when they arrived this afternoon. It is appreciated, but as we discussed, the intelligence all of you are gathering is invaluable. There is no need to compromise such a valuable resource," Henry said.

"This is it for now then?" said Franz. "How about a light snack before we retire?" Franz glanced at me but gave Henry a knowing look.

"Now that my friend, is a brilliant idea," Henry said.

I stood, thanking Henry profusely, "See you in the morning then," I said, and the two of them headed for the kitchen.

In the morning, I was up, bathed, dressed, and enjoying coffee long before anyone else in the house arose. The smells of breakfast were escaping the kitchen as Franz and Henry both strolled in. They were engaged in light conversation, taking their seats across from each other. Two food gladiators meeting on the field of battle. "Good mornings," and "slept wells?" were exchanged, and coffee poured. Moments later, the platters were on the table. The warriors looked around cautiously, saw no polite company in range, and engaged. They both managed a second plate before the genteel sex arrived with flawless manners. Both immediately assumed perfect posture and manners. All of us stood to seat the ladies.

Pleasantries were exchanged all around again. Young Gideon began piling food on, only to be scolded. All the men assured him it was quite all right to return to anything he liked more than once after finishing a reasonable first plate. This won us the gratitude of the sisters and the brother. Touché. Franz, looking straight at me with eyes full of mirth, called for his plate to be removed.

"My compliments, Klaus, but I simply could not suffer another bite I am that full."

Seeing Klaus's eyes filled with the same mirth I was feeling, it was all Henry and myself could do to keep a straight face.

Golda looked at each of us in turn and said, "When dining with you gentlemen, I often feel at a loss."

Franz and Henry both looked at me like wolves caught in a trap.

"Just pretend you are sitting at the table with a few additional brothers, understand?" I replied.

"Ah, yes, I see," said Golda and resumed her meal without the slightest glance toward either Henry or Franz.

Again, laughter was stifled. As gentlemen, we all sat and sipped coffee while making polite small talk. Henry heard the chimes of the clock in the Foyer.

"May we retrieve your luggage in preparation?" Henry asked.

"Thank you, that is quite thoughtful, however, Gideon brought it all down to the foyer while we were preparing this morning," Golda replied. That brought a round of "smart girl" looks.

After breakfast, we escorted everyone to the foyer.

"Please let us know of your success as soon as possible," I said to Henry as we embraced and shook hands.

"It has been a real pleasure, Jim, do invite me back for holiday. Truly a grand place, Jim, just grand," Henry said.

I whispered back, "If this goes well, it may become your second home." He took my meaning, slapping me on my back.

Henry stepped over to say goodbye to Franz as I reached Golda. Taking her hands gently in mine I rolled a small bag from my sleeve to my palm. She looked at me, shocked, and began to refuse. I pressed it gently into her palm.

"You'll need this, get a good start so your parents have a safe place to come to when the time arrives." Her eyes began to moisten, as I backed away and bowed.

"Miss Eigner, my cousin, and I wish you all a blessed trip and happy life," Franz said as he appeared beside me. He also bowed, walked over, and perfunctorily kissed both ladies' hands, then stepped back.

On cue, an old, beat-up car pulled into the circle drive. Further waves and well wishes were made by the Bauers, and everyone went away.

We watched them drive away. Franz turned to look at me, vocalizing my thoughts.

"I do not recall the last time I truly felt I have done something completely worthwhile, until now."

"I could not possibly agree more with that feeling," I said, then added, "did you want to finish breakfast or are you unable to suffer that?" We both laughed on our way back to the dining room.

Both of us had packed before breakfast, and we carefully retrieved only what we knew we needed from the safe in the study. Franz brought Klaus in and shut the door.

"Klaus we just wanted to have a frank conversation before we leave for Innsbruck, if you have the time," I inquired.

"Of course, Mein Herr," Klaus said as I motioned for all of us to have a seat.

"We could not possibly express our appreciation to you or your family for playing servants to us these past days." He started to protest but I stopped him. "Truly, you have played a large role in what we all pray is a safe trip and new life for that little family. You are receiving a significant bonus, Klaus, and no, this is not a negotiation. You have earned more than you know. We are arranging for a new car, big enough for your whole family. Keep it gassed up at all times, please."

Klaus interrupted, "Mein Herr, we do not need anything, we have a fine home, a sturdy truck, good land to work, plentiful livestock, and quite a savings." I waved my hand in understanding but continued.

"I understand, Klaus, but we would ask you to take the risk of doing this again. Understand, our actions endanger both your family and you. If something were to come of it, you must promise me that you will plead innocence. You must say we are cruel employers who do not keep you informed and simply demand. Do you understand?"

Klaus looked for all the world as if he would cry. Finally, he replied, "Yes, Mein Herr I understand, and my family, we know what you do. By doing God's work you allow us to help these people too."

It was the same feeling Franz and I had. I grabbed his hand in a type of celebratory handshake.

Franz added, "Everything must always be kept confidential, Klaus. If you need to escape, you take your family in the car and go to Vaduz. There will be no questions, do you understand?" Klaus nodded in affirmation. Franz continued, "you said the neighbor is your friend, if his family is in danger, we will help him. There are more Nazis flooding into this area making it their playground. When Austria is taken, keep him around the farmstead, try to get him to allow you to do his town errands for him, but protect yourself and your family first." We sat back as Klaus absorbed all this information.

"Do you have any questions?" I asked. Klaus shook his head no. "We will be back in a few weeks, possibly sooner. I am having a telephone installed for you, it will allow us much faster communication."

Klaus smiled a guilty smile and said, "We had one installed this summer, Mein Herr. I thought the Elder Gräf had informed you, my apologies."

I laughed and said, "No apologies, Klaus, please, we owe you a debt of gratitude. Keep the money safe, my friend, use it in any way necessary. Please arrange for a telephone in the main house as well."

Everyone stood, hands were shaken, as Klaus was leaving the study, he turned and looked at Franz.

"Mein Herr, we have prepared a basket for your trip. You will find it in the larder. I will bring the car around now."

CHAPTER 6

All necessities, including the basket, were loaded in the car. With such a short trip it seemed a waste, however, Klaus would be disappointed if it were left. I had drawn the long straw and was firmly in place behind the wheel, much to Franz's displeasure.

"Next time, besides, it is such a short trip, just enough time for a nap," Franz said, moving into a comfortable position, I just laughed.

"Don't get too comfortable, we need to get that wire off to The Earl. When we get to Jenbach, I will stop at the station there," I said, elbowing Franz.

He replied with a grunt and mumbled, "I fail to see how that affects my nap."

"Do you want to come to the house first or shall I drop you off?" I asked.

"No, my mother requested I stay with you tonight," Franz said.

"Then my mother will be expecting you for at least one night? Strange though, Father hadn't said a thing on our last call." Looking at Franz as I said it, I wondered if I should have asked Klaus if there had been word, but surely, he would have said something.

"Your house first then," Franz said.

Instead of obsessing about the lack of information, I turned my attention to the machine Henry had left with me. I had inspected it the other night, alone in the study. It seemed quite straightforward. I could only guess the function of some of the controls though. Without another machine or a manual, it would be hard to work out.

The highest peaks were hidden by ominous-looking clouds as the weather moved in. Since our arrival, we had only received a few scattered snow showers in the valley. We were due for a good round of snow, although I would be just as happy if it would wait. We could squeeze in a short ski trip while we were at Innsbruck. I admonished myself, thinking of all those people in work camps. The plot is playing out to seize my homeland. The tyrant breeding hate, desperately trying to push it throughout Europe. My thoughts turned dark like the clouds rolling along the peaks. So much senseless death and violence, for what? Because someone was a different religion, color, nationality, spoke a different language, wealthy? Why are we unable to look at each other and see fellow human beings? Navigating life carries enough pitfalls without trying to annihilate one another.

Therein lies the caveat though. The problem is not with the other race, religion, or nationality. It lies with the perpetrator, with their ego, shortcomings, trauma, wounds, and self-worth. When you break it down to the very base and look at the raw emotion of self-loathing being reflected in another human, there is almost pity. If only monsters wore signs that read, "I hate myself for (insert reason). Therefore, I will take that out on another human being in (insert the action) way." Alas, the monsters rarely show themselves in the way we believe until it is too late. The sciences of the mind were just putting out such theories and yet it all seemed too glaringly obvious.

Well, now, this is not any better a line of thought than worrying about Father and Mother. The miles sped by, and I tried to focus on the long-term goal of saving those that needed safety. What that looked like, how to accomplish it, the resources I would need, and deciding whether to return to Munich or stay in Vienna. So many forks in the road with no road signs to help. Germany would try to take Austria in the next few months, it was simply a matter of dates now. Convincing Kurt to leave would be folly. Our most valuable contribution would be continued intelligence, as Henry stated. Hopefully, we will be able to prevent bloodshed in some way. Vienna seems the logical choice for now.

"Please, God, when this is over, I would prefer not to attend Vienna again," I said under my breath.

"I would like to second that, God, Amen!" Franz added from where I thought he was asleep in his seat. Sitting up straight, we both made the sign of the cross at the Amen, and light laughter ensued.

There was a sense of excitement to be so close to Innsbruck. We were winding around KaiserJager Strasse, passing cross streets, just one more street, a quick left and there it was, my parents' home. Yes, my home too, but for me, we just left home. The Meadows was home, Innsbruck was the vacation. Innsbruck meant theater, opera, dancing, dinners, socializing, University, Fraternity, mass at St. Jakob's, uniting for common causes, Fatherland Front, skiing.

The Meadows meant comfortable days, runs, skiing, picnics, snowshoeing, hunting, horseback rides, sleighing, fishing, reading, hours in the library on chilly days with hot drinks and fresh baked treats, chess, or of late, planning the safe egress of peoples from Nazi brutality.

Pulling in through the gates and around the drive, Herr Liberman, Frieda's father, opened the front doors just as we stopped. Franz waved him away as he tried to open the car door for him. He immediately headed for the baggage in the trunk. We met him there to retain the small lock box.

"Herr Alexsander, Herr Franz, we are overjoyed you have returned home. Gräf Otto and Gräfin Alexsandra await you both in the sitting room."

We left Herr Liberman to deal with the rest of the luggage. Franz had taken possession of Bauer's basket of food from the backseat and was peaking in it as we entered the house.

Next to the vestibule table stood Frieda, her face crimson, her lips pressed tight. She walked straight up to us. We both braced ourselves for what might come. However, to her credit, she maintained her composure.

"Allow me, Herr Franz," she said as she relieved Franz of the basket. She then turned on her heel and headed down the hall. I looked at Franz, he at me, and we both thought the exact same thing. It would have been better in the long run if she had slapped us.

Entering the sitting room, Mother and Father both stood and greeted us warmly as we crossed the room. Father gave nothing away, but Mother bore a look of repressed tension at the corner of her eyes. We were offered refreshments, everyone was seated, sitting room conversation began things. The weather, Frieda's safe arrival, the "miraculous recovery" of her mother, Mrs. Baumgarten's roses won again this fall, recovery of the local economy although slow was progressing. The conversation continued and time slipped quickly away.

"I am certain both of you would like to freshen up after your trip. We will expect you for dinner in an hour." Mother said it as a statement, which meant go upstairs, clean up and get dressed.

Dutifully, we did as we were told. Arriving upstairs in front of our rooms, I motioned to Franz. We both entered his room, shutting the door quietly behind us.

"Oddly tense, awkward even?" I asked in a hushed tone.

Franz looked around as if the walls were spying and replied,

"Interesting, almost as if there is concern of being overheard?"

We stood uncomfortably for a few minutes wondering what was going on.

"See you in the dining hall shortly," I said in my normal voice. I headed toward the door. Franz nodded, and I slid out and crossed to my room.

Once there, I saw that everything had been unpacked, luggage had disappeared, and personal items were laid out neatly on the vanity. I walked over to the bed, rolled onto it, and lay staring at the elaborate tapestry on the canopy above. It matched the draperies pinned back to the headboard. My mind thumbed through all the conversation, postures, and sideways looks between Mother and Father. There was something amiss. My eyes followed the patterns above while my mind tried piecing all those things together. Then I suddenly recalled seeing the edge of some rough wood poking out from under a drapery across the room. There had been a few pieces of straw on the floor by it. At the time it seemed odd, but I naturally assumed it to be some new item collected by one of them. Packing crates, why were there packing crates hidden behind the draperies?

Where was Frieda? Normally she would have come in by now, ensuring my clothes were hanging properly, buttons, cuff links, shoes appropriately shined....

Well, I was probably running late. I undressed, moved to the bathroom, cleaned up quickly and began to dress when a familiar knock came.

"Enter at your own risk," I said.

Franz stepped in looking around a little surprised.

"Did you dismiss her already?" he asked.

"No, I haven't seen her since we arrived." I shrugged as I answered. We both raised our eyebrows.

"More intrigue is tantalizing, but when it is your daily fare, it isn't nearly as appealing in your safe places." Franz stated snidely. Laughter escaped my lips, and I did not try to suppress it.

"Did you happen to notice the packing crates behind the draperies?" Franz shook his head indicating he had not. The wheels of thought spinning. "Let us see if answers are on the menu, shall we?" as I finished my tie. Downstairs, we were indeed late arriving at the table.

Father gave us both the eyes but said nothing. We seated ourselves, placed our napkins properly and bowed our heads in unison. Father said grace, "Bless us, O Lord, and these, thy gifts, which we are about to receive from Thy bounty, through Christ our Lord, Amen." Protocols observed all around, we turned our attention to the meal. The soup was first served by Herr Liberman. Frieda would deliver items to the dining room, never looking once at either of us, leaving as quickly as she came. Which begged the question of where the missing servants might be? Dinner passed in much the same manner as our time in the sitting room. Somewhere between dinner and dessert, Franz tapped my foot subtly under the table. I looked up without moving my head and caught the direction of his gaze. In the far corner, there was a small wooden crate next to the cabinet holding the antique ornate China pieces passed down from generation to generation. The cabinet, it seemed, no longer held anything in it. There was a slight eyebrow raise, but we said nothing. We retired, not to the sitting room, but to the library, Mother joined us.

"Would anyone care for something?" Father asked as we were taking our traditional seats, everyone declined. An indication everyone was ready to get down to business without saying it. "Alexsander, Franz, we are leaving Innsbruck within the month. We shall pass the new year at the estate in Vaduz." Father paused, awaiting questions, there were none yet, and he continued.

"The Nazi party is firmly entrenched in Austria's political landscape.

Spies are everywhere inciting sedition, reporting on fellow countrymen. Both of you are well aware of the plight of our country and the dark days it will inevitably face going forward." He paused, went to the liquor cabinet, found his favorite liquor, and poured a few fingers before replacing the bottle. He left the cabinet open and took a small sip before continuing. Something passed between him and Mother, and he returned to pour her a smaller amount, delivering it into her hand then kissing her forehead.

"Above all, I will keep my family safe. Something I see as impossible to do remaining here. Franz, we prefer your parents to speak with you, but as you are here, and we are in the thick of it, your family will be accompanying us to the estate." Father looked Franz straight in the face waiting for questions. Franz simply nodded; Father took this as his cue to continue. "The bulk of both family's assets are now out of Austria's hands, as we soon will be. We would urge you both to follow us as soon as possible. I understand how important your work is to you both. Please consider the possible cost it may exact. The price is one neither of your parents' wishes to see you pay." He stared hard at us, took another swallow, set his glass down and retrieved some papers bound in leather jackets. There was one for each of us. "You will both find sufficient assets to keep you well in this country, or any other. We pray you join us soon; however, provisions are made for you both, regardless. Alexsander as you know, The Meadows is yours, there are several documents in the study I will need your signatures on, both of you as soon as we are done here. I would caution you both to keep Klaus and his family foremost in your mind when bringing danger to your door. My dear, would you like to add anything?"

Mother took a sip from her glass, cleared her throat, and began her obviously practiced speech.

"Although it pains me to leave either of you behind, we are aware of the work you are trying to do on Austria's behalf. As important as it seems your family is equally important. I beg of you both to follow us as soon as possible. We have decided to leave this house provisioned sufficiently for use, but all our staff have chosen to accompany us. Your father has indicated the need for you to choose your own staff for security purposes. Of course, you both understand why we must bring everyone away from here. Those who can travel to Vaduz without an escort have been sent ahead to prepare for our arrival. Franz, you who are so very much my son too, your mother and father will shutter the Innsbruck house indefinitely. You are to share this house with Alexsander as you see fit. We pray the allure of this lunatic will pass over quickly and we will be home in time to open the houses up for summer." She finished, shaking her head from side to side just slightly. Acknowledging her disbelief of the events happening in her life.

Franz stood, slowly walked over to Mother, and kissed her hand, saying, "You are as dear to me as my own mother, Auntie, thank you." He headed for the cabinet, pouring two rather generous portions of schnapps, then placed a glass in my hand without inquiry and returned to his seat, taking a bracing swallow from his own.

"Father, do you believe Vaduz will be safer than here? Lichtenstein is an easier target than Austria, perhaps it would be better to acquire a property in Switzerland?" I asked.

"It would seem so, Alexsander, however Lichtenstein is comfortably under the Swiss umbrella. An umbrella painted very clearly neutral with no tolerance for transgression. My sources to date are still reliable. Lichtenstein and Switzerland are both resistant to Hebrew immigrants, as are most in the current climate. Still, there will be no hesitation if they are with our family." Father exuded the confidence of his alliances, many of those through blood relation.

The whole situation brought my blood to boil, and my voice burst forward despite itself.

"The Fatherland Front, the Christian Social Party, even the damn Social Democrats are fighting tooth and nail to keep Hitler at bay." Everyone stared at me as my train of thought raced out of the station. "We have the utmost faith in your conclusions, Father. However, I am compelled to point out the Chancellors' continued diplomacy with President Motta to allow, at the least, Tyrol to fall under this same umbrella with no encouragement from the president hereto. The knowledge is not salon talk, but the interference from Reich pawn Guido Schmidt has undermined every effort with Switzerland. If the Swiss will bow down when Austria is on the verge of being led to the slaughter, who is to say the umbrella of neutrality is not a ruse to mollify Hitler? Falling before the curtain of fascism when push comes to shove. I believe Motta will protect Switzerland at all costs, but Lichtenstein may well be a piece on the board he is willing to sacrifice."

Father stood his ground, his wheels turning as he took in the information.

"Alexsander, Franz, your efforts are not unappreciated in any monarchist household. The danger you have put yourself in these last years does not go unnoticed. The war and make no mistake, we understand this as its own war. The battles you are fighting every day, buys Austria precious extra time." He paced for a moment, finger in the air warning everyone to allow him his thoughts before continuing. "There are no guarantees we will not settle into Lichtenstein only to face the tyrant full on. However, it is the best chance I can offer any of our families to escape what I am afraid, no, what I know, from all your hard work, will be the horror of war. These last years we have prayed those that forced us into acquiescing to the Treaty of St. Germain would hold to their word and not leave us defenseless in the face of tyranny. Whether they turn from us due to the atrocities of the Great War, or as I believe, their fear of the Reich, is not for debate. The fact is, they have turned away from us. France,

England, or America could have intervened at any point since 1934. They not only abandon us, but my colleagues tell me they whisper we are complicit with that little madman. I believe as you both, Austria will fall, and God protect the Chancellor and all Austrians when it happens." Father concluded his views.

"History, I fear, will tell a much darker story than the truth. In all the research being done in the background, we find that although all Austrians are still seeking positive results from these last twenty years, less than a quarter of the country believes Nazism will help. In Tyrol, it is far less than that, as much of Tyrol and the far South continue to be Monarchists. The Chancellor continually reaches out to anyone, even the tyrant to the South, for help, but he is rebuffed at every turn. He has become the anvil being beaten by the hammer; his tempering is failing with every stroke." Franz spoke from the heart, a heavy sadness in his words.

A reverent hush fell over us, a silent salute to a man we all cared for and respected. One who had only Austria's best interest at heart but was far too kind for the job before him. Every one of us would continue in our ways to support him though, until the end and after.

"Franz, your mother asked you to stay with us while you are here. The house is in disarray it seems. They will be over in the morning," Mother said, breaking the spell, the compassion showing clearly on her face.

"Thank you, Auntie, your home has ever been my second home." Franz's voice gave no hint of the sadness I knew he would feel not being able to go home. With another generous swallow of Schnapps, I could almost hear him saying "Damn Nazis!" in his head.

The rest of the evening's conversation involved the logistics of moving an entire household. Seven families in all had met and agreed to work together. If the Nazi presence continued to increase, or lasted for a length of time, anything left or stored could easily be lost. Several held properties in Switzerland, several in Lichtenstein, and those that did not have a property in either location was offered homes on the aforementioned estates. The few that were not relatives were long-standing business associates or brothers in arms from days gone by. All were financially tied to each other. Everyone with Jewish servants or relatives was taking not only themselves but their families with them.

The Von Grünne's estate was here in Innsbruck with a sizable house in Mayrhofen. Much of the furnishings were being transferred to the Mayrhofen property, the rest were being sent to the guest houses in Vaduz.

"Paperwork is the last thing I would care to attend to, however, let us be done with it," Father said.

Mother spread kisses to cheeks, hugs, and wishes for a good night's sleep as she excused herself. Then the men proceeded to the study. A few papers were an understatement. There were directives, deeds, letters of credit, business transfers, note transfers, and the list went on. Father's agent had already "witnessed the signatures," and Franz and I made a joke of thanking his invisible presence each time we signed until the joke wore thin and the paperwork overtook all of us. Father was exceedingly tolerant of all of it, as he was of our choice to remain.

"Father, are you certain you have left something for you and Mother?" I jested as we finished signing the last.

Father sat back heavily in his chair, sipping the last of the drinks from our earlier time in the library.

"Originally, I set out to build on a substantial amount of inherited and earned wealth. Enough to support both of our sons and their heirs and so on. When we lost Otto, it did not detour me from my original intention.

Franz simply took Otto's place over the years. You are both my sons, and you will have the wealth I built for my sons. Our family has a vast number of holdings you still know little of, either of you. Trust me when I tell you, I would never allow your mother, who is also the love of my life, to want for anything. She shall suffer no hardship if I draw breath. That includes my brother and sister-in-law, your parents, Franz." He stood, came around to both of us in turn, and shook our hands, slapped us on the back, and said. "I would never condone the frivolous spending of money! Though, you two gentlemen should go support the local economy tonight, while there is one. No one will be waiting up, so if you do grace the house again tonight, do not wake your mother!" With that, he gingerly crossed the study, and went out the door.

Franz and I stood in the study staring after him.

"Who was that?" he asked.

"I haven't the foggiest idea," I replied shaking my head. "Change into your street clothes, I'll meet you in the vestibule," I said, already heading toward the hall.

CHAPTER 7

As we headed out, not a word was said. I have always wondered if our ability to communicate without words was from growing up together. Or if we operate in some type of parallel reality no one understands yet. Or a little of both. The walk took about twenty minutes at our leisurely pace. Over a year had passed since either of us had been in, and I found myself hoping to find Madame still running the show. We were barely through the door when she saw us both.

"No!! No, no, no, it cannot be!" Madame almost screamed as she rushed over giving both of us hugs, and blatantly kissing us in turn. Entwining her arms around each of ours, she pulled us along into a private receiving room.

"Ages, just ages, why have you deprived us for so long? Brenna, bring the best Schnapps, Lily, hors d'oeuvres" The house has the most beautiful additions since you were last here, my loves." Planting kiss after kiss on each of our cheeks, we were deposited on a large, overstuffed chesterfield. Uncommitted ladies filed into the sitting room, flowing around us and each other. Madame sat between us using a peacock plume fan to give the girls direction, moving them this way and that. A particularly good Schnapps was placed into one hand while a beautiful young girl used my free hand to caress her.

"Stop! Stop! You little minxes, back up, back up, let us see you. My darling Franz and my darling Alexsander are not mere sausages to be flung between your thighs. Tch, tccht, the art of seduction, ladies, the art of seduction. Yes, much better, much better. They are young, you know, difficult to teach patience and finesse to young ones sometimes."

"Well, our darling Alexsander's smitten with an adolescent himself these days," Franz said laughing.

He finished his glass and extended it for more. The glass was instantly replaced with another full glass. The empty was removed and refilled, awaiting.

"No!" said Madame, slapping me with her peacock plumes. "Tell me this is not so, you are my gentleman, my moralitas! You have become a deviant? A young siren has bewitched you. Have you stolen her virtue? Who has done this to you, my darling?"

I rolled my eyes with as much emphasis as possible at Franz. Finishing off my drink, it was of course replaced with another.

"I assure you, Madame Eva, I have yet to deflower an innocent. Although to hear Franz, my horns may be sprouting forth at this very moment. However, the spell was broken by the gallant Franz and my honor was maintained." At which point we all broke out laughing so hard I spilled my drink, which was immediately replaced by a lovely young girl, younger than the one I was accused of deflowering.

"Nonetheless, our dear Alexsander is in desperate need of attention, as are we all, of course," Franz stated with all seriousness.

"We are always at your disposal, my loves, you know you have just to raise your finger and point to be taken to ecstasy for as long as you desire. Franz, I trust you have everything you need right in front of you, but you, my Alexsander, I am afraid the years are piling up. Perhaps we can find someone younger to bring you pleasure." Madame spoke with all seriousness, at the last part, she looked at me longingly, but with a hint of disappointment.

"Madame Eva, I sit beside my desire even now." Madame's eyes lit up like a teenager just asked to prom. Another round of drinks was had while Franz sorted through and found the ones that looked like what he longed for but would never have. I had barely touched this drink, waiting for the preliminaries to be finished. Franz was taken off to the depths of the house, the requested Schnapps and 'hors d'oeuvres' in tow with the three giggling ladies. Madame had one of the girls pour her a small Schnapps.

"Oh, my darling Alexsander, what incredibly different lives we lead. Yet you are so often my desire. It truly has been too long. I am like the virgin herself since last you were here. Often, I reminisce about our first time together, when we were both young. Do you recall?"

"Indeed, I do, just a young pup, wet behind the ears. Completely lost except for my urgent need. Until I saw you, there was something about you, Eva, there is still something about you. You said no mere child would have the favors of the Madame. Off you sent me with that young girl." The words poured from my mouth while my mind was lost in her eyes.

"That silly thing, her yelling because a young man became too aroused his first time, silly slip of a girl." She clicked her tongue, running her fingers through my hair. I handed my drink to the only girl left in our sitting room and we snuggled together like a young couple in love.

"I was so humiliated, and I knew Franz would never let me forget it. You came in, chastised that poor girl, snatched me up in a robe, and dragged me off to your room. It was a night I shall always remember," I whispered to her sweetly, wrapping my arms gently around her waist. Our lips met, passionate, longing, the kiss of two who are intimate with each other's desires and needs. Releasing her, I stood, reached down, and scooped her into my arms.

Always the Madame first, she said, "Perhaps we should bring Olga in case I am unable to fulfill your needs."

I shushed her, glanced at the girl looking hopeful in the chair, and said, "Olga, your mistress will not need you to attend to her any further tonight." With that, I carried Eva up the stairs to Madame's Boudoir.

The morning dawned with a bluebird sky. I lay with Eva in my arms pretending for a moment we two had a different life. Eva was my only regular indiscretion. When I was younger, I had tried again in Munich, Vienna, Switzerland, and of course, the year in England. Each time I had come away feeling cheated somehow, not just for myself either. I felt it for them too, like I had forced them somehow to choose to make their living this way just by utilizing the service. After the first two tries, I stopped for years. Whenever I knew Innsbruck was my destination, I found myself hopeful that Eva would still be there. When love had escaped me all those years ago, and I had finished drowning in sorrow, I ran to Eva.

There was a light knock on the door. Eva sighed and begrudgingly approved the entry. Olga came into the room with a tray of coffee and pastries. She moved a small table next to her mistress's night table, setting the tray on it; ensuring everything was within reach of her mistress. I caught her casting curious glances at me and quickly looking away.

"Herr Franz left a message, he would see you at home later, Herr Alexsander," Olga said quietly, then curtsied, and left the room.

Eva poured coffee into a cup, and I propped myself up in bed, taking it gratefully. She rearranged her pillows and poured herself one, then nestled back toward me. I knew the routine and had my coffee in my right hand already, my left arm curling around her as she lay back. We both sighed audibly, giggled like children, and relaxed into sipping our coffee.

It was I who broke the silence, "Am I amiss in believing Olga is perplexed by my being here?"

Eva drew herself up just a bit as she replied, "One would say she was unaware of her Madame allowing anyone to breach the sanctity of the boudoir."

Something in her voice stirred something within me. I set my coffee on the night table and gently took Eva's cup, placing it next to mine. Rolling her toward me just a bit, I wrapped her in my arms.

"Eva, how long has it been since you have engaged in a liaison with another man?"

Eva looked shocked, and something else I could not discern. Instantly, she was out of my arms, out of the bed looking for something to put on, all while cussing in French. Much of which I understood, however, she did throw out a few new tidbits. As she played her charade, the veil of it fell, and I saw clearly what I should have seen years ago. Madame Evangeline had always been, and still was, in love with me. It was like lightning, why had it never dawned on me? The passion, the tenderness, the caressing, at no other time had anyone ever engaged in these physical delicacies with me. They were all the things I had longed for with someone I could never have. When I let that go, I let it all go, determined to stay alone. The idea that I might have everything I wanted, everything I needed in front of me the whole time.

My side of the bed faced all exits, sliding out quickly I came toward her. She saw me and launched into a new tirade in French.

"You insolent child, how dare you try to manipulate your way into my heart? You petty little prick, get out of my house this instant!"

I grabbed her gently around the waist and kissed her. She feinted pushing away, even punching me lightly in the chest and arm. Then we melted into each other, I gingerly tossed her on the bed and the fight became a passion we both could now openly release.

In the early afternoon, I sent a message to the house that I was detained with business and would not be able to attend supper. The timing was inappropriate, but I did not care. Fresh coffee showed up, and we both enjoyed a toilette together in the giant bathtub usually reserved for patrons. Comfortably dressed in silk loungewear, we got cozy in her small private sitting room and enjoyed an incredibly late breakfast. Well, late for me, Eva, by profession, was required to keep quite late hours. However, she said she would retire at 2 am and kept the habit of being up with the sun to finalize anything needing to be tended to. She would set the schedules for personnel, and doctors' inspections, as she insisted on keeping a "healthy harem" as she put it. Meals were planned, shopping organized, outside entertainment, special guests, etc. Then she would retire for a long nap around nine am, and at two in the afternoon her second day began.

She had been chatting about trivial things when suddenly I felt the need to know. I very simply said, "When?"

She set her plate aside, went to the ewer, washed her hands, and came back to sit in a chair opposite me. She reached her hands out to mine, and I wrapped her deceivingly fragile-looking fingers between my long ones. She cleared her throat, hesitated, and then began.

"When you attended here the very first time, I knew you were dangerous for me. Even then, the ability to separate me from you (heavy sigh), well it was impossible." She stopped, removed her hands from mine, and motioned for a glass of water, which I poured and handed to her. "Still, it was easy enough to fool myself. In those times, you would often be gone for years, and I had a business to run. My… charms, shall we say, have always commanded a much higher price than those of my proteges. Being formally trained at Le Chabanais in Paris has provided gifts that allow me to be a commodity here. In the beginning, it helped me to be actively engaged in my business. Learning to block out what doesn't suit the moment is a helpful skill." Eva sipped some water, set it down, looked at me, then got up and strolled over to look out the window. "When you came to me, brokenhearted, and poured yourself out to me, it shattered any shred of defense my heart had left. Those weeks were some of the happiest and saddest moments in my life. To know that I would never be able to be that love you were mourning was unbearable at times. Being with you, though, brought me such joy I often forgot that you would be gone in the blink of an eye again. It was then that I began to exercise extreme prejudice when offering my skills. Even so, it never again took place here, always in one of the suites. After a time, even that came to a stop. There have been a few times with clients I have had since even before we met, but very few, and only for an obscene price." She turned to look straight into me. "When you were here those weeks, I had a new mattress made. It is the same one now, no one has ever lain in this bed with me but you. Olga has been with me just six short months, therefore seeing you in my boudoir, let alone with me, would have been a shock. This is my sanctuary, where only you and I are ever together." She moved back to sit across from me holding her hands out to mine again. "I am not some foolish young whore who thinks there is a chance for us. I know you will not ride up on a white horse and rescue me from my life as a courtesan. They say the nobility went away in 1919 with the damn treaty, but everyone knows it is not so. You are a nobleman, descended from royalty on both sides, and I am a woman, sold into Le Chabanais at seven years old and trained in the art of pleasure. Sold to the highest bidder when they deemed me an 'appropriate age.' Our love will be kept here for us in safety until I sell this place and find a new chapter for my life." A tear escaped and rolled down her cheek. I quickly reached up and caught it with my finger, kissing it away.

"Please, come here with me." I gathered her to me on the small lounge and held her for a long time. The soft silent sobs slowly died away. I handed her my small linen towel from our breakfast and felt her dry her eyes, sniffling softly. Pulling her close, I quietly said, "No, there is no grand church wedding where we invite half the country, and you walk away the new Gräfin Evangeline Von Rieser. However, there are other ways for us to live happily if you are willing to settle for less. We may still be married, we just would not be able to do it in the eyes of God, which I do not believe requires the church or a priest. It also would prevent you from carrying any titles, however…"

Eva broke in to say, "I don't give a damn about marriage or titles, most of our clients are married, many are nobility."

I hugged her a bit and shushed her, continuing, "A mistress is quite a common thing, even among Catholics, as you well know. If you wish to continue your business until you decide you are done, that is also an option. There are no conditions on my feelings, Eva." I swung around to look her in the eyes saying, "and no judgments at all, I love you for you, Eva, all of you, all of it! I fell to my knees, took her hands, and said, "Evangeline, will you spend the rest of my life with me on your terms?" Eva fell into me crying, and I held her until we collapsed on the floor.

After supper, we went out for a stroll, sneaking out and around the avenue to come from a more appropriate place. It was the first time we had ever been outside of the property together, yet it felt perfectly natural. Eva's steps matched my stroll. Light snow began to fall, flakes slowly drifted down, kissing her face before they disappeared. Over the day I had completely forgotten everything in my life. Walking outside, the spell of being alone with Eva lifted. The reality of the world and the game I play in it interfering. Of course, if she were to be a more serious part of my life, she needed to understand the position in which I would be placing her. As we strolled along the Inn River listening to the gently moving water, a better opportunity was unlikely.

"Eva, there are some things you must know. Please allow me to explain most of this before we discuss anything. Everything I am about to disclose must remain in confidence. In 1934, a group of us was approached to assist in gathering information regarding Germany's newest Chancellor. Our group already had a vested interest since an incident in 1923, for reasons I will not elaborate on now. Therefore, when we were approached about doing this for our country, it simply meant moving our focus a bit. With the attempted coup, our focus was already shifting, so it all went hand in hand. There are things I am unable to tell you, not because I do not trust you. On the contrary, I trust you implicitly, but in this case, the less you know, the more believable you would be if pleading innocent should it become necessary." I stopped and turned to look at her under a streetlamp. The beauty of her eyes still captivated me.

"Franz and I, as well as several others, are in harm's way and will continue to be. There is no help for it, we are in the thick of things now. The Nazi threat is very real, and they will take Austria, sooner, I fear, rather than later," I concluded in a very low tone.

We began walking slowly again. She nestled farther into my arm.

"Are you cold, my dear? We will turn back whenever you like," I said, concerned.

She smiled and replied sweetly, "The hands of Monsieur Frost are nothing. It is bliss to walk with you here, together, pray continue."

"There is every reason to believe within the next few months the Nazi presence here will grow significantly. It is of the utmost importance to help those of Hebrew descent find ways away from here while they still can. Even now, countries are turning Jewish migrants away. Finding places for them to go is becoming the hardest part. England and America are some of the best options, but both require traveling through other countries to obtain passage. I will not bother you with logistics. I just need you to understand the danger we are all in. You see, my darling, our precarious social situation may not matter one bit very shortly."

Bringing her under the safe harbor of a large conifer, I looked down into her eyes, with the best pleading look I could manage, and said, "Above all, I would like you to stay safe, therefore please consider what I am asking. Would you be willing to leave the country?"

Her mouth parted, her face showing a stunned look, something I never thought to see.

I continued quickly, "Of course, we will have someone look after the business for you. I should just like to see you safe. Leaving the country may be too much to ask right now. You could stay at my estate just a short way from here. Close enough to run things, but not actually be in the city."

Recovering herself immediately, she pulled my face closer to hers. Placing a light kiss on my lips, she hovered there and began to speak, under her breath.

"Alexsander, do you not see the leverage my business gives you? The Nazis will frequent the brothel, as they already do when they come on holiday. Men say many things when they are properly motivated during the heat of sex."

I stared at her, stunned. It had never even crossed my mind.

"It would be far too dangerous, my dear, if caught..."

"Men do not even remember the things they say when the time is right. Think about those moments when you are on the brink and then pulled back, over, and over," she cut me off.

She looked into my eyes as I thought deeply about what she was saying. She was right, overall, it could serve as the strangest most covert interrogation technique we would ever devise. It might be possible to determine troop movement, unit deployment, and future targets. The possibilities were laid out before me like a road map. I filed this information away to contemplate later. We looked around subtly, saw nothing, and stepped out from the conifers.

We resumed our walk, enjoying the still quality the snow brought to the night. Approaching St. Jakob Cathedral, Eva slowed. I was admiring the architecture as always; however, I sensed a different feeling entirely coming from Eva.

"What is it, my dear?" I inquired.

"It is nothing, amour, we shall go back now."

Taking her hands in mine, I faced her.

"Secrets will not do, we have wasted years already, let us treasure the time we have together. Honesty, always, there is nothing I would judge you for Eva. Please, confide in me what bothers you as we stand here in front of St. Jakob."

"May we?" she said, motioning toward the Cathedral.

I was a bit surprised but escorted her up the stairs, we both stopped to light a candle in the vestibule and proceeded in. In perfect time, we both knelt slightly, made the sign of the cross, and stood looking at each other. She smiled a sly smile, I wanted to pat her on the rump, but under the circumstances.

She chose a pew close to the back, we sat quietly next to each other. Each in our thoughts. Where the vision came from, I could not say, suddenly I saw Eva at the age when I first met her. Clear as day I was standing at the front of the church, Franz, Karl, and Wilhelm beside me. We were surrounded by hundreds of relatives, colleagues, and friends. In my vision stood Evangeline, dressed in the loveliest pink gown, veils, bows, ribbons, and a plunging neckline framing a large bouquet of star lilies. The pinks in the lilies matched perfectly with parts of the dress, tiara, and veils. At that moment, God was acknowledging what should be able to take place in his house.

I looked at Eva and saw tears streaming down her face. I handed her my handkerchief.

"Let me describe to you the vision I just saw. I am there, just to the right of the altar, wearing the finest formal suit money could procure here. The church is full to the brim, but the only vision I see is you. You begin toward me carrying star lilies in a large bouquet. Every part of your luxurious gown matches some part of the pink in the lilies. You are wrapped in lace, bows, silk, ribbons, and veils. On your head, you wear a tiara, made just for you, ringed in pink gemstones. Your lustrous hair is piled high on your head but falling seductively in just the right ways. There has been no more beautiful bride throughout time. The love you spark within me consumes me."

Eva sat, slightly aghast, tears gently falling from her eyes, staring at me. Suddenly, she threw her arms around me and held me tight, her face tucked into my shoulder. Then she wiped her eyes, stuck my handkerchief in her sleeve, and stood up, waiting for me to escort her out.

The walk back began quietly holding each other, reveling in some mysterious moment of magic we had been blessed with. Suddenly, she broke away and ran to some bushes. It caught me off guard, still slightly under the spell of the church, until I was hit squarely in the face with a snowball. Running into the little park by the river Inn, I gathered snow and reciprocated. We played in the snow until we were laughing so hard neither of us could breathe. Eva complained of the tightness of her corset. I generously offered to divest her of it there and then.

Upon arriving in the boudoir, hot cocoa, and peppermint schnapps were ordered with a light snack. Olga delivered the tray as we finished changing, piling pillows up by the fireplace. We spoke long into the night about the things lovers speak of, also of conspiracy and clandestine operations.

In the morning, the day started in bliss, we were out of bed at dawn. She had to begin her morning tasks and I needed to get back to the house.

The house was in all-out chaos when I arrived. Everything was the opposite of the polite facade put on for us when we had arrived the previous day. Crates were being packed everywhere. Movers were making quite short work of it. I found my father in the study with Franz, hiding, it seemed.

"Ah! There he is. Were you able to save the world?" my father winked at me and went straight on sorting through a pile of papers. "I had thought to leave books at least, but upon further contemplation, it doesn't seem prudent if those rascals go crazy once they take over." Father looked up at me as if in inquiry, although I knew he truly was not asking.

"Yes, I quite agree," I said, and looked over at Franz who still seemed a bit off. "If you gentlemen will excuse me, a bit of exercise and then a change of clothes are in order," I said, winking at Franz.

"If that exercise involves a saber, I am right behind you," Franz added eagerly.

Off we went to our rooms, and after changing, we went to the atrium with our gear and got to it.

"Sabers at the ready," I said, presenting.

Franz countered with, "En guard!" followed immediately with, "Allez!" He lunged straight in allowing me a quart touch. We went through that routine three times, on the third, he finally allowed one parry before I scored Septime. Walking over to the table, I removed my mask and set my saber in place.

"Would you care to talk about it or would you rather I continue to kill you? Fencing would imply we fence, not just stab the same person over and over. Hardly any challenge in it for me currently." I said.

Franz walked over to the saber rack, forcefully set his mask down, placed his saber in the guard, and turned suddenly.

"Yes, bad form, Sandy, perhaps boxing would have been the ticket!"

"Fritzy, something has been eating at you since Vienna. I know you well enough to understand some of it, but not everything."

Franz stared at me hard, anger, hatred, and sorrow all playing through his eyes at once. Then he turned and began pacing again.

"Wilhelm has arrived in Vienna to keep an eye on things until our return, Sandy. The news is bad, in addition to the forced appointment of Nazi officials, Ribbontrop is threatening a forced takeover if a peaceful transition is not on the table soon. That would all seem quite enough, however, Wilhelm is onto another assassination plot. The others are coming in from Munich, Karl will be in tonight." Franz ran his hands through his hair, frustration plain on his face, he continued though. "The meeting went well this morning though; my parents are leaving at the end of the week. They asked me to accompany them of course. Mother used tears to tug at my sense of duty. I agreed to escort them to Vaduz but assured them I would need to return immediately." He continued his pacing, stopping occasionally as if to reorient himself.

"Well, we knew they were ramping up efforts," I rejoined.

I heard footsteps approaching, we switched to a casual conversation about our fencing or lack thereof. Herr Liberman approached us.

"Herr Alexsander, a telegram has just arrived."

"Thank you!" I replied. Upon handing me the telegram, he immediately returned to his duties.

DEAR JIM, THE GIFT YOU SENT IS BEING DELIVERED IN THE MORNING STOP IT MUST HAVE BEEN IMPOSSIBLE TO PROCURE MANY THANKS STOP DANGEROUS WEATHER BREAKING LOOSE HERE WILL CHECK IN SOON STOP

"Some good news at least, the Eigners are safe. He is right about the weather though. Then you will leave at the end of the week... You should stay with your family for a while, Fritzy, and take a break. With Christ Mass coming and St. Stephens, our families will be thrilled if you stayed. Things are liable to be rough these next few months. Some rest certainly is in order," I said, folding the telegram and placing it in my scabbard for now.

"I will consider it, Sandy, but only if you stay away from Vienna until I return." Franz stared hard at me, continuing, "On your honor, you will not go anywhere near Vienna without me."

I considered what he was asking, there was the possibility that it would be necessary to return before he could. With Karl, Wilhelm, and the others in Vienna, it seemed unlikely though.

"Well, Fritzy, I will promise you this, I will not leave for Vienna without telling you first, will that do?"

Franz hesitated, stuck out his hand, and we shook on it.

"You should come along, Sandy, it would do you some good too." He looked at me as he was saying it and leaned in, squarely eye to eye. "Family gatherings would seem to pale in comparison though when faced with a choice between a certain level of ecstasy and listening to our families for two weeks." He broke out in laughter, I grabbed my mask and saber and stepped around.

"Sooner or later, Fritzy, you have to get it off your chest, or I may kill you, en guard!" I said, and we spent the morning getting the workout we both needed.

I would regret those words the next day.

CHAPTER 8

As both houses were being furiously packed up and shipped off, we found ourselves in the way. Fritzy suggested some exercise up the mountain. The summit was reporting a fresh ten inches with pleasant weather through the afternoon. Franz's prodding and temptation won out at last, and I found myself on the way up the mountain in full gear. Frieda still had not uttered a word to either of us, but as we were leaving, a basket full of food appeared. Judging from the contents, it was the basket Klaus had sent with us. I had sent word to Eva hoping she would sneak away, but she declined, requesting another trip a little farther away. I sent word back to plan a trip to Mayrhofen for the coming week, as her schedule allowed.

The conditions were ideal, we took the low run first for a warm-up. On the second run, we went all the way to the top, wagers being made the entire ascent. The sky was a clear baby blue, the powder on top perfect. With Fritzy having already taken the win for the first run, I had the determination to take him on this one. We started at a count of three.

Flying down the run, I felt free for the first time in months, years. Straight lining brought me down faster than I wanted to admit possible. Before I realized it, the run-out was in front of us.

"YEAH!" I shouted, barely crossing the end marker before Fritzy face-planted me for my trouble. It was worth it though. Like two kids, we could not wait to get back to the top.

Early afternoon brought clouds massing on the peaks north of us and marked an end to the trip. Truth be told, we were beat and happy for the basket of food and a beer. Being Austrian, my aversion to beer seemed almost criminal, but it simply never appealed to me. When necessary, I could push myself to drink a half pint or so. It took some real effort on my part though. Instead, I would opt for other libations. Just now, water was sweet nectar from the gods.

We made short work of our lunch and headed back to Innsbruck. Franz drew the straw for the trip. I almost passed out in the passenger seat when he dropped the bomb.

"So, you finally figured it out."

He said it like I understood exactly what he was talking about. I lay against the seat trying to decide if I wanted to sit up or just engage in a relaxed position. Better judgment warned me to sit up. I stretched my overtaxed muscles and sat up, ready to duel.

"You have baited the hook, accept this gesture as me grabbing your line and running upstream," I said, looking at the clouds rolling along the peaks, edging their way down the slopes.

"You dope! Eva! You finally figured out why you couldn't stay away from her."

I sat up farther, moving my left leg onto the seat and turning my body so I could look full on at him.

"Fritzy, how the hell do you know anything about Eva?" Considering our track record, it put me off thinking he knew or had known for any amount of time.

"Only twice in our entire lives have I ever seen you pining for a woman. Anytime we are away for more than a few months you start… 'When we get back, I'll go see Madame, I wonder when we'll be back so I can go see Madame, I wonder if Madame is still there.' It does not matter that there are houses at your disposal all over Europe, you only want to be here. I thought you would never figure it out!" Franz said, rolling his eyes.

"You knew, you knew, and you never said a word? You knew when, when...." My throat closed off; I could not say it. My throat burned like liquid fire tears were behind my eyes, and rage swelled in my chest. "Stop the car!" I said in a voice that did not even sound like mine.

Franz pulled over. I got out, grabbed my coat, and started walking. Fritzy drove up beside me with the window down.

"Come on, Sandy, get in the car."

I ignored him and kept walking. I do not know how long it was before he gave up and drove off.

Women were a problem when we were younger. Inevitably, we always fell for the same girl. In time, we would let the girl choose, of course, the girl had no idea, or if they did, they never let on. There was never anyone serious, as usual with us, the competition and the challenge became the catalyst. At 26, in the middle of a ski holiday, we met her. Amalia Maria Magdalene Von Steiner, the most beautiful woman I have ever known. Fritzy felt the same way of course. There was a meeting over hot schnapps in front of the fire in our suite. All bets were off, every man for himself, and luck to both! Her Brown hair glistened, her lips were perfectly shaped, and her hazel eyes showed the light of a million stars. Listening to her voice brought a feeling of love to my chest, words fail me even now.

But Amalia fell madly in love with Franz.

Franz understood my plight, he struggled with the hurt I felt, mingled with his love for Amalia. I left for Innsbruck immediately, truly wishing him the best but needing to escape. Months went by, I took a sabbatical from my internship at Innsbruck University. Franz reached out often, genuinely concerned, even offering to walk away. Absurd! The blessing of love is a raffle we often do not win. Franz and Amalia both won a gift not to be discarded. Within that first month, the dreaded question came. Best man, best man at the wedding of the woman haunting my mind. Of course, I would accept the obligation of best man. When was the wedding? Where? We must celebrate the bachelor's holiday before. Fortunately, it would be months away still, with two families from minor nobility, formalities would drag the timeline like a tiny barge tugging an overloaded ship.

Eva lingered in my mind in those dark days, but somehow, I could not bring myself to go to her. Instead, Switzerland became my immediate destination after the wedding news. Unbeknownst to me, my parents followed close behind. The entire world seemed in crisis, a mirror of my embodiment. My continuing goal inadvertently became transmuting myself into a bottle of alcohol, no matter the type. Less than a week after my arrival, Father, accompanied by his manservant and several other gentlemen I had never seen before, barged into my suites, packed me up, and pushed me into a carriage, gifting me and my screaming head a seemingly endless ride to the Villa we would be staying at. I was pounced upon, hauled to a large bath, scrubbed head to toe, dressed, given hair of the dog, thankfully, and presented to all just in time for supper. After supper, my mother forgot her normal departure and joined my father and me in the drawing room. Surprisingly, a very generous portion of honey liquor found its way to my hand courtesy of my Father. He had acquired a taste for it in his youth. Rarely had I observed him partake, but tonight he held an equally generous portion. The shock came when he handed my mother the same. A memorable family moment was about to happen in 3, 2, 1... Father's posture became statuesque as he began the practiced speech.

"Son, you credit the name Von Rieser. The actions you have taken throughout your life serve as a model for others. We take considerable pride in your life and the achievements thereof. The recent developments in the Dolomites are unfortunate on your part. However, as your parents, we have ever sought to impress upon you the unforeseen consequences of the wrong left turn, as it were. We are led to understand the young lady betrothed to Franz never had intentions for anyone else?"

It was obvious from the tone that this was posed as a question, and they both looked at me waiting for a reply. The words hurt as they passed my lips.

"No, Amalia never made any pretense of having the slightest interest in me."

The pain must have been visible as Mother averted her moist eyes and Father, very discreetly, cleared a tightened throat.

"Alexsander, your recent lack of standards is understandable had the young lady trifled with you at any point, love is something we deeply understand," he cast a glance at Mother, "but we also understand the damage it may wreak under these circumstances. Therefore, you shall convalesce here at the Villa for as long as necessary, out of the public view. Your Mother and I will remain with you for any support you may need; but Alexsander," he dropped his voice low and looked straight into my soul, "do not drown in your sorrow. The body requires breath to live."

As if emphasizing his point, both downed the entire contents of their glasses. Mother, slightly breathless, came over, kissed my cheek, and whispered in my ear.

"We will retire now, we love you, Alexsander."

With that they were gone, shoes clicking up the stairs.

I took my glass, finished filling it, as the honey liquor had become a favorite of mine also, and stepped out into the night air to drown. The moon was almost full, sleek, and lovely in her grace. Turning a lounge chair toward the moon, I sat down to look forlornly at another lady I would never touch. Halfway through my glass, my father's manservant inquired after my needs. I assured him there was nothing he could satisfy, and he retired for the night.

Only when Otto passed had there been a deep sadness from either of my parents. Tonight, would indeed be one for the records. Throughout my life, they had supported, suggested, and spun tales regarding morals, consequences, and outcomes. The solemnity of what had just transpired was anything but lost on me. I rose and walked to the edge of the veranda, looking longingly at the white lady in the sky. I slowly poured the rest of the expensive glass of honey liquor over the railing. Whispering to her, "My only true love."

I entered the drawing room, turned the glass upside down on the tray, and went up to bed. I lay on top of the covers with the curtains wide, bathing in the love of the lady that would ebb and flow through the rest of my life. She took pity on this poor mortal man as he bathed in her caresses, falling asleep in her embrace; perhaps Amalia was an infatuation made more appealing by her unavailability. I prefer to believe my lovely lady moon healed me in exchange for my expression of devotion. Whichever it was, the morning dawned on a ravenous appetite and the question to my parents in between bites.

"May we please just go home?"

A look passed between them never observed by me before, it felt like love jumping into joy's arms.

I had taken up my post at university again when I returned to Innsbruck, but not before taking comfort from Madame for a few weeks. Then off and on for some months after. Looking back, he was not wrong, my core feelings for Eva were almost identical to my feeling for Amalia. With a caveat, my feelings for Eva were intimate, solid, and unwavering.

To this day, I still feel the same way for Amalia as I always had. Now though, in the light of the truth, those feelings had always been there for Eva. I simply knew being with her was impossible, therefore I never took the time or the chance to entertain anything more.

"Jesus, Mary and Joseph, I am such a child," I said to no one.

Looking around for the first time in what seemed forever; I tried to get my bearings. Christ, it was raining, how long had it been raining? Irritated, chilled, and a little off-kilter, I stopped, and just took a few breaths for a minute. My eyes closed, and I heard the distinct sounds of an ale house. Just down the road a bit. I was just walking across their lot when my car pulled up next to me.

"Sandy, just get in will you, we'll work this out," Franz said.

I looked at him, but the rage was burnt out, gone. I climbed into the passenger side feeling cold, wet, and betrayed as we headed home. How the bath was hot and ready for me, I do not know, but it was. I saw no one when I came in, went upstairs, stripped, and climbed into the bath. The comfortable warmth enveloped me. Then Fritzy barged in pulling a chair and table up to the tub. He retrieved a tray prepared by the same mysterious person I assume prepared the bath. He gingerly set the tray on the table and took a seat.

"We are bathing together now?" The words took on a snide tone as they left my mouth.

"Well, if you'd like, but it will be tight, let me get undressed first," Franz said as he stood up and began taking off clothes.

"Stop, please, Franz, just leave me in peace."

"No, Sandy, no I will not leave you in peace, I will not leave you period, just as you never leave me when I need you," Franz said with fierce determination, staring at me. "Here, just drinks the damn thing!" Franz said, handing me a hot peppermint Schnapps.

I had to admit it hit the spot.

"How could I know, Sandy, how could I know how you would feel about her too? Neither of us could know. At first, I thought it was infatuation. If you could see the way you are when you are with Eva. On some level, it did not seem possible to feel the way you did for her and still fall for someone else. Then, when it happened, when your depth of feeling hit me, I realized you had no idea about your feelings for Eva. None."

I started to interrupt.

"No, let me finish my thoughts, it has taken years to find the words. I love you, Sandy, you are my brother, my twin, the other half of me. How was I supposed to tell you that you really love another, and you cannot have her either? Even if by some fluke you had listened, what would you have done? What could you have done? You are thirty-five, Sandy, you are secure in yourself, your station, your faith, would you have been able to love her at twenty-six?" Franz sat back as he finished speaking. He ran his hands through his too-long blond hair, poured another schnapps, and leaned back heavily in the wing chair he had dragged in next to the tub.

Suddenly, like a madman, I was struck by the scene. Me, naked in the tub, Franz in a wing chair crammed in next to the tub, and a reading table with a platter atop crammed in between the tub and chair. Laughter consumed me, all I could do was laugh, before I knew it, Fritzy was laughing right along with me. We laughed until we cried, stopped, started, and laughed some more. Our ribs hurt by the time we were able to stop. We sat quietly, staring at each other. Franz spoke first.

"Sigmund Freud has some interesting theories on what just happened."

"Let me guess, a minor psychotic break resulting in an uncontrollable release of penile frustration?" I said.

We both started to laugh again but had to stop.

"For God's sake hand me a towel and let's find some food!" I said, draining the tub and standing up.

We ended up at a favorite supper house by the plaza. Orders were placed, and we relaxed in the quiet corner we had asked for.

"You know me better than I know myself in some ways." I was looking across the room as I said it, watching people interact with each other. Spotting their habits, their patterns, and nervous behaviors.

"As you do me," Franz replied, also observing the room.

"I would have destroyed her, would have blamed her, accused her of...of tricking me, trapping me, wanting my wealth. Anything that would have driven her from me forever, knowing I couldn't be with her, couldn't bring her home, marry her, parade her around in the way she deserves." I looked over at Franz as I said it, shame filling me, I went back to observing the room.

Franz swirled his drink, still watching everything around us.

"If it had gone the other way, you would have devastated them both. Eventually, Eva would have overshadowed her. She would never have been able to live up to the goddess firmly entrenched in your heart." He sighed a heavy, hurt filled sigh, continuing, his voice almost breaking, "Her very temperament was a gentle summer breeze. Eva is a whirlwind of fire; it would have broken you after you broke both of them."

He swallowed the contents and motioned for another. The thoughts formed into words behind his eyes.

"When you went to Switzerland," he continued, "I had the ticket to follow you, but Uncle Otto said 'no,' he would not allow me to go. 'Spend time with your betrothed,' he said, 'enjoy the chaos of insanity you are both about to experience before you settle down.'"

Franz's drink arrived with the hors d'oeuvres we had ordered. He woofed down several and resumed.

"Uncle Otto did not know, but we were set to call the whole thing off if you and I were unable to overcome the wedge. I would not settle for one or the other. We made a promise to each other, you, and I, when we were young, a promise that has carried us through everything in our lives. As long as I breathe, my oath will remain whole." He stared at me, laughed, and looked back at the people getting on with their lives. "I hear what you're thinking, Sandy, we both know you would have done the same for me. So, climb down from the cross you are erecting in your soul. Christ already owns that property." We stared at each other; a small laugh escaped me.

Dinner came with a beautiful steak, side dishes covering the table. The thought we would never eat all of this was on the tip of my tongue. However, our last meal was a light snack on the slopes. I even made a good showing, wiping out the steak and finishing several helpings of sides. The waiter came back to check on us and looked surprised. "Skiing!" I said, and he assured us they were able to provide additional items if needed. We both chuckled as he moved away.

I gave up while Franz scraped the bowls clean.

"A heavy burden to carry for nine years," I said as he pushed his plate back.

"Is it, Sandy? Is it heavier than the burdens you carry for me?" Franz replied with a question, looking at me intensely.

"I suppose it isn't, Fritzy, but it certainly makes you a disagreeable fuck at times."

We both laughed, relaxation slowly seeping back in. Much to Franz's delight, the dessert tray arrived, leaving one of each, at his request. For an unknown reason, this caught the attention of all the patrons in the vicinity. We both smiled our most brilliant smiles, and everyone turned away. Which prompted more laughter from us. The waiter returned to check on us, bringing a hot buttered rum for each of us, compliments of Herr Schumacher's table, current Governor of Tyrol.

Franz inclined his head, as Schumacher was in his field of view.

"Looks like both of our parents, along with other members of the front are there. They are just off the main dining area in a private salon." Franz said, smiling and talking.

"I quite prefer to remain seated here, thank you." I said watching Franz for cues.

"Well, no one waved us over or inclined we should volunteer, oh there we are, they have closed the doors, off the hook." Franz said, his shoulders relaxing.

Time ticked by the crowd had thinned, and we were both enjoying coffee. Still occupying our spectators' playground.

"Will she renounce her lifestyle and seek absolution from his holiness?" Franz threw it like a trump card.

I stared at him, unsure of how to reply. I had not even thought of it. Second, I doubted very seriously she would feel she needed to be absolved of a life she was forced into. Lastly, and more importantly, marriage was not a condition she seemed inclined to.

"Gaining absolution may not be a pursuit she finds worthwhile." But even as I said it, I realized where he was headed with this.

"Yes, I will be your best man, regardless of the official capacity of the relationship. However, take the time to consider all the implications and the people they will affect. It is easy to take on, the you-and-me-against-the-world persona when you have nothing to lose in life. However, we are not afforded that luxury. We will not stop being held to standards because we are in love."

Franz sounded so very much like my father as he spoke the words. But he was correct, I glanced back at the closed doors of society behind me.

> *I too pass from the night,*
> *I stay a while away O night,*
> *but I return to you again and love you.*

Why should I be afraid to trust myself to you?
I am not afraid, I have been well brought forward by you,
I love the rich running day,
but I do not desert her in whom I lay so long,
I know not how I came of you,
and I know not where I go with you, but
I know I came well and shall go well.

I said it quietly, only Franz to hear the truth of it.

"Perhaps, if we form a united front and speak with her together, she will understand the gravity of the situation," Franz said.

"'Our love will be kept here for us in safety until I sell this place and find a new chapter for my life.' Those were her words to me, she understands the situation all too well, she has for years."

The bill was paid, and we began the walk home. The air was cold, we walked in silence, pulling our coat collars up and our hats down. Upon arriving, we both went to the study, built up the fire, and pulled the lone remaining chesterfield close to the flames. We lay back, each at our own, established end. So much still needed to be said, discussed, and worked through. I still had not relayed Eva's idea for extracting information from those patrons belonging to the Reich. I also needed to discuss the possibility of needing to move two Jewish girls who worked in her establishment out of the country. My mind worked through all the things we needed to talk about.

CHAPTER 9

The face before me was laughing, an evil, menacing laugh. He had something I needed, but what? He just kept taunting me with his laugh,

"Who are you?" I insisted.

He was shorter than me with blue eyes and blond hair. He just kept laughing, and I grabbed him by the shoulders, shaking him hard.

"Who are you?" I screamed.

"Sandy, wake up, SANDY!" Fritzy was saying as he flew backward to dodge my punch. I came clear off the chesterfield, swinging for his face. He approached me slowly, hands up in a gesture of acquiescence.

"Easy, Sandy, it's me, you understand? It's Franz."

I sat down, dazed. He approached me slowly, watching. He left for a few minutes before returning with a glass of water. I gulped it gratefully, trying to remember who the face belonged to, and what it looked like. Do I know this person?

"You spooked me there, you were screaming at me, 'who are you?' I woke up, and you just kept saying it louder and louder, thrashing around," Franz said looking concerned, visually checking me.

"I think there is a little too much going on in our lives right now. I'm not suggesting you come with me, I'm telling you, come with me to Vaduz."

Franz stared at me as he squatted down in front of me. We were both still in our dinner clothes, what time was it?

"No, I'm....I'm good! It was just a nightmare. A weird nightmare, I have had it before, it just seemed so real this time. What time is it?" I asked.

He stood and backed off a little way looking down at me.

"It's half of 7, we passed out, it seems, and slept the whole night," Franz said looking at his watch.

My watch, yes, I looked at my watch, it was 6:37 in the morning, wow.

"How about some coffee in my room?" I suggested.

"I'll meet you up there."

Franz watched me for a minute before heading off to the kitchen. Hopefully, he was having someone make it, his coffee either ended up burnt or light brown.

As I made my way up the stairs, I noticed from the mezzanine window that the fog had lifted. Sore muscles complained about sleeping propped up and skiing. After some coffee, I would stretch them out. I made my way to the bathroom, undressed, and had a brief toilette. I was shaving when Frieda appeared with the coffee. She came straight to the bathroom, brought her face around to mine, looked me over, said nothing, and then left. Well, I suppose that meant we were gaining ground with each other. I dressed in fresh clothes, poured a cup of coffee, and walked to the window. Oh, thank the Lord, Frieda had made the coffee. I sipped at it gratefully while looking out at the new snow delicately blanketing the street below.

After my second cup of coffee, I rang Karl up in Vienna. They were having considerable luck baiting Nazis with the R.H. Plan 3documents that had been gathering dust, waiting for my cousin to deal his hand. We had

---

[3] Rudolph Hess, the Führer's Deputy, planned coup accusing Chancellor Schuschnigg of multiple violations of the Austrian-German agreement.

procured copies by nefarious means, knowing the manipulation that had been occurring with some of the officials closest to him. What his kindness stopped him from seeing, we saw all too clearly. Where his heart drew lines not to be crossed, we straddled them dragging traitorous scum out of their nests to be used, reformed, or disposed of. Unfortunately for fanatics, reformation was rarely an option. The news was the same, three plans still in play with the intelligence still pointing to Hitler accusing Austria of violating the treaty and Hess beginning to stir up riots, at which time, Germany would benevolently swoop in to rescue poor Austria.

On the positive side, we were finally getting firmer dates. February was beginning to emerge as a primary target. Which meant unrest would accelerate by the end of January.

It was already December 11, 1937, our clock was ticking quickly. We needed the family settled so we could focus on helping to quell the threat, or at the very least, getting as many of them out as possible. I rang Eva up before she would turn in for the day and set up a meeting with her to go to Mayrhofen, asking her to decide to stay until Monday. We set up a plan that would allow her to get away under cover. Then a call to Klaus to have The Meadows ready for the short stay. I wrote several pieces of correspondence and prepared two telegrams, both to The Earl, but one expressly meant for Henry. I went about some general stretching and then sat down for some breathing and focus.

Franz walked in just as I was getting back up. He looked around.

"Well, I see you are quite recovered. Get me up to speed, would you?"

I ran over everything I had discussed with Eva. His parents were not leaving until Wednesday, so he would join forces with me at Mayrhofen. Then we spoke of the possibility to use Eva's ladies in our efforts, and the two Jewish young ladies in her establishment who needed safe passage. We came up with an idea to get them out immediately, although no one would like it, including them. He went over the telegrams from me to ensure they were properly coded. Then I phoned them in.

"Frieda popped in with more coffee.

"I told her you were shell shocked upon waking and asked if she would be able to get your coffee up to your room as soon as possible. She looked at me with a concerned look and waved me away, not a word. She also did not look at me like she was going to skin me either, progress."

I paced the window saying, "We are going to have to find at least one staff member when they leave, someone we can trust implicitly."

"I'll put some feelers out," Franz was saying, he looked at me and added, "in all of this information, what are you not saying?"

I turned to look him in the eye, "I need to get back up to Vienna, just for a few days." Figuratively, he shot me, using a look, and walked out of the room.

When we were young, Li, the master our fathers had brought in to train us before we were taken off to gymnasium,4 would dump an entire jar of mustard seeds on the floor and walk away when we quarreled. We then would have no choice but to pick up every single one, with no container to put them in. It took both of us, one to hold the seeds and one to pick them up. If we cheated, he would knock them out of our hands, and we would begin again. He would even use us against each other, but in the end, we were taught to rely on each other. Not just on the physical being but on opinions, hunches, and feelings. These were the lessons that guided us through our lives, war, schooling, friendships, espionage, and even love. At this moment, Li had just knocked the seeds out of our hands, because I had cheated.

---

4. Gymnasium is a term in various European languages for a secondary school that prepares students for higher education at a university. It is comparable to the US English term preparatory high school.

An hour later, Father rang for me. I found him in the sitting room with Mother.

"We were told you had an episode this morning. Are you quite all right?" Mother said, coming over to give a cursory examination.

"Just a nightmare. I assure you, nothing to worry about," I replied.

"You have never been prone to nightmares before, except for the war, I suppose, but that is to be expected." He was eying me too, not concerned as much as suspicious.

"Why has Franz cancelled the escort of his parents to Lichtenstein?" my father asked. They were both staring at me, waiting. I began to answer when my father squared himself and said, "And Do Not Put This Back on Him!"

I sighed heavily and walked slowly to the fireplace.

"Things are transpiring currently in Vienna. Franz swore me to an oath that I would not go to Vienna until he returned. However, the vermin refuse to wait until our family's plans are concluded to continue their systematic subversion of Austria," I said, trying to keep all emotion from my voice.

"Austria's requiem is coming, and we shall attend it as a widow in mourning for her lost love, with remorse, reverence, and respect. Pray we will not have to attend yours beside her," Father said and left the study.

Mother was dabbing her eyes and starting to follow Father, she slowed as she approached me.

"When have either of you been wrong about the danger to the other?" she asked, grabbing my forearm as if she had tripped. Tears ran from her eyes. She straightened and continued after her husband.

Leaving the study, I stopped and truly looked around for a moment.

Although my room and Franz's room were still intact, the rest of the house was becoming a skeleton of its former self. I went to the sitting room; a lounge, two chairs, a drum table, and a game table. No paintings, few rugs, no porcelain, no piano, no cello, one small clock, and one small barometer. The receiving room empty, dining room empty, the kitchen still held quite a few items and the servant dining quarters were still intact. Additionally, the servants' quarters were left with the necessary furniture and linens. Everything else was packed and gone or being packed. The library was empty, not a book left on a shelf. Everything was tidy and clean. Two wing chairs, one table with a chessboard, and a liquor cupboard. I went upstairs, the other bedrooms were bare, even the beds were gone. The atrium still had basics, but just enough for Franz and me, and that was it.

"My house is even worse," Franz said from behind me. "Even the draperies are gone, Sandy. Mother and Father have moved to the former royal apartments until Wednesday while everything is completed. My understanding is your parents will join them tonight."

I walked over to Franz, fishing in my pocket for the mustard seed I had taken while in the kitchen. I reached out, and he opened his hand. I dropped it into his palm and we both looked at it.

"I don't know why, I just know you cannot go to Vienna without me, so I've canceled my trip," Franz said, closing his hand over the seed.

"No, you need to go with your parents. This is devastating for all of them. My mother shed tears today." I touched Franz's shoulder. "On my honor, I will not leave for Vienna without you, go to Vaduz. Once I settle things with Eva, I may join you."

Franz took my legs out from under me, catching me with one arm as I fell.

"That is for being an ass!" He laughed while I regained my feet.

"Get a haircut, you greaseball!" Now I laughed.

Upstairs, I packed a bag for Mayrhofen, then took it out to the car. I decided to walk down to post the letters myself and went back into the house to retrieve them. As I passed the study, I heard crying. The doors were closed, but it was my mother's voice.

"Our home..." was all I heard her say as I hurried on. These were private moments I had no business intruding on, but it did strengthen my resolve to go with them.

Out on the street, clouds skittered by, but overall, the day was fair. Enough sunshine was coming through to make you feel the linger of fall with the promise of winter. I decided to take Maria Theresa Strasse back and swing by the cathedral. More tourists were around than you would think, given that we were not quite close enough for Christ's mass holidays. Germany's tax for entering Tyrol was not having the effect it once had.

As I approached a group of very Bavarian-looking young men, I excused myself and passed between them. I counted ten of them as I passed through. They were gathered around the window of a shop. These were not Bavarians, they were Nazis. The banned swastika lapel pins declaring loudly just who stood in the strasse. I slowed my pace and moved to linger by a window next to them. Feigning interest in an item, I listened. "Munich," "führer," I heard them say something about wanting to be stationed at the camp. They would be able to ski whenever they were off.

After studying the window display, I once again politely made my way through the group and entered the shop. It afforded a better look at them. I left the door cracked just a bit, and words filtered in on the crisp air. Yes, yes, they were around the right age, was it possible? Were these the Hitler youth squads?

Behind me, the shop owner said quietly "...more and more of them, the emperor needs to come home before it is too late."

"If only it were so easy, good sir." I placed a gold piece in his hand

and closed it gently into a fist over the piece, motioning for his silence. He smiled in pure gratitude and went about tidying the shop.

Leaving, I continued slowly browsing in windows until my opportunity arrived to turn off the main strasse. Backtracking, I made my way back around the plaza and headed for the house. I stopped for a moment and wrote down every word I could remember.

Once home, I went directly to my room. I rang Karl and gave him the coded message about a camp here in Tyrol. He would investigate it, it would take time, as usual. There were two messages on my writing desk. I opened the one that was so obviously in female writing first:

> *Dearest,*
> *I will await you on the corner by the Inn river,*
> *at the prearranged time.*
> *My deepest love,*
> *E.*

Wonderful!" Father sent the second letter:

> *We reside at the royal apartments, you may find us there if needs be. Please*
> *meet us at the train depot at 8 sharp, Wednesday the 15th.*
> *Father.*

So that was in place, but where was Franz? It would be time to pick up Eva shortly. I went through my things once more, checking for anything I may have forgotten. Everything was in order. I went down to the vestibule to wait for Franz. A few minutes later, he appeared, dressed for travel, clean-shaven, and agitated.

"Sandy, there are Nazis in the square, a lot of them."

"I know, we'll have to talk in the auto," I said.

"My bag is ready, start the auto, I'll shut the house," Franz said over his shoulder as he bolted up the stairs.

Out to the auto I went. Klaus's basket was in the front, loaded with goodies. Frieda? So, she must not be to upset. I started her up and was just getting anxious when Franz slid in.

"Frieda?" he asked, looking at the basket in the back.

"Must be!" I said.

We were off, it was nearly dark, the late fall sun was setting low behind the mountains. I went around where KaiserJager Strasse meets the Inn River and there she was. I pulled up next to Eva. Franz was out of the car in a flash, opening her door before I had even made a complete stop. I got out of the driver's seat and took my place in the back seat next to Eva. Franz finally had carte blanche to chauffeur us to Mayrhofen and beyond.

We were out on the open road within minutes of leaving the city. Eva lifted her veil and wraps, looking so beautiful it hurt. I moved the basket to the front for Franz. We were quiet, just looking at each other. It was another first being in a car together, being chauffeured away from the city. No prying eyes, free to sit next to each other openly. I wrapped my arm around her shoulders, and she snuggled into me. We settled in for the drive, fingers entwined. The first quarter moon was heading into full. The beauty of it was magnificent.

Franz had the grace of allowing us the better part of the trip before breaking into our bliss.

"It pains me to break into these tender moments, but we need to address the situation from today."

Eva looked from me to the back of Franz's head. I looked at Eva.

"There were a group of young men in the square today. If you put them all together, there should be ten. Judging from the conversation they are Nazis," I said.

Eva smiled saying, "Yes, these boys are all blond, some blue eyes, some brown, muscular, tall, I know these boys. They are Nazis, they are here on holiday. They arrived at the house yesterday evening wishing to sample Austrian hospitality."

"My favorite kind!" Franz added.

"As we discussed, my Alexsander, they say so very much when properly motivated. I have with me all the notes from the ladies they sampled. All my darlings sat with me the other morning after you abandoned us. We spoke at length in the ways of prompting a lover's secret nothings from their lips." Eva laughed with pure joy.

"Our little aspiring führers will all be returning to give more of their little knowings away. All will have contacted at least one of my ladies by the end of the night. My two best people are taking care of the house this weekend. Andre will be running the house while I am gone. Of course, from behind the scenes. Renee is playing the role of Madame; she is quite good. I have been grooming her for some years now to replace me when the time comes. Do not worry, my darlings, any information available will be coerced from their minds before they leave our beautiful Tyrol, with not a single one the wiser." Eva laughed again, while Franz and I stared at each other in the mirror.

Never had any of us, in all our years, been able to get such a plethora of information without finding a cache. Even interrogation could take months with varying results. Eva had done in one night what would have taken us months.

"I have left you both speechless?" she inquired, "I will take that as a compliment."

"Madame Eva, it is truly a compliment," said Franz, looking at her in the rearview mirror.

"Speaking of Madame, shall we say Mademoiselle, or would you prefer Frauline, Frau?" I asked.

"Oh my, yes, etiquette, what do you gentlemen feel is best?" Eva asked.

"Perhaps first we should address your formal name first, your surname," Franz said.

Eva suddenly looked stricken.

"Eva, what is it, my dear?" I asked.

"Madame..." she said, her voice trembling slightly, "we take the name of our house. I have never known my surname. My only name is Madame Evangeline Le Chabanais." Eva's voice broke just a little at the end.

"Scheisse!" Franz and I both said at the same time. Eva sucked in a breath, I squeezed her hand and looked at her.

"It is alright, just give us a moment. What is the fun of life without those puzzles you must immediately solve."

"Allard!" Franz said triumphantly, "Mademoiselle Evangeline Allard."

"Allard, noble, yes, I believe... let me practice for a moment," Eva said, trying all the different versions, playing it out on her tongue. "Frau Evangeline Allard, Fraulein Eva Allard, Frau Eva Allard, Mademoiselle Eva Allard," she went on like this for some minutes.

"Easily solved, and for family history, we shall stick to the truth that you are an orphan. You were sent to the convent," I said.

Eva broke out laughing so hard she began to cry. She was drying her eyes with her kerchief.

"My darling, you have a twisted idea of the word truth," Eva said. "Who am I meeting? I will adjust the story accordingly."

"Only the steward for The Meadows and his family for now, they will not ask any questions, your name will be the only thing necessary here," I told her.

She nodded looking relieved. I looked at Franz in the rearview mirror. The gravity of our future was hitting home. His words from dinner last night played out before me. If I had tried to be with her at twenty-six, it would have devastated us both.

CHAPTER 10

Of course, Klaus was out to greet us as we pulled around.

"Franz will put the auto away, Klaus," I said as I extended my hand to Eva as she exited. "Klaus Bauer, may I present Mademoiselle Evangeline Allard, Mademoiselle, Klaus Bauer, steward of our dear Meadows. He and his family are kind enough to perform lesser duties for us of late to preserve The Meadows privacy in these difficult times." I bowed slightly to Klaus.

"Gräf Alexsander, you do myself and my family much honor." Klaus bowed in military precision, continuing his greeting, "Mademoiselle, we hope you will find everything to your standards."

This statement brought visions to my brain that I fought to suppress, a great smile found its way to my mouth despite my best efforts.

"Herr Bauer, it is with sincere gratitude I find myself in the generosity of you and your family's care."

In the foyer, we went through the change to fuzzy boots, with Franz arriving just in time to relay the story to Eva. One of Klaus's sons appeared to carry all the baggage to our rooms.

"Otto, would you please place Mademoiselle's things in the main suite," I said as Otto struggled to get the three of our bags in one try.

"Yes, Herr Gräf," Otto replied.

"Just Herr will be fine Otto," I said after him. He turned quickly, bowed in acknowledgment, and headed up the stairs.

"Supper will be served in an hour, Mein Herr. Messages have arrived for both you and Herr Franz. They have been placed in the study, at your request. A light snack is awaiting you in the sitting room. May I attend to anything else for you?" Klaus said very formally.

"As always, Klaus, you have thought of our every need." I said in reply, giving him a wink.

"Thank you and thank Frau Greta," Franz said pushing past me to shake Klaus's hand.

I turned to Eva, "Would you prefer a tour, or shall we retire to the sitting room in anticipation of supper?"

Eva was blushing, judging from Franz's expression it was something neither of us expected to ever see.

"A tour, if you please." Her voice was the voice of youth, much like what I would imagine she sounded like before circumstances stripped away her innocence.

As always, I allowed Franz to place her on his arm and tour her through the house. He was much better at it than I was; he always remembered the distinct types and styles of stone masonry, woodworking, and architectural terms. We were both true admirers of architecture, understanding it in a way impossible for me to articulate, the terminology just did not stick with me. But ask me to explain how something works and I will give you a complete discourse.

Guaranteed the full hour for the whole tour, I excused myself and went to the study where a message from Henry, in code, awaited me. I would need to decipher it. A message from Karl also needed to be deciphered. I left Franz's messages and went to the desk to puzzle out these two. The feeling of comfort as I moved into the room enveloped me.

"I love this room!" I said to no one, before sitting down at the desk, and getting to it.

After a quarter-hour, I believed the messages had been worked out. Henry would be returning indefinitely after my last message if accommodation were available. Karl's message also bore a more hopeful note. There was a glimmer of hope coming from Mussolini's camp. He and Hitler had a bit of a falling out it seemed. After all, how many fascists could one continent hold? At last count, we were up to three, plus a communist dictator, perhaps they were ready to start eliminating each other.

Italia was offering a small olive branch to the Chancellor. A holiday with his son to celebrate Christ Mass & St. Stephen's with a visit to his eminence Pope Pius XI. At least that would be the headline. The underlying truth was some discussion with at least an emissary from Mussolini. The dictator had already been instrumental in carving out a large chunk of what was once Austria, and is now considered Italy, which never inspired trust in me. It might even be said no Austrian was foolish enough to believe any good would come from that camp. He was, though, for all intent and purpose, the devil we knew. The same could not be said for the fascist above us.

After putting together, the necessary replies, I began the painstaking process of translating them into code. Each one uses a different cryptic. Having two people working on it made it so much easier, but I was managing my way through on my own.

Hearing Franz, I tucked the correspondence away for later. Putting on my best smile, I opened the door just in time for them to enter the study.

"...The piping originates here behind this hearth. This hearth holds the largest tanks in the house, providing heat and water for the closest lower rooms, as well as the master suite and bathroom above it. These are the very same tanks we just observed in what you took for the closet around the corner. We saved this room for last," Franz concluded.

"I believe that is the fastest tour you have ever given. We need to set you up for several a day at a schilling a piece!" I said, winking as we laughed.

"Alexsander the house is, une oeuvre d'ingenierie et d'art, très impressionnant."

"Mademoiselle Eva, vous êtes très gentille, but it is le monsieur Gräf that deserves your admiration, as he is L'architecte," I replied with my very rusty French. Speaking with Eva was the first opportunity I had to use the language in some time.

Eva looked at both of us in confusion.

"The tanks are what keep this room so cozy? It is like the womb, as if it wraps itself around you."

"Indeed, it is the warmth in the stone itself," Franz answered her.

"Would you care to await supper here or move into the sitting room?" I asked her.

"There is food in the sitting room, I am afraid I must be a scoundrel and insist the lady accompany us lest I injure Frau Greta's feelings," Franz said, offering her his arm. This of course brought a round of teasing from Eva and me.

Upon entering, Eva began to move toward one of the side chairs, Franz swooped her around to one of the love seats and deposited her in the middle.

"Mademoiselle, may I offer you an apéritif?" I asked, slightly bowing in front of her. Another blush, this is who Evangeline truly is, I thought to myself, an excited young girl, deserving of the kindest, loving treatment one could provide. Here is who I am truly in love with, not the Madame, but this creature with the beautiful soul before me. The Madame is the facade she wears to provide for and protect herself.

"You are always too kind Alexsander, wine, if you please," she said smiling her prettiest smile at me.

Franz, surprisingly, selected only a small plate, though it was very crowded with slices of cheese, meats, and crackers.

"Eva, would you be offended if I were to forgo the niceties?" Franz asked, batting his eyelashes in jest.

"Cher Franz, please do not starve yourself for me!" she said giggling.

I delivered Eva's wine, then broke out the BarenJager honey liquor for Franz and me. I was feeling celebratory having the three of us here together. Sitting almost inappropriately close to Eva, we all breathed a collective sigh. As we sat relaxing in the house, Eva and I watched Franz devour the first plate, returning for seconds, he motioned to both of us. Eva waved her hand in declination, but I could not help but poke a little fun.

"I fear, Herr Franz, there is not nearly enough on the tray for you to be so generous as to offer a share to others."

Franz rolled his eyes, swallowing quickly to get in a sarcastic laugh. He resumed his seat, took a swallow of the bourbon, looked at it approvingly, and continued his small snack.

"I will speak candidly, gentlemen," Eva stated, looking fondly at both of us. "Thank you, both of you, this whole evening is wonderful. I am not ungrateful for my fortunes, but being here with both of you is the first time in my life I have felt at home. As if all is wiped away, a glistening chrysalis cracked open before me, my wings drying, about to take flight." Her face showed an almost ethereal light as she spoke the words. It was as if the divine were intervening, and it was not lost on Franz or me.

"Eva," I turned, reaching out for her free hand, "if you would choose to move into this life, where you belong, pray, would you consider seeking absolution and baptism officially?" I hurried my words along while she was still slightly stunned. "Neither of us believes you need absolution for anything in your life, dearest, please do not misunderstand. Absolution would simply be the vehicle allowing us to be married in the church, affording you every courtesy you deserve in life."

There, the question was posed, and I held my breath. From the look on Franz's face, he too was holding his breath, his plate set aside, he sat forward in his chair.

She sat as still as a statue, her face gave nothing away, nor did her eyes. Finally, after what seemed an hour, she took a long deep breath, set her wine down, and rose. Franz and I glanced at each other uncertainly. She moved to the fireplace looking forward, never glancing at us.

"I was baptized by the priest who came to Le Chabanais. Although I never witnessed it, I was told he came to sin once a month to prevent himself from worse transgressions. Now I believe the priest did not come to sin at all but was in some way related to my maître, and these were his monthly attempts to bring her away from the life she had chosen. Maître entraineuse insisted I attend catechism, then mass and confession every week until I was deflowered. Is absolution possible in such circumstances as mine?" She stood staring into the fire. I saw Klaus approaching out of the corner of my eye, I quietly waved him away.

"Do I cast aside the opportunity to help both of you, help the country I have made my home?" She turned to search our faces as she said it.

"Perhaps your role simply changes, my dear, from Madame to entrepreneur," I suggested. She looked hard at me and hard at Franz, both of us trying to offer reassuring looks.

"May I be allowed time for consideration or is the decision to be urgent?" she asked.

I rose and came to take her hands in mine, looking into her eyes I said, "Evangeline, you may take all the time you need, my love." She squeezed my hands tightly, looking down at them.

"Your kindness, as ever, fills my heart, but enough sentimentality for now! Herr Franz, you are wasting away, when might we expect supper?" she asked, intentionally changing the subject, lest she lose her battle with the tears pooling at the corners of her lovely eyes.

"You, my dear, are a woman after my own heart! All is ready if the Gräf will do you the honor of escorting you," Franz said, coming over to kiss her forehead.

Supper was an extravagant affair for which Franz was exceedingly grateful. How Klaus had procured shark, I couldn't guess, but it was superb. There was a fresh green salad, evenly sliced tomatoes with cucumbers. If I had not known better, I would have thought us at the Italian Riviera, certainly not the Alps in December. Klaus was beaming with all the praise, as well he should. Dessert, a gelato with fresh fruit, finished me off completely. After profuse gratitude was poured upon Klaus and his family, we moved to the study with the request for coffee.

Offering Eva, a spot on the Chesterfield, I sat beside her.

"Franz, I left your correspondence on the table. Mine is just under the lamp there on the desk if you would be kind enough to check my work, incoming and outgoing," I said.

Eva seemed to be taking in all the different things in the study. Elsa, who had not made an appearance until just now, brought in the tray of coffee. She placed the tray on the large table, excused herself, and closed the door behind her.

"Ah, yes, she is quite the beauty. Am I remiss to guess this is the young creature who beguiled you so easily?" Eva said, looking me in the eye with a playful glint in hers.

"Beguiled might be a stretch…" I was saying when "Pffssshhhhtttt" was exhaled loudly from the desk. Franz pretended to be completely engrossed in his work, never looking up. Eva laughed at me but patted me on the arm reassuringly. She then went to the tray and was kind enough to pour for all of us. She waved us back to our seats and delivered our cups, but continued to wander around the room, becoming familiar with different objects and examining the photos and paintings.

"Yes, Sandy, they are all correct. Interesting news from both parties. Mine is as well. Eva, you understand the confidence involved here of course?" Franz looked at her to confirm she understood his statement. He then continued, "The Reich is gathering troops along the border with Austria, more specifically in the Salzburg area. Nothing excessive as yet, but building, nonetheless. There also seem to be regular sightings of Luftwaffe, patrols going over every two to four hours during daylight," he finished.

"Information which corroborates what we understand of the timing in play," I said, having also risen from my seat. I walked over to the fire to stoke it and add a log. "Fritzy, would you add to both? Would you ask them if we are able to gain any firm information on troop strength, equipment totals, or anything of that nature? It would be nice to have enough decisive information to share with the Chancellor that supports the need to ignore the treaty and begin a defensive troop build-up," I said.

Franz countered, "I quite agree, but sadly it is a line I believe our cousin will not cross. However, it wouldn't hurt for all of us to be armed with the information."

"Might this be a good time to review the notes recovered from last night's guests?" Eva asked.

"Indeed, this would be an excellent time," I moved my coffee over to one of the chairs facing the desk, as Eva followed my example. Before seating herself, she reached into what I thought was a pocket. However, I could see her hand moving around freely beneath her skirt. Then I heard rustling paper as she produced several folded pieces. She smoothed these on the desk and took her seat.

"How shall we proceed? Would everyone like their own or shall I read them to you?" she asked.

Franz peered at them from a distance, "In the interest of thoroughness, please read them and we will take notes."

He handed me some paper and a fountain pen, as we would inevitably find different things of interest. Sliding a latch on the chair I produced a type of small writing desk. Eva looked over, astonished, I pointed to a latch off the arm of her chair. She flipped the latch and pulled. The desk practically flung itself across her lap, she broke into laughter, giddy with excitement, she placed it back and then brought it out again several times. I was delighted in watching her fascination. She looked over at each of us, realized we were watching her, and cleared her throat.

"Please excuse me, I am ready to continue."

"Uncle Otto designed them," Franz said.

"Many hours of writing have been performed on them, we can assure you," I added. Eva smiled at us both, organizing her papers.

"'While licking his sausage, I inserted one finger. As he was holding back, I inquired about him being here in the future to enjoy my ability to please him. He was having trouble forming sentences. I did get him to say he wants to be stationed at the work camp they were going to build. That way he could ski and fuck me whenever he is off work.' This one is from Sally," Eva said and grabbed the next one.

"My dear, you may leave out the method used to extract the information, if you please," I suggested placing a hand on her forearm before she began the next one. Eva looked at me, looked at Franz, and shook her head.

"Oh, yes, I see, very well," and continued. "One seems to be saying it will be a concentration camp built close to Salzburg, but he will come as often as he can on the train." She turned the page and scanned another. "Here he is talking about when they free us, us being Austrians, we will go with them to free the Polish Czechs while the Führer punishes the French oppressors. Again here, 'we will save you and then save the Czechs. After that, we will put down the Judes and French, who conspire to subjugate all Germanic tribes. The true race must overcome the filth being mixed within it like a cesspool.' Again, this one speaks of maintaining the purity of breeding and the elimination of filthy Jews. My dearest Ida, she is Jewish, he was saying this to her. I wonder how he would feel if she had told him right in the middle of...please excuse me." Eva leaned back and rubbed her temples.

"May I have a few minutes, gentlemen?" she entreated, placing her papers on the large desk, putting the small writing desk away, and rising.

I rose too, "Would you like me to accompany you?" I asked, placing a hand on her forearm.

She took my arm, "Yes, please, Alexsander."

I waved behind me for Franz to continue reading the letters. We left the study and stepped out into the great hall. Eva stopped to take a deep breath. When she began to step forward again, I led her to the lavatory just to the left. She excused herself and went in. As much as I wanted to linger by the door, I stepped away to afford her some privacy. At one moment, I heard a sob, but heard nothing more after.

A brief time later, Eva appeared, looking quite her usual self, perhaps a little strained around the eyes. As I escorted her back, she looked at me in a way that was different than any way I had ever seen her look at me before. I stopped, concerned.

"Evangeline, what is it, dearest?"

"My poor Alexsander, you and Franz, you are privy to these atrocities every day? The hate, the disregard for thousands of human lives, the megalomania, how do you tolerate the blind injustice? Why are we not told of these things? Where is the outrage, the rallying cry to defend ourselves?" Eva's voice was rising with every word. "I am of course used to a certain level of darkness and depravity, but this is genocide."

I led her back to the study and seated her on the chesterfield. I waved at Franz, who immediately poured a healthy quantity of Schnapps into a glass and brought it over to me. I gently placed it in her hand as she stared into the fire. He nodded at me, and I nodded back, he went and retrieved two more. Sitting with her, I pushed the glass a bit, and she took quite a swallow, sputtering just a bit, having not realized completely what was in the glass. She shook her head slightly, looked toward both of us in turn, and sat back into the cushions.

I repositioned myself to the table across from her with Franz.

"My apologies, to both of you," she said, the businesswoman sneaking in. "My behavior was uncalled for; I hope I have not disturbed the household."

"No one is here but us Eva, the Bauers will all be home tucked in bed by now. Even if Klaus is still around, he feels the same as we all do," I said.

"Now you see why only he and his family are here. Our most trusted servants are with our families. We dare not risk bringing anyone in, although the service his family is providing is far beyond his duties," Franz added.

"For many, this is a game to be played, and Franz and I were once also of that mind. We played the game well. But no longer, now we see the human lives in which we are dealing. The Chancellor too feels this, we all strive to protect and preserve those the coming storm will wipe from the earth. Your horror at the realization is a pain we have all had to come to terms with. Please do not feel an obligation to bear such a burden, my dearest, no one will think less of you. Allow me to show you to your room, my darling, we will finish this nasty business, you rest," I suggested.

"Oh my, Alexsander, thank you for wishing to shield me. No, I must do my part, I just needed a moment."

Franz reached out and placed a hand on hers saying, "Eva, I have read all of the letters, we have everything we need for tonight. Tomorrow we will all review them again with fresh eyes for anything we may have missed. Please allow Sandy to take you to your rooms, please."

Eva sat forward, kissed Franz on the cheek, and stood up. "Of course, you are both right, Alexsander you will retire with me?" She looked up at me, hopefully.

"It would be my pleasure!" I said, offering my arm again. We said good nights to Franz and made our way up the stairs.

We arrived at the door to my parents' bedchamber, and the strangest feeling came over me as I opened the door to allow her in, like a child caught sneaking the cookie, he was just told he could not have. The Meadows was mine now, the papers filed, Klaus in my charge, but I could not help but feel my parents look at me entering their bedchamber with the woman I love, unwed, unmarried, a sinner in the sight of God. As if God did not show up at Eva's establishment.

Still, these momentary sentiments were easily overcome. I helped Eva undress, kissing her neck, she smelled of vanilla and cinnamon, I lay my cheek against hers. Once she could manage to relieve herself of the rest of her cumbersome attire unaided, I stepped into the closet to hang my clothes. When I stepped out, my eyes were delighted with the vision of her dressed in silks. She handed me a set, climbed into the exceptionally large bed, and patted next to her. I pondered why we were wearing silks to bed, but I dutifully put them on, turned on the bedside lamp, and shut off the rest of the lights. I climbed into the bed and pulled her into my arms.

"Alexsander?"

"Yes, my love?" I replied.

"If I am absolved, would I be considered a virgin again?" Her voice asked the question with such a serious tone I repositioned to look at her.

"Well, I am not certain, but it will not hurt to ask." I reclined into the pillows again.

"Alexsander?"

"Yes, my love?"

"Would you be disappointed if we did not engage in carnal pleasures tonight? It is not that I do not desire you, it just feels wrong somehow." Her voice was so apologetic.

I took her in my arms and kissed her face softly, slowly ending at her lips in a long passionate kiss. Then I pulled my face away, just enough to look into her eyes.

"Evangeline, if we were never able to have sex again, I would still love you with my whole being, please never doubt that," I whispered and snuggled her into me.

She was asleep within minutes. I was not so lucky. I lay as still as possible, she slept on. An hour later, she rolled onto her side, I slipped a pillow up next to her back, and slid out of bed rubbing some circulation back into my arm. Slipping on the fuzzy boots, I went downstairs to the study. The door was still open, lights on.

"You have to read these," Franz said as I entered.

"How did you know I would be back down here?" I asked, staring at him incredulously. He stood up, stretched, and reached for a glass of water.

"Well, I knew there was no possible way you were having sex in your parents' bedroom while unwed. She was in no state to be dragged off to your room, and your sleeping is always negotiable, when stressed, the only place you are sleeping is right here," he pointed at the Chesterfield. "Right here!" he said pointing to my place on the couch. He walked over, grabbed up the notes, and we sat going through each one. He read them and I made notes, then I read them, and he made notes. Then we compared and compiled notes.

"Well, Fritzy, we certainly have information to pass along."

"We certainly do, Sandy, we certainly do. In the morning we will prepare the messages, I am exhausted, sleep well!" Franz left the room as he was saying this.

I found myself saying, "sleep well" to the closed door. The fire had burned down, I stoked it, putting quite a large log on. The clock read 2 am, better try for some sleep. Next thing I knew he would be down here ready to go out for a run. I spread out, grabbing a throw from the back to pull over me. It felt so good to lie down.

CHAPTER 11

"Good morning, my darlings, what a wonderful night's sleep. Am I too late for breakfast?" Eva arrived in the dining room dressed in a lovely green and white brocade dress, her hair perfect, eyes sparkling. None of the sadness or despair from last night seemed to linger.

"Good morning, you are lovely, yes, we are just enjoying our coffee. Would you care for some?" I asked.

"Oh yes, please, shall we finish the correspondence after breakfast? I have something I would like to attend to after." She had a bit of a sly look as she said it.

"It is complete, reports are already on their way to the appropriate people. Our gratitude and the gratitude of all those whom you have helped, Eva," Franz said.

A look of relief flitted across her eyes like lightning. If I had not been looking at her that instant, I would have completely missed it.

"Franz, is there a church anywhere nearby?" Eva inquired.

"My dear, this is Tyrol, you would be unable to throw a rock without hitting a church," Franz replied, his eyes filled with mirth. I tried my absolute best to stifle a laugh.

"If I may ask you to drive me to a local priest so I may speak with him?" she said, looking at Franz. My curiosity was piqued, why would she be asking Franz? But absolution is quite serious in itself; for Eva, it must be a difficult prospect indeed.

"My pleasure Eva, we shall go after breakfast if you like. I believe the Priest in Brandberg would be the best choice, just up the road. Wouldn't you agree, Sandy?" Franz said, looking at me for approval in more than one way.

"Yes, I believe that's a wise choice," I said smiling at them both and returning to my coffee.

At that very moment, a breakfast fit for royalty appeared, much to everyone's pleasure. Eva made a particularly strong dent in the pastry, which she compared to the finest in Paris in between bites. I looked up in time to see Greta beaming through the door as Klaus made her come to listen to the compliments. After breakfast, Franz retrieved the auto, Eva procured boots and a heavy coat, and they set off.

I took the opportunity to cover the estate with Klaus. We went over all the repairs, plantings, stock, budgets, buying, and selling for the last quarter and the coming quarter. We also discussed the servants' quarters. The decision was made to use it for any Jewish refugees needing a place to stay or hide. We discussed plans for who we would allow to use it, how they would notify us, contingencies if for any reason we became suspect, and so forth.

When we were done, I changed into some mountaineering gear, grabbed my pack and snowshoes, and headed up the trail to Maria Hilf. The climb was familiar and not too far, but going anywhere here on foot unprepared in December could be a disaster. Many tourists make those mistakes without ever getting an opportunity to rectify them. The day was lovely, cumulus clouds skittered along here and there, giving way to plenty of sunlight. The snow turned deep quickly, so I stopped to strap on my snowshoes and grab my poles. When I arrived, there was no one nearby. The door and walk needed to be cleared a bit from the last clearing. I took my small shovel and scraper and spent some time clearing it all out.

Being born at The Meadows, my parents were close to the Priest at the time. He had afforded them the honor of christening me here in a very private, small ceremony. I had always felt tied to this place somehow. I removed my boots before entering the little chapel. God always felt present here in this tiny little chapel, an overwhelming feeling of love spread over me. We spoke at length about everything, my worries, transgressions, hopes, dreams, my health, I asked for strength and protection for all of us, everyone who would ride out what was coming. I asked for absolution for everything but the three things I could not promise I would never do again; make love to Eva, lie to protect another, and defend unto the death of another. Somehow, my heart felt right, like God was honoring my truth. It had never been in me to try to gain absolution through a lie. I knew many who did, and that was between them and God, I could not.

Evening came on quickly, as it always does this time of year, but I found myself unable to go quite yet, as if something were holding me back, embracing me in that feeling of love. I moved to the outside, tidying up what I could see as the light faded. Suddenly, the sky lit up with the last rays of the sun, and they somehow cast on the little church, although impossible from the position, the light was brilliant and blinding for just a moment.

"Thank you!" I said aloud. My heart full, I felt ready to head back.

The fading light brought the feeling of the hunt. Being out in the brisk fall twilight. The last light was surrendering to the blue black of night, making my progress slow. Coming through the back of the property, meadows now bleak as winter spread her blanket across the earth, my feet crunching down the dry vegetation, I thought of Persephone brought into the underworld with Hades, tricked into consuming the pomegranate. Her mother, Demeter, was devastated by the loss of her daughter for ingesting those six seeds. In her wrath, abandoning the earth to darkness for the six months her daughter was confined to hell with her husband. Allowing all to wither and die before her lovely daughters return in the spring.

I came round to the front of the house, finding Klaus's son, Alexsander, waiting for me. He relieved me of my gear and informed me a beverage would be brought up to my room while I changed for supper. He was gone before I had the opportunity to ask if Franz and Eva had returned. I headed upstairs to my room and found a wonderful hot mint tea awaiting me. Lovely after the chilly trip down. I removed my clothes and placed them in a basket to bring downstairs. I enjoyed a nice hot bath and dressed for a casual supper. I set the basket outside the door, retrieved my mug, and was turning to go downstairs when I heard voices. At first, it was hard to pinpoint where they came from. I moved back into my room across the shared lavatory into Franz's bedroom. I cracked his door to the hallway and made out the voices clear as day. One voice was Eva, I was certain, the other sounded like Greta, Klaus's wife.

At first, a twinge of guilt made me start to shut the door, but that same feeling that kept me at the chapel held the door cracked as I eavesdropped.

"My Klaus felt the same way, dear. It is not for you to decide. You could easily go before a priest right now, and they would never know, but you are choosing to go with a clean soul. Pray to St. Mary of Egypt, she will guide you in your penance and clear the way forward." Greta held Eva's hand as she spoke.

"Bless you, Greta, thank you for sharing your story. To see that someone not only left a life of sin but is happily married with so many beautiful children is the greatest gift of all. I pray Alexsanders parents will accept me when I tell them," Eva said.

"Gräf Otto and Gräfin Alexsandra never once looked down on me or treated me badly. They are fine people who faced their own challenges to be together, they will not forsake you, Eva. Just be certain to follow the priest's direction, my dear. Now I must go finish dinner before the children ruin something." I slid the door closed as Greta finished what she was saying to Eva.

Walking slowly over to a side chair, I sat for a moment to work this through. Greta just told Eva who she was, no, but yes, it must be. Why would she say the things she was saying if it was not true? St. Mary of Egypt? It had been a long time, but then I remembered we had a book on saints in the library. My parents probably couldn't remember them all either. Eva wanted to tell my parents; I suppose that meant the church was willing to absolve her? Well, for the time being, I would just go to the library to see if I could find that book.

I went out my door and the basket had disappeared. Darn it, Greta must have seen it and taken it down.

Entering the Library, I was able to locate The Book of Saints without much effort. I found an account on page 158   5

"Her career of infamy in Alexandria...lifelong penance..." I read aloud to myself.

"St. Mary of Egypt, is there a reason we are researching saints?" Franz asked as he walked into the library. I turned like a shot, feeling caught at some nefarious misdoing. "Oh, yes, I see, let me shut the door," he said, walking back over to shut the door and slide the latch.

"You remember who St. Mary of Egypt is? How do you remember that?" I asked him.

"Honestly, I am not certain I remember her as much as I remember the phrase, 'career of infamy' from somewhere. Perhaps I read it or saw a

---

5. The book of Saints: a dictionary of servants of God canonized by the Catholic Church. By St. Augustine's Abbey, 1921.

painting in a gallery with captions," Franz answered.

I relayed what had transpired upstairs, including my less-than-gallant behavior in continuing to listen.

Fritzy laughed, saying, "Well it is not as if we do not spend much of our time trying to gain information using less than honest means."

"Do you know something from the trip today?" I asked.

"Nothing substantial, we made small talk on the way up. A parishioner brought me home for coffee and cake."

"Of course, she did!" I broke in, Franz continued.

"I never said it was her, but it was. After coffee, I returned to the church and waited another hour or so. Eva came out of the church with the priest, which meant I had to go pay my respects since it is still the same priest." Franz shot me the 'I couldn't believe it' look and went on, "Every part of me wants to say he didn't recognize me, but we know he did. They spoke a little longer and we left. Eva seemed a little nervous but in good spirits. She thanked me profusely when we arrived and ran upstairs."

I handed him the book, opened to page 158 with the small paragraph about St. Mary of Egypt, then began walking around a bit, thinking it through. Fritzy slammed the book shut, found where it belonged, and placed it back in its home. Opening the Library door, he left, then quickly returned with two glasses, the bottle of honey liquor, and sat at the chess board, motioning to me to join him.

An hour later we were at an impasse and slightly high. The honey liquor is now sitting at the game table with us. Klaus and his son, Alex, had brought chairs over and were engrossed. Frau Greta appeared at the door.

"Supper will not keep forever, what is happening in here?" she asked as she made her way over to the board. She looked at both of us and said, "Whose move, is it?" Everyone pointed at Franz. Greta reached over, moved the pawn, knocked over my king, and said, "Checkmate, please eat supper." Then she bustled out of the room like nothing had happened.

Horrified at the loss of the game, we all looked at Klaus, he shook his head, knowingly. We all laughed, got up, patted him on the back, and headed into Supper.

Eva was not in the dining room. I began to turn and head up to look for her but was stopped by Klaus.

"Herr Alexsander, that was what we were coming to tell you. Frau Eva will be in her room this evening in prayer. She has asked not to be disturbed." I looked at Klaus, then Franz, but no one offered an explanation.

Slowly, I went to my seat at the table. Elsa appeared to serve dinner with Klaus. It was a quiet meal.

After dinner, we returned to the chess board to play another game. We both chuckled as we looked at the board, left with the ruined game. The pieces were reset, and we resumed thinking drinking.

Returning from our morning run, we raced up the stairs to beat the other to the lavatory. As we rounded the corner, Eva was just approaching the stairs. I managed to throw my arms around her just as we collided, rolling her on top of me as we fell. My head slammed into the floor. Franz had veered hard to the right, hitting the wall with a distinctive thud which threw him back on top of us. There was a collective moment when everyone froze, waiting to see if their body was injured. Eva responded first.

"Franz, if you are quite alright, would you be able to get off of me?"

Franz rolled over with another thud as he hit the floor. Eva carefully made her way to her feet, assessing herself as she went. The world was spinning, I tried to look over at Franz. The motion made me instantly sick, and I pushed myself to the other side, just in time to lose my stomach. I heard Klaus, then Eva talking, Franz was suddenly there, bleeding on me. Why was he bleeding? I could not tell. He was feeling the back of my head, my neck, my spine, moving my shoulders. It felt good, I think I said. Then suddenly the left side of my head was killing me.

"Who are you?" I kept asking the man in front of me. He would not stop laughing. He was trying to kill me. "Hey what are you about, who are you?" Everything went black.

My eyes opened a little, and the light was soft, I moved my arm to my head, but the searing pain was not there. It did ache though, just at the base of my neck. My arm and back were both sore.

"Eva! Franz!" I said, and instantly heard them both beside me. I opened my eyes the rest of the way, they were there hovering over me, looking dreadful. "You both look dreadful, are you alright?" I asked, my voice croaking a bit. They laughed, looking relieved, and began asking questions.

"Tell me about the pain in your head, Sandy, you said your head was killing you before you lost consciousness."

"Did I, I don't know, it just feels sore, my whole body feels sore," I said, shifting my weight a little. Eva moved to adjust the pillows and they both helped me sit up a bit.

"Take it very slowly, my love." Eva said, caressing my forehead gently.

Wow, I felt like I had been thrown from a horse. Of course, I took the force of my weight and Eva at whatever speed we had been going, so in a way I had.

Franz had a light and was moving it in front of me. He handed it to Eva and showed her where to hold it. He was looking at my face, poking, prodding, checking my eyes, tongue, and hearing. Then we started body movements, and small movement abilities, he made me get up, which was not enjoyable. Squats, arms, everything, he even made me come to the lavatory and evacuate my bladder so he could check for blood. He then put me back to bed, telling me to drink water and left the room.

Eva was fussing, helping me get situated.

"You would think Franz was a doctor the way he acts," she said, smiling at me.

"Well, technically, he is, but that is a subject for another time, my dearest," I said very quietly.

She looked at me with wide eyes but acknowledged my request and took my hand in hers.

"We were quite scared, Franz said something about a concussive blow." Eva looked at me with a question in her eyes.

"When the head is hit with enough force it can cause the brain to be, well jostled really. It is not well understood, but it is thought the brain bruises in a way, which may cause a lot of things to happen. There are also cases where the fluid will pool up in the skull and put pressure on the brain. Those are what he is concerned about," I replied, causing her to look even more concerned. "Not to worry, I'll be sore for a few days, but I am just fine," I said, trying to reassure her.

"Why would he watch you make water?" she asked.

"He is looking for blood to see if there was damage to the systems that control those functions. Kidneys in a human being are in the back of the body, he is just being cautious," I explained.

Franz was back a few minutes later, standing vigil at the end of the bed.

"Broken?" I asked,

"No, just bruised, bled like it though," he laughed.

His nose was visibly swollen, and he looked to have acquired a bit of a black eye on the side he hit the wall.

"How about a glass of water to start?" he added.

I was not up to the argument and took the glass of water Eva handed me. She rose to help, and Franz chastised her gently, he wanted her to let me do it for myself as he was still assessing my primary movement functions. After I finished the water, I turned to set it on the night table. A telling act with which my body showed me exactly how much pain I was in.

"Let's get that nightshirt off, Sandy, and get you over here by the window." A minute later, Franz was examining my back, each rib, vertebrae, neck, and head again. Eva came around to watch and gasped. I tried to look behind me, alarmed at her reaction. Franz held me still.

"It is simply a bruise, I know it looks dreadful, but it is the force of hitting the wood floor with his own weight, your weight, and my weight on top of him. It is quite common for someone thrown from a horse or auto accidents. Even falling from trees, rocks, or buildings. Now you know what his bones look like inside him." Franz laughed, but Eva did not seem to find it funny.

Now I understood, my bones had bruised an impression on my skin. It could be disconcerting if you did not understand what you were seeing.

I dressed and went back to bed just in time for the knock on the door. Klaus, Greta, Elsa, Otto, and Alex came in. Thankfully, the rest of the children were not present, however, they had drawn a picture of me skiing. Greta set a tray down with broth, crackers, cheese, buttermilk, some type of pudding possibly, and a small slice of bread with butter. They looked incredibly concerned, Franz reassured them. They visited for just a moment, assured me they were seeing to everything, bid me rest, and quietly filed out of the room. Franz followed them a few moments later, I am certain he was procuring food for himself. He left strict instructions with Eva about what I was allowed to eat off the tray.

Eva offered to read to me while I sat propped up, sipping broth, and dunking a soda cracker occasionally.

"If I might make another suggestion, would you be uncomfortable speaking with me about your trip yesterday? There is no pressure, of course, but I am anxious for information if you are ready." I said, trying to suggest it as gently as possible.

"Oh, Mon Cher, forgive me, I was coming to find you this morning when this terrible incident happened. Yes, I wish to tell you everything, may I?" She edged up onto the bed to touch my arm. I set my broth down, taking her hand. "The Priest was so very kind. We spoke at great length. He tested me on my lessons, I do not know how, but I remembered everything he asked. He..." Her lip began to tremble just the tiniest bit. I reached my other hand over to brush her cheek, she reached out, bringing it to her lips, she kissed my fingers, took a deep breath, and set my hand down, "He said to me that because I was sold into sin as a child, it is different than if I was a grown woman choosing that life. He explained the blessed sacrament of marriage and sex between a husband and wife. Did you know of this? I did not know of this. Now I am even more disgusted by the men and women who engage my services. Once I am granted absolution, my choice will be made for the life I have ahead of me. He heard much of my confession, when I am ready, it will be completed. Have you been through absolution for your mortal sins?" She asked the last part very timidly.

"Yes, but I have never asked to be absolved of laying with you, nor will I until you are my wife. Yes, I do know of the holiness of marriage, and I do believe in it. If I did not, it would be extremely easy to allow you to stay doing and being whomever, you care to be. In truth, I am prepared to do just that if you should choose. However, I believe to my very core the vision I had in St. Jakob was a blessing, allowing all the doors to open for us to be married. I am not justifying or condoning any of my behavior, but I will not seek absolution for something I have every intention of doing again!" I said.

She looked down at our hands, "You understand that I will need to tie up loose ends with my current life? I would also need to remain chaste until our vows have been witnessed by the priest?" She peeked through her lashes waiting for my reaction. I took my hand from hers, placed my fingers gently under her chin, lifting her face so she was looking straight at me.

"I meant what I said to you the other night Eva, I love you unconditionally, but if you wanted to have sex this very moment, I would not be able to resist you. Until we are married, I will not seek confession, but you may stay chaste forever if you wish, as long as I may kiss you and hold you," I said tenderly.

Tears filled her eyes as her hands cupped each side of my face kissing me.

"I have already sent messages to my financiers and to the new Madame Renee and Andre, they are seeing to my things and arranging the paperwork. They had the finances to buy most of the business for some time, but I did not know what to do with myself. My new profession will be as a boring old wife!" She laughed with joy.

"Believe me, my dear, your position will be anything but boring." I said. "Then you are saying you will not need to step back into that life for any reason?" I asked cautiously.

"None at all, mon cher, none at all, Madame will continue to collect information, and other means may be used to obtain it than me procuring the documentation." She beamed as she said it. I rose slowly going to the writing table.

"Please have Madame deliver all your personal effects to this address. Including your two personal maids of Jewish descent, you understand my meaning?" Opening a drawer, I selected a card with the Innsbruck address on it and placed the card in her hand. "Please finish what you need to with the priest, my dear. You will be leaving for Vaduz from Innsbruck Wednesday at 8 am, accompanied by your maids." I leaned over and kissed her before finding my way back into the bed.

"Oh merde, I will need a ride to the church. Franz will not leave you." she said excitedly.

"Ask Klaus, my dear, he will arrange it," I said laying back feeling more relaxed than I had in days. I drifted off to sleep as she left the room.

"I feel you staring at me, you know?" I said.

"Eva told me the basics, marry her now before we leave for Innsbruck, Sandy," he said.

I opened my eyes, slowly moving around to get out of bed. I needed to start stretching or I would never be able to move.

"No priest ever born is going to marry us in less than six months, you know that, Fritzy. Don't you think I would right now if there were a way?" I shot him a hard look as I said it.

"I'll drive up and see how much it will take for him to bend the rules," Franz said, heading for the door.

"Stop, Fritzy, just stop, she is going to be with us, she is going with us to Vaduz, and we will make sure she stays in Vaduz when we leave. She will be safe!" I walked over to him and put my hand on his shoulder. "She'll be safe, our mothers will fuss over her and spoil her, and she'll be fine."

He walked over and sat down in the chair by the bed. I walked around for a few minutes, making myself squat, bend, damn it hurt, then went back, and propped myself back up in bed. He looked at me, his eyes filled with pain.

"I thought that too, when I took her home," he said, just staring at me.

"I am so sorry Fritzy; I should have been honest with you and explained the horrible feeling I had about her returning home. If I could go back, I would force you to keep her at your parents' estate and not just suggest it. It must have seemed like I was being selfish, trying to keep her near me too." I was sitting on the edge of the bed, anxious to find some way to make up for that terrible error in judgment.

"No, it didn't occur to me that you were trying to keep her near you. I knew you had worked through it, it just seemed ridiculous to prolong the process by keeping her away from home. I thought the sooner she went back, the sooner she would be mine." He stared at me, holding back the tears and hatred.

I waited until he came back to himself and asked, "Do you have a feeling we need to be wed now?"

"No, I just, I have a feeling something is going to happen. Maybe it is Vienna? When I think of Eva, the feeling is not there. Only when I think of you going alone to...well honestly, Sandy, lately when I think of you going anywhere alone. I wish I could explain it," Franz said, looking at his hands.

"You don't need to explain it, I trust you implicitly. If you say we need to travel together, then we travel together." I reached over and grabbed his shoulder reassuringly as I said it, damn that hurt.

CHAPTER 12

The following morning, we were fed, packed, and loaded in the auto as the sun was rising. Goodbyes were exchanged, Greta and Eva's were more private and involved a few tears, which we all ignored. If withstanding pain builds fortitude, then my cup was full. Franz was thrilled to be driving but recommended that I sit in the front for less jostling. Wanting to sit with Eva, I ignored his advice and spent the first half of the trip in misery. Every bump, bend, turn, and jostle, a test of my fortitude. Halfway back I gave in. He pulled over and I occupied the front passenger seat the rest of the way. It still bore pain, but not nearly as much.

We arrived at the house to find all of Eva's things, including her two "maids" in the sitting room being interrogated by Frieda. Franz and I were both perplexed by the fact Frieda was there, which added to the chaos. Eva marched over to the two ladies, who immediately stopped speaking. She told them to take a seat and keep their mouths shut until they were spoken to. Frieda immediately walked up to Eva.

"Just who are you and what are all of you doing in Gräf Von Rieser's home?"

I was not sure if she was referring to Father or myself, but it made little difference.

"STOP, please!" I said, standing in between Frieda and Eva. "Frieda, I appreciate you protecting the house, however, what are you doing here?" Frieda assumed a defensive posture at once. Launching into her explanation.

"Although you and Herr Franz do not deserve my services, I would not leave you to fend for yourselves. Therefore, I stayed behind when the Gräf and Gräfin removed themselves to the royal apartments. These women, who are obviously not who they pretend to be, showed up with all these belongings saying they were here for Mademoiselle Evangeline Allard. Which, as I explained to them, there is no such person at this home," she glared at them and continued, "they need to take these things and themselves and remove them immediately before I contact the authorities!" Her voice took on a higher pitch as she went.

"Frieda Liberman," I stressed the next part, "who is my personal housekeeper and attendant," Frieda shot me a less than pleased look, "I would like to introduce you to Mademoiselle Evangeline Allard, my soon to be betrothed." I looked hard at Frieda as I reached out for Eva's hand, Frieda looked like she might faint.

"My pleasure, Fraulein," Eva said sincerely.

"These two ladies who will be posing as Mademoiselle's maids for an undetermined amount of time are in need of safe passage, Frieda....just as you are. Ladies, I am afraid I am at a disadvantage for your names," I said.

Eva went to each lady in turn. "May I present Ida Frisch and Sara Mann, Fraulein Liberman."

Frieda acknowledged both girls but still looked extremely pale, the girl gave an awkward wave at Frieda, ugh, not a good start at all.

"Franz, would you..." I barely started to say it and Franz presented his arm to Frieda and whisked her away. Schnapps would be in her future if my skills were still sharp. I took a large breath, stretching my muscles a bit before the next round.

"Oh my, you must be..." Eva began, but I gently motioned for her to allow me to continue.

"Ladies, after your recent exposure to the German elements invading our area, I am certain you understand the urgency of removing you to a more accommodating climate. To do that, you need to pose, VERY CONVINCINGLY, as Eva's maids. You will be receiving a crash course in how to do that. Tomorrow morning, upon rising, you WILL be Mademoiselle's maids, understood?" Both girls fell over themselves with assurances. "Eva, please take my room, at the top of the stairs turn left, first door on the left. You will need to begin lessons at once; we will work on proper attire. Ladies will you help your mistress with her things?" I said, leaving no room for argument from anyone.

Lord, my body hurt, onward, off to the kitchen where I found Franz and Frieda at the servants' dining table with a bottle of Schnapps and a partially full glass in deep conversation.

"We do not expect forgiveness for our transgression. You are a stubborn woman and we both knew the only way to get you out of Vienna willingly was our ruse." Franz was speaking in his most sincere voice.

"If you would have but been honest with me," she was trying to say.

"You would have insisted on staying with us, would you not?" Franz asked.

"Yes," she said, lowering her head.

"Stubborn, but smart and tough, and now we need your help to save those two Jewish girls. You must be very, very tough to have gone through what they go through. Do you think you could help them?" Franz was amazing at bringing women around to his point of view. "Help them have a chance at a good life, a chance to not die in a Nazi work camp a few months from now or worse?" He finished her off with the last sentence.

"Herr Franz, I will try my best to teach them what I know," she said, rising to go off to help.

"Frieda!" I said, she turned to see me and smiled just a bit, "Please contact the dress shop, we need at least one if not 2 seamstresses here immediately."

"Yes, Herr Alexsander, right away," Frieda said.

"You will find all of the ladies in my rooms, Frieda, fully outfit them if you please, including luggage, all of them," I said.

"Yes, right away," she said, and walked away like the captain she was.

I found a glass, walked over to the table, and sat down, a small moan sneaking out.

"Working out the soreness I see!" Franz said, laughing.

"Shut up and pour me a decent amount of that would you?"

He started laughing again as I pushed my glass over to him. He poured the glass half full, grabbed Frieda's still half full glass and touched mine with it.

"Zum Wohl!" he said.

"Zum Wohl!" I tapped his newly acquired glass and drank the whole thing.

"You gave her your rooms? I take it you are planning to bunk with me tonight. I will try not to molest you in my sleep," Franz joked.

"I was going to stay in the study, but under the circumstances your bed, preferably without your advances, might be more comfortable." I started laughing as I said it, but lord it hurt.

Frieda unpacked us and repacked us both, dragging Ida and Sara along, forcing them to help with everything. Teaching them how to choose things, how to fold things, on and on. In the early afternoon, the dressmakers arrived complete with two racks of ladies' clothes, boxes of lady's necessaries, shoes and more. They went to work on both girls.

Frieda was overjoyed to find out she was included in the fittings and schooled both ladies in proper etiquette of being professionally fitted. Eva enjoyed watching the fray until she was also made to join. An immense amount of arguing about too many clothes started it off until I asked exactly what "type of clothes" were packed for Vaduz. I followed up with a list of what the bare minimum requirements would be for daily life there.

"Oh my!" was uttered and not another disagreeable word was exchanged.

More items were sent over, more were taken back. The luggage arrived; Frieda had chosen very well. Items were sorted out into sections of the room for each lady, to be packed in the proper luggage. Eva, of course, would have the bulk of items, her maids needing only 2 real types of clothes and Eva needing everything from day wear, to riding, skiing, evening, lounge wear, formal, informal, supper, etc.

Franz and I stayed clear most of the day, playing chess, with an occasional trip out to check on things. Eva found her way into the library at one point, looking sheepish, Franz said. I was studying Franz's last move and without looking up, inquired about what was wrong.

"If I may be frank," she hesitated.

"Darling, money is of no concern, if you want it, buy it, if the ladies need it, buy it, if you think you might need it two years from now, buy it," I said, still studying the board. Franz was looking at her I could feel him gauging her reaction.

Somehow, Frieda had managed dinner in the middle of the madness. We sat at the servants' table, the dining room an empty shell. I made everyone eat together as equals, but not until Frieda taught the girls how to serve. Then they were allowed to sit and eat, manners kept in check every step. It was not the most pleasant thing to watch, but Frieda was patient, kind and repetitive. After they ate, they were made to clean, do dishes and so on. The three of us made our way out to the sitting room, which was organized chaos.

"It is so much, Alexsander, I don't know!" Eva was saying. I cut her off.

"My love, please stop, it is what is needed for Vaduz. We do not expect the transition to be easy for you, but if you allow the three of us, Franz, myself, and Frieda, we will guide you, as well as Ida and Sara. Allow us to make the transition of these coming months smooth and gentle for you. You have been the lady of a house for many years, now you will be a lady of minor nobility overseeing multiple households. Honestly, it is much the same, even the pitfalls. Please relax, enjoy the scenery, allow someone else to steer the ship, so to speak." I held her hand raising it to my lips as I finished, reassuring her.

Franz, in his classic style, added, "Trust me, my lady, this is nothing, if our mothers were overseeing this, you would not be able to see the color of this room for all the items being procured for the trip."

We all found the few spots left to sit, making ourselves as comfortable as possible.

"Frieda tells me the servant's quarters are still fully intact. Your ladies will be housed there for the night. She will ensure they share the same room in Vaduz," I said. Eva looked relieved, probably thinking they would all be sleeping in the same room. "Was there anything else you needed to tend to, my dearest?" I inquired about Eva.

"I believe everything is in order. Two couriers came today to finish some legalities. Money is being moved to Vaduz for me. I put the latest 'notes' from Madame Renee on your desk in the study. I will excuse myself from them under the circumstances. I am concerned about Ida and Sara though." She stopped speaking and looked at me as if unsure how to approach what she wanted to say.

"Please express your concerns," I assured her.

"Ida and Sara are concerned about their future, um, employment."

Eva looked a little amused.

"Have they said what they might have in mind or are they thinking to continue in their previous line of work?" I inquired.

"They have indeed, they have asked to continue as house staff in the future. Requesting to continue training with Freida."

I looked over at Franz, what would we do with them? The only staff we needed now was here. The one place they could not stay.

"Originally, my thought was to have Frieda oversee things for you, however under the circumstances…" I drifted off, getting up to stretch and change positions. I paced the room a bit, stretching out and thinking. With Eva becoming my wife, we would end up with a household, so eventually we would need staff. "Are either of the ladies able to cook?" I asked.

"No, I don't think so, I would have to inquire though," Eva replied.

Franz grinned; he already knew what I was up to. I rang Frieda, she along with her two new shadows appeared in the sitting room.

"Frieda, the ladies feel they may like to continue employment with our family. Therefore, I will leave it to you to train them thoroughly. The entire household, kitchen, laundering, all of it. Would you be willing to take that on?"

I watched her expression change as I said it. Frieda understood well what I was saying. This would put her in charge of her own staff. Establish her solidly as housekeeper for my household.

"Indeed Herr Von Rieser," Frieda said proudly.

"Very well, thank you, Frieda."

With that Frieda chased them back into the kitchen.

After what had seemed like an eternal day, my sore bruised body found itself in bed.

"You better not be au natural, or I'm throwing you out forcibly," Franz joked, coming over to climb in bed.

"Don't worry, I won't rub it on you, much," I snickered at him.

"Thank God you have night clothes on."

"Fritzy, come on, you really think I would invade your bed naked?"

"It wouldn't be the first time, Sandy!"

"We were a little younger then, and I only did it to annoy you." I laughed, trying to find a comfortable spot.

"So, how do you want to play this out tomorrow with our parents. Are we going for the immediate chaos of telling them Eva is going to be your wife or shall we drag the satire out slowly?"

"After running through every possible scenario about a dozen times the last few days, I'm going for the long game." I just hoped it was a practical choice, but I knew Fritzy had played it out too, so here was where he would or would not be devil's advocate.

"I agree, except for one problem, Frieda knows."

"Scheisse! I'll talk to her in the morning."

"I already did, Sandy, she has no desire to tell anyone. Her maids sing like little canaries, so Frieda is well informed about Evangeline. She has also threatened for them to disappear if they breathe a word of it to anyone else. That woman would die for you, Sandy."

I rubbed my face with my hands, a new problem.

"Oh yes, I'll just bet she is thrilled to find out her new mistress was a Madame, Fritzy," I sighed.

"Actually, Sandy, I am not certain Frieda will look down on her at all. She has always been very fair about judging people by the way they treat us, not by who they are. It has made her an asset in our work, time will tell though. Get some sleep, old man, we are going to have one hell of a role to play tomorrow morning."

"The better part of valor is discretion, my brother."

"Amen, brother!"

Two cars arrived in the morning. Bags were loaded, ladies were loaded, the property was secured, and we were off. During the war, it had always impressed me the efficiency with which equipment, supplies and men were moved. Today, I felt none of that efficiency in our lives, although Franz assured me, we were doing quite well. Father had arranged for a parlor car, instead of a passenger car on the train, thus accommodating both families. Therefore, accommodation was adequate, even with the additional passengers. Evangeline was introduced as a fellow traveling companion of Franz and me, and we left it there to begin with. Frieda squared away the two "maids" and we began the trip settling into coffee.

I loved the train, and this trip particularly. The scenery on this route is spectacular every time. A body would have to be dead to find no joy on this trip, if only it was longer. Franz and I were sure to sit on either side of Evangeline so she would not be cornered by herself by any of our parents. Our mothers were already plotting, probably working out a series of questions worthy of the inquisition if we knew them and we did. Eva had been warned, and with her skills, we had no doubt she was more than capable of outwitting them both. However, we strived to put it off as long as possible.

Around eleven, a lovely brunch appeared, my father literally pushed us both out of the way physically, he then gracefully offered his arm to Eva. There was nothing we could do, farewell to thee, my love. Each of us took the other's mother, it was a tactic we had long employed to keep them in check. Eva was placed between both of our fathers, and like the professional she was, had them eating out of the palm of her hand before the first bite of the meal.

Our mothers, sisters in every respect, tried everything to pin us down.

Who is she? Who are her people? Where are they from? Are they nobility? Is it a family we know? Are they related in any way? Why haven't we seen her before? What circles does she travel in? It was a solid hour of deflection. As they were our mothers, lying was out of the question. We would both be caught immediately but deflection, we could pull off.

"I believe Innsbruck, possibly Paris, I am not familiar with a family by the name, are you, Fritzy?"

"No, have you met her people, Sandy, no?"

"We certainly could be related, Fritzy, do you know?".

"I believe she is quite private, preferring a simple life, do you know Sandy?"

By the time we were done, the resounding opinion was the young lady had pushed her way into our car by batting her eyes at their sons. We must have been momentarily smitten with the young lady and just asked her to share our accommodations.

Our fathers came away with an excess of information. She is incredibly intelligent, a businesswoman from a strong French family, minor nobility, and from money, too busy for marriage early in life, now ready to find the right man to settle down with. None of these things were said to them by Eva, simply implied. Enamored of her, they simply drew their own conclusions without her having answered a single direct question. So went the trip to Vaduz.

Arriving at the train depot in Schaan, automobiles and staff who had come ahead weeks before were on hand to handle bags, staff, and family. Off we went to Vaduz, Franz, Eva, and I in our own auto. Both of our mothers tried to gain entry, but to both of our father's credit they escorted them to their auto.

"Is it too soon to re-board the train and head elsewhere?" I inquired about them both. Eva laughed nervously.

"We could continue on to Switzerland, perhaps the Villa," Franz said jokingly.

There was a collective sigh as we prepared for act II. Our plan was for Eva to retire almost upon arrival, needing a rest and opportunity to freshen up. Unknown to Eva, Franz and I had a date with a jeweler of some renown.

The parents were distracted by the chaos of arrival, so we took the opportunity to spirit Eva away to her room and inform everyone she was not to be disturbed. Frieda, of course, would see she had everything she needed. Franz and I went back out to the auto and left.

Herr Bergman awaited us, his skill as a master jeweler was phenomenal. I described the tiara to him, and it was as if he could see into my mind. Pulling out a sketch book, he drew a sketch almost identical to it. He brought out the most beautiful pink diamonds, they were delicate, perfect for the tiara. He had just acquired them two weeks before. He would fashion it from white gold, using the pink diamonds on top of each of the five points, small diamonds encrusting the band connecting to each point. It would be magnificent, an exact replica of the one I saw her wearing in my vision. Even Franz got caught up in the excitement of it. Herr Bergman swore secrecy, and we set off back to the house.

Slowing down a bit, I asked Franz, "Any suggestions on how to proceed from here? Our mothers will not become less adamant regarding their uninvited guest."

"Short of coming out with the truth now, no."

"Fritzy, did Eva share with you what still needed to transpire with the priest? I was not quite myself at the time. She had Klaus arrange transportation, but I did not follow up after." Overriding my discomfort was my priority that night. Getting everyone prepared, packed and out of Innsbruck overrode private conversations regarding our betrothal.

"You were asleep when she arrived home late that evening. She seemed quite happy, but after the conversation you and I had, I did not pursue the outcome of her meeting. Not quite myself that night, Sandy, my apologies," Franz said.

"Not at all, well I need a private word with Eva to plan accordingly. Fingers crossed everyone is still busy."

Better than busy, everyone had retired to their respective boudoirs until supper this evening. We were both able to speak with Eva in her private sitting room.

"Oh, my Alexsander, these rooms, they are magnificent. So many, a whole family could live here quite comfortably. Are you certain these are all for me?" Eva's excitement warmed my heart.

"Yes, they are all for you. I assure you; these are only guest chambers; our rooms are even more extravagant. The Von Rieser's side of the family is the origin of the Estate. Father will be extremely happy to relay the history, I am certain. Franz's parents will be living in the guest house, which is the equivalent of The Estate in Mayrhofen," I replied, watching her admire her surroundings.

"The treaty of St. Germain served as a catalyst for our families, through Uncle Otto's direction, to consolidate much of our holdings. The bulk of both families' fortunes are in Lichtenstein and Switzerland. The properties in Austria are few, and Uncle has liquidated several more of those in the last few years. He has anticipated the power grab for Austria for some time," Franz explained.

Eva seemed fascinated but we had more pressing matters.

"If we might change the subject for a moment. The priest in Brandburg, were there directions for our arrival here? Any instructions on the next steps needing to be taken?" I inquired.

Eva seemed overjoyed to be reminded. "Confession is complete, the priest instructed me in penance." She excused herself and went into her boudoir to retrieve an envelope. "I am to speak with the parish priest, Josef Henny, here, at a St. Florin. He will receive these documents and advise us from there."

"Advise us?" I asked.

"Yes, he said we should attend the priest together," Eva answered.

"Anyone feel like a drive?" I asked.

As we approached the Cathedral of Saint Florin, Eva was captivated by its beauty. Franz relayed the history for Eva as we entered.

"The Cathedral's design and erection are credited to Viennese architect Friedrich Von Schmidt. The build took place when Austria was still whole under Emperor Franz Joseph I in 1869. At that time, Liechtenstein was still considered a sovereign country under Prince Johann II, however they fell into the Austro-Hungarian Empire. The royal family still lives in Lichtenstein castle near Vienna."

While Franz showed Eva around, I sought out the priest, Josef Henny. He brought Eva and me into his office, introductions were made, the envelope handed over, and we were asked to take our seats. The envelope held quite a thick letter and a document of some sort. Sitting patiently across from him watching his face was akin to being at the theater. Emotions played across his features as the pages were read. He inspected the certificate, stood, walked over to his fireplace, and threw the letter onto the fire.

"Those things are behind you, my child," he said approaching Eva. She began to kneel, and he took her elbow, "please, no, my dear, you have no need to kneel before me." He brought his chair around from his desk to sit facing her. "You choose the holy sacrament of marriage?" he asked.

"I do, forsaking all others," she replied quietly.

"Continue your penance, my child, seeking the guidance of our Lord in all thoughts and actions. St. Mary of Egypt is your patron saint, seek her counsel as well.

You are the young man wishing to enter matrimony with Evangeline?" he asked, looking at me.

"I am, Alexsander Jakob Wallner Von Rieser," I said.

"Ah yes, I know you now, we shall receive your parents at mass then. They are here with you. Yes, of course, please deliver my blessing to the family." He whispered something in prayer and continued, "I am given to understand the two of you have known each other for many years. You have broken moral law together on more than one occasion. Have you sought confession for these and other transgressions?" he asked.

I felt like my father had just cornered me doing something terrible. Of course, the only way forward was truth.

"No, I have not sought confession for my defilement of our bodies. Nor have I taken communion since the first time," I said quietly.

"Do you intend to seek confession and the holy sacrament of communion before the witness of your vows?" he asked.

"I do!" I replied.

"Very well, I will see you both every month until May, you may choose a date after May for your vows to be witnessed. I will see you in January on this same date. You will both need to make confession and then partake in communion in May," he said.

He prayed with us and expressed his joy at Evangeline's new path in life. We thanked him, said our goodbyes and were on our way. The box was checked, our secret could be let loose.

Driving home, Fritzy was staring at me, "Fifteen years, how did I miss that?" he said laughing.

"Excuse me?" I asked.

"Well in my defense, it was not my intention to eavesdrop. I came looking for the two of you and just happened to show up at the right moment," Franz pleaded, hands in the air.

"If you must know, I would always walk up behind all of you. Everyone would be making their way back so they would not even realize I was not taking the body or the blood. The priest would bless me and typically whisper something about confessing," I said, laughing at my ruse. Although I felt the guilt of it too even as I laughed. Eva looked slightly distraught, "Don't worry, my love, you are worth the sacrifice of my immortal soul!" I said, joking, only for her to burst into tears. It took almost twenty minutes to get her back together again and continue home.

Once in her room, I called Frieda. "Frieda, please draw her a bath and perhaps some hot tea. If she is still not recovered, please let me know." "Eva, darling, Frieda is going to draw you a hot bath. Please allow yourself to let go of the guilt, just let it wash away, my darling. Listen to the priest, my love, you have a new life, a new path." I kissed her forehead trying to reassure her.

If I were in her place, I am not certain I would be able to overcome the guilt with which she was wrestling. She had never said, and I had never asked, but my guess was she began as a courtesan somewhere between 12 and 15.

"Please, St. Mary of Egypt, release her from the guilt of a thousand men and women's souls," I whispered as I left for my room.

CHAPTER 13

Frieda had followed me out the door, I sighed and let her come along behind me. I entered my room and turned, waiting for her to close the door, and come out with it.

"Herr Alexsander, I have Ida in the kitchen for the week and Sara in laundry for the week. I will then switch them when they are going well enough."

"Frieda, you have never asked me about any household decision that involved someone performing a job. What, pray tell, is it that you want to speak about?"

She hesitated, I turned and went to my wardrobe room. She followed, grabbing my items as I removed them and laying them on the chair.

"I apologize for my behavior at the Innsbruck residence, Herr Alexsander. Both girls will be simply fine, I am certain. They are lucky to have someone who gave them the opportunity to have a better life. Everyone, you and your family have helped are most grateful."

I turned to ask her to turn so I could go to the lavatory, but she was gone. The door to the bed chamber closed behind her as I walked out to look for her. Going in to run a bath, I sat on the edge of the tub and took a deep breath, and another. There had been too much emotion for one day, and we still had supper to go. Scheisse, I might pretend to be indisposed and stay in my room tonight.

In the mirror, I saw my back. Slightly terrifying, my ribs bruised into my skin but the rest quite normal. A nice, long soak would ease my soreness and hopefully my nerves. I lay in the steaming tub, grateful for the quiet, mulling over the entire day. It seemed like several days in one. All the tasks could have been spread out, but I felt an urgency to marry. Strange, as I had never had any inclination to marry. Even with my feelings for Amelia, marriage was never a thought. And the tiara, I desperately wanted to place it on her lovely head before I left for Vienna. A promise of the life ahead, the life she so deserves. The open declaration of commitment leaves no question of my intentions. The warm water enveloped me. I dunked under holding my breath, lifting out just enough for my nose to take in the air. My whole-body becoming part of the water.

Restored, all the soreness, emotion, anxiety, and guilt washed down the drain, I extracted myself from my haven to dress for supper. Luckily, I had the towel wrapped around me as I exited the lavatory. I had not heard Father come in, but there he sat at the reading table, his favorite crystal decanter of BarenJager sitting with two partially filled glasses.

"Thank you, Father, for bringing me a libation. Am I to be the sacrifice before dinner or after?" He stood up and walked to the window.

"Oh, Alexsander, let us not engage in any drama. Your mother and aunt will have that quite in hand tonight I suppose. I prefer you in the role of your namesake, a conqueror, a man who makes his own destiny, as you always have."

It was not lost on me, he removed being named after my mother from the picture.

"Allow me to finish dressing and we shall toast like men off to the trials of war then," I jested.

"That, my boy, may be close to the truth."

I was just starting my tie when he came around and finished it for me.

"I remember when you were quite young. We would practice tying your tie every night before dinner. Anytime I was away on business, your mother would always tell me of your trials tying it yourself. 'He will not allow me to assist him,' she would say, 'he tells me it is his father's right to teach him.'" Father laughed and motioned to the chair. I sat, we toasted, "zum wohl!" "Zum wohl!" We both drank the contents in one swallow and father poured it again.

"So, how do you plan to announce it?" He looked me square in the eye as he asked. "NO, men to war remember. No drama, your rules."

This is where I should tell him he should be a gambler, but he was, if it was not for his abilities, our families, like so many others, may have been left with worthless titles and a pauper's bank account.

"It is complicated, Father." I took the new glass and swirled the honey-colored liquor around.

"You mean because of her former profession?" I stared at him, not knowing what to say. "Oh, come now, Alexsander, do you really think I did not know about your extracurricular activities? You are my only son, I am aware of Franz's indiscretions also, all of them!" The look on my face brought the next statement, as my father waved in the air. "Good God, no! I would not share those items with his father, do you think me a tyrant?"

I stood, swallowing a bit, and setting the glass down. I walked over to the window, preparing for the duel.

"No, Father, I will not let her go!"

My father started laughing, grabbed my glass with his and came to the window with me. He handed me my glass and, as we looked out, surprised me yet again.

"Alexsander, you have been in love with her, I believe, since your first row with her. I knew about Eva before Amelia because that shocked me. I thought you would grow out of it in time. She would move on, you would move on, but you always went straight back as soon as you were home or in Innsbruck. These last years, I assumed you two would just continue the pattern until, for whatever unfortunate reason, it ended." He paced the room, thinking, putting together what he wanted to say next. Although I wanted to question him, I knew my father, all would be answered before he was finished. A knock came at the door.

"Come!" we both said at the same time. Frieda came in and looked at both of us, unsure of whom to attend first, I waved her in. She came over, looked at Father then at me.

"The lady is quite recovered; she will be dressing for dinner in a few minutes."

"Thank you, Frieda, please let her know I will attend her sitting room shortly to escort her to supper," I said.

Father raised an eyebrow, Frieda hurried from the room, shutting the door behind her.

"Not to repeat myself but how do you intend to announce it?"

"I was just going to announce it, Evangeline refuses to marry under the ruse of a lie and plans to tell the truth when push comes to shove."

Father whistled, "That, my son, is one brave woman." We stared at each other, and he turned to resume pacing. "I have done my own investigation, but tell me her story, from her view if you would indulge me?"

I laid out the story, not in depth, but the necessary details. Father swallowed down the rest of his drink. Poured some more, brought the bottle over to me, and refilled mine.

"I believe I have a solution that will settle this nicely." He grabbed me by the shirt but motioned for me to grab the bottle. I did as I was instructed.

Down the hall we went, arriving at the door to Eva's sitting room, Father tapped gingerly. A few moments went by and then we heard "Come in, please." Father swept into the room like a knight charging a dragon and made straight for Evangeline.

"My dear, you look ravishing, please come sit down for just a minute and humor me if you would," he said, taking her hand and leading her to a chair that faced the entire room. She looked at me for a clue as to what was going on. I motioned to her to hold on and she seemed to understand.

"My dear, I must admit to the charade of knowing both who and what you are about for the last fifteen years." Pure panic hit her face, again, I motioned to her, wait. "I do not hold with the idea one human being is better than another. There is simply good and there is evil, and you, my dear, are not evil. Even then, they are both of God, or how could they exist? I will rely on you not to repeat this to any priest, bad for business, you know," he chuckled continuing, "our problem is how to present you to the entire family honestly. Therefore, I would like to propose the following!

You were sold into bondage as a young girl, truth. Throughout your life, you were subjected to degradations, truth. As you grew older, the prospect of another life never seemed possible due to the evil you have always been subjected to, truer than not. Until Alexsander shined the light of possibility upon you, allowing you to break out of your bondage and return to God. As you are absolved, what, when and how do not exist."

Eva and I were both staring at him, struck by simplicity and truth without disclosing untoward details of her life. Once the Absolution card hit the table, any questions would thereby be considered an affront to God's judgment in absolving her.

"Frieda......Frieda! I know you are in the other room, please go retrieve Herr Franz, thank you," I said.

"Now would you like me to announce the betrothal before or after dinner?" Father asked.

Evangeline stood up, walked over, took my father's hand, and got on tippy toes to kiss his cheek.

"You, sir, are a scoundrel and an angel," she said.

"I assure you, Mademoiselle, I have never been accused of the latter," he said, laughing.

I went over to shake his hand, he set his glass down and gave me a hug, congratulating me on choosing such a fine match for myself. It was the first hug I could remember since graduation. Franz came rushing in carrying his shoes.

"Frieda wouldn't even let me get my shoes on, what is going on?"

Father ran through the plan, Fritzy looking perplexed that Uncle Otto had charge of the conspiracy. He kept looking at me for confirmation, which I nodded at the appropriate moments. He set his shoes down, shook Uncle Otto's hand, and was also subjected to a hug.

Father made his exit saying, "I cannot tell you how excited I am." Grabbing the bottle, he went through the door, charging into the battle of wits about to ensue in the sitting room below.

We all came together in relief; Frieda cleared her throat.

"If I may inform your two maids about your situation?" Eva went to her, taking both hands in hers.

"Of course, my dear Frieda, thank you so much for everything. I truly understand how Alexsander and Franz cannot do without you, you are such a blessing." Frieda blushed and excused herself from the room. "If you two do not mind I still need to finish pinning my hair, I'll be out in just a moment."

"Evangeline, you look absolutely stunning just the way you are," I said as she moved out of the sitting room.

With all the excitement from Father I had not had time to really look at her. She wore a dark green evening gown, matching the color of her eyes when her passion was up, lovely silver earrings, and a necklace accenting décolletage.

"Well, there is my shock for the week. Do you have another one of those, Sandy?" Fritzy asked, pointing to my glass. I handed it to him and walked into the other room.

Eva was pinning the last strand of hair on her head. I turned her around gently and kissed her passionately. No explanation for the feelings coursing through me. The kiss left us both slightly breathless. We must have looked half mad to ravage each other. Her eyes glowed dark green, and it took every ounce of my effort to back away from her, while she pushed me away.

"Alexsander," she said breathlessly, "my goodness, you are not making my vow easy."

"My apologies, I am overcome," I said back toward the door.

She giggled a little, "Yes, I see."

I flushed red, turning away, I readjusted my ego, "I'll meet you and Franz in the hallway in just a moment." I returned to my room, and after removing my tie, I folded my collar under and freshened up with some cold tap water. If Franz had not been there, Eva and I would have been on the sink, the floor, and who knew where else. Lord give me strength, this was going to be a long six months.

"Hail Mary full of grace."

"You okay, Sandy?"

"Yep, right here."

Pulling myself together I grabbed the dinner jacket only to hear something fall to the floor. I bent over retrieving a case with the family crest emblazoned on the front. I opened it, inside a jewel encrusted broach of the family crest. Specifically, the family crest of the Gräfin (Duchess). Father must have brought it. I placed it in the jacket pocket, grateful to have a betrothal gift after all.

Father beamed as we walked into the sitting room. Eva once again became the focal point of all. Franz and I, as a joke, kept taking turns placing her on our arms. Our mothers and his father continually trying to figure out if either of us considered her a love interest. My father became the epitome of the cat that swallowed the canary. Dinner followed the same pattern as brunch on the train. Eva took her place next to my father, Franz seated on the other side of her. His father to my father's right, which kept her well insulated from our mothers. With a full staff again, dinner became a leisurely and pleasurable affair.

Franz caught Ida peeking out from the kitchen once to get a look at her former Madame and all the fancy people she was with. I wondered if it had dawned on her that she was now part of those fancy people too. I knew what her former profession paid after deducting room, board, the house's cut and so forth. They would be pleasantly surprised to see their new pay structure. Here she would not be charged for her needs. They would both be free to seek employment with other households if they became unsatisfied here or seek new professions altogether. Well trained household staff commanded a very decent wage these days, which was why the profession could be quite cutthroat among truly wealthy families. Once a household obtained skilled staff, you were unlikely to be let go for anything less than theft or assault. When we had encouraged Frieda to obtain a position with a lady, she was receiving offers for double her salary. The position was only as a lady's companion, not running a whole household as she had been doing for me. Frieda, being highly intelligent, understood the references she gained by staying put and running a household. It took most people far into their later years to be in such a position. To be well established at that by thirty was an achievement to be proud of.

Dessert went by, and we fairly held our breaths waiting to see when Father would fell the blow. It was now or never; the ladies would return to the sitting room and the men to the library or study. I saw father speak to the head butler, here we go. I winked at Franz, and we slid up on either side of Eva, each taking an arm.

"Ladies, I believe we will all join you in the sitting room," Father said, offering mother his arm. She eyed him with suspicion as they took the lead of the procession. Once in the sitting room, we seated Eva in the love seat between us. Everyone assumed their traditional places. The head butler and footman arrived with Champagne and glasses. Mother started to say something but opted to watch her husband reveal what they all suspected. The butlers began pouring champagne and the cat spit the canary out.

"Everyone, take a glass if you please, come on, come on, the bubbles will be gone at this rate. My darling Evangeline, would you attend me please?"

Evangeline looked unsure but rose, and with her glass in hand, made her way to my father. He gently took her hand, turning her out to face the four of us.

"Evangeline, long have we wished for a daughter to grace our home, and I could not have chosen a more perfect addition to our family. It brings me the greatest pleasure to announce your betrothal to Alexsander. Congratulations, my dear!"

He passed her back in my direction, and I received her with my arm around her waist. We all drank the toast at Father's lead and chaos ensued. The old rascal loved every minute of it. How long have you known? Why didn't anyone tell us? Tears flowed like champagne. Mother and Auntie swooped upon Eva, pressing for a date, what would her colors be? What about her family? Truly realizing the implications, I think the conversation with my father earlier in the night really came home for her. Father stood back and watched, and then at the precise moment I almost pulled her away, he tapped on his glass getting everyone's attention.

"If you please, I have words that must be shared with my family before we go further. Please take your seats, all of you. Before we proceed, and with your permission, the story of Mademoiselle Evangeline Allard must be told so as not to subject her to undue strain." He nodded to her for permission, and she returned his nod, then looked down toward the floor. "Mademoiselle was sold into bondage at the tender age of seven, she was just a young girl. Throughout life, she was subjected repeatedly to humiliation, disgrace, dishonor, and debasement of the evilest sort. As she grew older, the prospect of another life never seemed possible due to the evil to which she was constantly subjected. Until Alexsander and Franz were able to show the light of possibility to her, allowing her to break out of her bondage and return to God. Our dear Evangeline comes to us from St. Florin with confirmation of her absolution. Bless you, child, for persevering, we welcome you into the love and protection of our family by the grace of God." Everyone broke into Glory Be. At the Amen, I then took the opportunity to solidify things.

Kneeling in front of her, I took her hand.

"My darling Evangeline may every day hold the grace of you within it. I beseech you to join me in the holy sacrament of matrimony, to forevermore be my wife, my friend, my lover. I fear your betrothal present is some time off, however, there is something more fitting to the station you will be assuming I wish to present to you." I placed in her hand the jewel encrusted family crest of a Duchess. "I present to you the crest of your family which will forever more protect and defend you, even unto death, the future Gräfin Evangeline Allard Wellner Von Rieser."

Evangeline fell into my arms, crying, as did Mother and Auntie cling to their husbands, dotting tears from their eyes with their handkerchiefs.

Most probably, their tears were memories from the men standing next to them pledging themselves and their families to them. Champagne went round again; everyone took turns congratulating. As things calmed down, Father gave me the eye, eventually excusing the men for a Cognac and a cigar. Eva, now safe from prying questions, was left to be doted on and fussed over as the daughter neither of them had.

CHAPTER 14

Evangeline pulled me into her sitting room. Closing the door, she wrapped her arms around me and pulled me to her lips. Her mouth was sweet, the taste of Champagne lingering on her lips. My hands took on their own purpose, navigating through lace and silk, Eva pushed me back reluctantly. Her eyes begged me to take her there in the sitting room. The words were soft, hesitant.

"Do you think, just this once? How are we to wait so long?" She pushed off me, turning away, not looking at me. "Just being near you, it is so difficult not to touch you, to kiss you. Why do we need to wait so very long just to have our vows witnessed?" She sat in a chair, frustrated, her hands between her thighs, closed off.

I squatted down in front of her. "I long for you too, but we will do this. We both know I must return to Vienna. It will be easier for you with me away. No, please do not look so sad, we spoke of this. We must do what we can to help in the time we have. Please, my darling, bask in being spoiled by my parents. Continue with the priest, we will persevere. In no time at all, I will be standing at the altar next to Fritzy sweating." I took her hands and kissed the palms of each one. I stood and bent over to kiss her forehead.

"Get some rest, it has been a very long week."

"Alexsander, I do not ever want to be without you again, must you go?"

She rose to kiss me. I kept it brief and wrapped her in an embrace instead, hoping to spare us both the need to stop our passion for one another. I heard her whisper, "I love you so very much!" into my chest and I whispered the same back into her sweet-smelling hair.

A light knock came on the door. We gave up our embrace as I said, "come!" Sara emerged, looking smart in her house uniform.

"Mademoiselle, Frieda has instructed me to assist you in changing for bed," Sara said, her eyes darting to both of us looking for confirmation.

"Thank you, Sara," Eva said. I wished them both a good night's sleep and excused myself.

I made my way down the hall to a room that suddenly seemed so empty as I entered it. Making love to her would have been so easy. Staying chaste with her mere steps away was going to require a great amount of fortitude.

Frieda appeared after a brief knock to gather my supper clothes.

"Allow me a moment, Frieda, and I'll change." She made herself busy pulling out bed clothes she knew I would not wear, turning down the bed, while I changed to shirt and slacks.

"Congratulations, Mein Herr!" she said while quietly gathering the clothes and leaving. I looked over as she closed the door to see quite a large grin on her face.

As distracting as the last week had been, it was time to get back on course. Going to my writing room, I retrieved the letters from Madame Renee. They were several days old now, but certainly of use. Frieda had placed some correspondence on the desk also. The correspondence that was household in nature I set aside for morning.

I read all the letters, beginning the second round to take notes when I heard Fritzy knock. He just came in, the knock being his signature warning. I laughed to myself.

"Well, I felt Uncle Otto handled tonight in his usual noble style. I have often wondered if he is not secretly a Hapsburg6 too, operating incognito," Fritzy said with great amusement.

"There would be no shock at all if we were to find truth in that speculation. Have you come to assist in the dirty work or are you here for another purpose?" I inquired.

"Oh, definitely the dirty work, how could I resist? Speaking of resisting?" He gave me an inquiring look.

"As chaste as ice, as pure as snow",7 I said. We both broke out laughing. "Honestly, it is a struggle, and I fear it makes it doubly difficult for her to have me nearby. We both came dangerously close to transgression tonight. If I had not lost control earlier, I do not think it would have been such a close call tonight."

"Anytime you use a line from Shakespeare to drive a point home; there may be no doubt you have definite feelings involved," Franz said. Taking a seat, he continued, "Look, the Chancellor is on holiday with his son, or so goes the ruse. Karl and Wilhelm are putting their plans in place. No word on Henry heading this direction?" He looked up to see my head shake in answer to his question, "No? Perfect. So why don't we take Eva sightseeing tomorrow? We need to do something to keep you occupied."

"Fritzy, I already know where you are headed with this, and no." I tried using the firmest voice I could find.

"Yes! Yes, you need to return to Vienna, but really, until Karl is ready

---

6. The **House of Habsburg** (/ˈhæpsbɜːrɡ/), alternatively

spelled **Hapsburg** in English and also known as the **House of Austria,** is one of the most prominent and important dynasties in European history.

7. Shakespeare Hamlet Act3 Scene 1, 145

and the Chancellor returns, you do not need to be there. Am I correct?" As usual, Fritzy knew the answer to his question before he asked. He had me cornered.

"No technically we do not, but if we were in place, ready to go..." I said.

"We can sit around all day staring at each other. Walking different routes, spying on who is coming and going. Everyone will be observing the Holidays Sandy, relax, please," he quickly countered.

"You know who will not be relaxing and observing the Holiday, Fritzy? The Nazi's!" I said, knowing the battle was already lost. "You read; I'll write," I said, handing him the stack of notes.

Happy to end the discussion, we took turns as we had previously. Each of us taking notes from the other's reading, we compared when finished deciding what if any information needed to be passed on.

"Pretty much the same as the other letters except this Ulrich. It is unclear if he is SS or training to be SS. He talks about a new law where they may detain or incarcerate anyone, they deem asocial or criminal without evidence. They are targeting Roma's specifically. Why would they target gypsies?" I asked.

"Worse why would you indiscriminately throw someone in a work camp? It seems like yet another way to get more forced labor," Franz said.

"Anyone saying anything against someone else could potentially be thrown into a concentration camp, without any due process." I meant it as a statement, though it was rolling through my brain like a question.

"Eleven o'clock already, let's take that bride to be of yours up to Gutenberg Castle in the morning, what do you say?" Franz looked at me, hopefully.

"Will you leave me alone if I don't agree?" I asked. Franz posed the most dramatically hurt face possible. "Then, yes I think she would enjoy the trip, now good night, Fritzy!" I told him as I got up and started heading for the bedroom.

Once there, I turned the lights out and opened the draperies. The moon was almost full, shining in to light up the whole room. She was magnificent, I left the heavy draperies on the bed open to enjoy the soft light. Removing my clothes, I climbed into bed, it felt so good, I seriously considered letting them go on the trip alone tomorrow. I would just lay here and let the soreness seep into the cushion of the bed for the day. It would never happen though; I would not last in bed that long. If Franz had not slipped me whatever he gave me the day I fell, I would have never been able to stay in bed then. Of course, he thought he was sly, but I do not just doze off sitting up. I watched the shadows play throughout the room, hoping for sleep, wishing for Eva to be there next to me, warm, inviting.

No! I began to think of the Eigner parents in Vienna for some reason. Perhaps they would be ready to make a break for it. I closed my eyes, letting best and worst scenarios play out in my head.

The next few days were spent in a whirlwind of activity, prompted by Franz, and supported by Eva's enthusiasm. Playing along became its own game of sorts. With all honesty, these things were the last I wanted to spend my time doing. However, the reality that this may be the last opportunity we had loomed in the background. Therefore, I threw myself into it with gusto. We even purchased a Leica camera for Eva and then took pleasure in teasing her about how much money she was spending on film.

Good to my word, we went to Gutenberg Castle and managed to procure a tour. The Paris church of St. Nicholas was just below for our next stop. Another day we spent in Schellenberg going to Obere Burg and

Untere Burg castle ruins. We made one day a day just for museums, and one for galleries. Eva was outfitted for outdoors and we tried a hiking trip, which allowed her to determine she prefers the automobile for her excursions, although she was quite content being outdoors just not traversing it. Additionally, she did not much like outdoor activities in winter. Fritzy and I both made attempts at teaching her the basics of skiing, which she solidly rejected. She was fond of sitting outside by the fire watching us though. I said nothing to Fritzy, but secretly I was grateful for her rejection of skiing. Eva looked nothing like Amalia, but any ski trip always brought her to mind.

The Holidays were upon us in no time. Herr Bergman phoned to notify me the tiara was complete and ready for approval. Father came into my writing room just as I finished changing.

"Alexsander, I understand Herr Bergman rang," he stated, but it was really a question. I came around to the room while tying my tie to greet him.

"Indeed, I just spoke with him, is there a problem?" I asked.

"No not at all, I have several things to pick up. If you are perhaps also going, I thought we might ride together."

"Of course!" I said.

"Very well, I'll have the car brought round, five minutes shall we say?" he asked.

"Perfect, Father, five minutes in the vestibule." I rounded back to the mirror to adjust my tie.

What a wonderful gift for Eva, it had all worked out for the best. The family crest for the betrothal and the tiara for Christmas, after all, the tiara was something she would wear for life, not just one event. As I walked across the writing room, I noticed the letters placed on the desk. I quickly went over to the desk and then stopped myself. Father would be waiting; they would keep until later. I went down to find him in the vestibule, a footman helping him with his jacket. I arrived just in time for him to turn to help me, but I waved him away with a thank-you.

In the automobile, Father told the driver to head for Bergmann's. Light conversation, primarily regarding the purchases the ladies made for servants during St. Stephen's after Christmas, began. Evidently, several pieces of jewelry were among the gifts which were part of what he wished to retrieve.

The tiara was exquisite, the band was laced with diamonds and a small central teardrop pink spinel lay in the center. Branches, it seemed, of tiny diamonds sprung from the central teardrop, weaving around to create the tiara, almost as if they were ivy. What looked like five crowns sprouted from the top of the tiara at even intervals, each surrounded by diamonds with a single teardrop pink diamond at the center. Throughout the entire sculpture, for that is what it truly was, small pink diamonds lay between placements causing the entire front to glisten a soft pink. It was enough to take your breath away.

"Herr Bergmann, a work of art, even the Bagration tiara[8] pales in comparison, you have outdone yourself!" Father declared.

"The design belongs to your son, bringing his creation to fruition is the only part I have played." Herr Bergmann said graciously.

I bowed to Herr Bergmann

"Without your masterful skills, Herr Bergmann, it would never have been made manifest. Truly, I am in your debt!" I replied.

"Alexsander, having seen your gift, I am now forced to change the gift I had chosen for her," Father stated, a little outdone.

"No need, Herr Otto, knowing the secret, I selected a gem to match

___

[8]. In 1977, the Duke of Westminster purchased a diamond and spinel tiara and matching set of jewels reported to have belonged to Catherine Bagration as an engagement present for his future bride Natalia "Tally" Phillips.

the tiara," Herr Bergmann said, bringing out a delicate looking bracelet that matched the tiara perfectly. One of the same beautiful pink diamonds graced the center.

"She will adore it, Father!" I said, admiring the two next to each other.

We spent the next hour going through all the items purchased for everyone, right down to Eva's new maids. Ladies poured from nowhere when the time came to wrap everything and prepare it. The offer was made to deliver everything, of course, but I could not bring myself to let the tiara out of my sight. Instead, Father and I enjoyed a coffee in the sitting room while all was prepared and loaded into the auto.

Arriving home, Mother and Eva came to oversee everything. Father and I slyly disappeared in the chaos, carrying our packages underarm. Franz must have been out at the guest house with Auntie and Uncle, there had not been a trace of him since the previous day. Entering my writing room, I went round to the wardrobe room and placed the package in the safe hidden in the tie cabinet. I hung my jacket on the valet stand, rolled up my sleeves, and returned to the writing room.

In the mail there was an envelope from Henry. Finally, a target ahead to move toward.

Dear Jim,

I hope the Holiday finds you safe. Planning to go abroad, communication will be much better as I travel. My former secretary sends her best, also doing well for the holidays. Let's schedule a trip when you are available. Perhaps after the first of the year, then we could do some duck hunting. All my best,

Henry S. Fletcher, III Esq.

London

Henry is on his way back, and he is bringing another machine, we will be able to get the communication network up. Well then, the Meadows on the first, now we are back in business! What a wonderful day, the tiara was ready, and Henry would be on his way at the end of the week. The news would keep until after St. Stephens though. Eva had made a little secret, she wanted me to give the whole business up and stay here with the family. Oh, still relay information and dabble, but stay out of the fray. There was an obligation to the Red and White, to my countrymen, an obligation I did not have words for. If I stepped back and hid here with my family, I would never be able to live with myself. After all, if I save just one person, haven't I changed the course of history in some important way?

I sent a note to Parish Priest Henny at St. Florin explaining the possibility of being detained on business past the meeting date set for January 15th. I asked if it would be possible to start on the 30th, as I was certain to have the next meeting on January 30th. Mother said Eva was at mass almost every day now. She and Auntie had taken Eva under their wings, so to speak, and were slowly tutoring her on the finer aspects of running a home of some means. As charity held a close place to each of their hearts, they were keen to establish Eva in their organizations. However, Lichtenstein did not have an impoverished population comparable to the areas of Tyrol, upper and lower Austria. Therefore, they used their efforts to raise funds and provisions to send back over the border. Much of their efforts were through the church, in the same ways they had helped Klaus and Greta after the war.

Evangeline found a passion for the work they do. As she was unfamiliar with losing a business deal, Mother and Auntie were enamored of her talents immediately. She seemed to be able to procure at least some type of donation out of even the stodgiest person, especially men. It was with a significant amount of self-control that Franz, Father, and I were able to stay quiet one evening, as the entire conversation from before supper to retiring centered on Eva's uncanny ability to procure money from men. What is more, she left them happy about it regardless of how miserly they had begun. I had teased her ruthlessly later in her sitting room, stealing a few kisses and running off before donating something I would not be able to take back.

Christmas Eve came, both families opted for the family to celebrate Christmas Eve at the guest house with Franz and his parents. Then St. Stephen's would be done in the main house allowing trees, decorations and presents to stay put. At Uncle Franz and Aunt Anna's, the tree was lit, carols were sung, and a light supper was served. The staff celebrated their personal holidays in the main house, less the few who insisted we could not fend for ourselves on Christmas. At midnight, all the members of the household who were Catholic attended mass as one family.

Mid-morning on Christmas day, a beautiful brunch was served, feeling full and content we all moved into the sitting room with the tree. There we began the rounds of presents. I received a lovely pair of white gold cuff links from Eva, and a new book for my travels. My first true present from her. I vowed to keep them with me, knowing realistically I would rarely wear them.

My favorite Christmas treat had always been the tangerines, feeling like a glutton after such a large breakfast, I managed three before anyone noticed. Everyone then laughed riotously and recounted different tales of my adventures with Christmas tangerines to Eva. Franz would trade his tangerines for peanuts every year and this morning was no different. We divvied them up, thrilled with our haul. Things were winding down and Father and I winked at each other. I retrieved both packages and handed him his, he pushed back and winked at me.

Mother and Auntie noticed the change in the room immediately, chatting stopped, and an air of anticipation crept over everyone. I went to Eva and handed her both boxes. The boxes themselves were wood painted white with pink cherry blossoms covering them. She opted for the small box first, she set the large box on a little table next to her. Sitting in a side chair, she lifted the latch and opened the box. Her eyes turned as big as saucers, she looked at me and I looked at Father. She had tears as she acknowledged the gift.

"Please do try it on, my dear, we are all waiting to see how lovely it will become on your wrist." Father said in his most charming voice.

Mother's eyes glistened a bit as I looked over at her admiring her husband. Eva took the bracelet from the box, looking to me for aid, which I readily provided. Everyone insisted on a close inspection, she made her way around the room ending back around to me. I motioned to the other box, which she had clearly forgotten in her excitement.

Lifting the latches cautiously, she opened the box. Pink silk covered the contents, gently she pulled the silk cloth away to reveal the tiara. The box began to slip as her hands began trembling, I reached over, quickly steadying the box, setting it on her lap. Tears were streaming from her face. I handed her my handkerchief.

"May I?" I asked.

She nodded yes and I removed the tiara from the box and placed it on her head. The ladies gasped, the men nodded at me in approval, especially Fritzy, his eyes lit up with knowing. She began to say something, but only a little cry escaped. I held out my hand, she took it, and I strolled her around the room so everyone could see. Then I took her to the large mirror over the mantle. When she saw herself, she stood stunned, tears subsiding. Looking at me in the mirror, she slid closer, straightened the tiara, and laughed with joy. She threw her arms around me laughing or crying, perhaps both, it was hard to tell. Everyone was staring at us with such love. My heart hurt for the love we were both so lucky to have.

Finally, she pulled her face from my chest, wet handkerchief still pressed to her mouth. I reached into my side pocket, having anticipated this, and pulled out a dry one to hand her. She took it gratefully, laughing at me. We came back over to the center of the room where everyone was up, admiring, congratulating, and Eva was expressing her gratitude over and over. Things began to calm down, more coffee was served.

I looked over at her and said, "I will expect to see that again on our wedding day, with a dress to match."

I leaned back a little and saw my mother, who gave me a little wink.

"As Mein Herr commands," Eva said with a little giggle. Smiling at me with her playful look, she was painfully beautiful. The day flew by, the house full of joy, gratitude, and happiness.

In the morning, I was roused by Fritzy, bright and early. Everyone was in the kitchen for St. Stephen's Day. All the staff were chased out to sit by the tree enjoying coffee. We all carried out trays of pastry, breads, and other treats. Some had been procured, some were made by Mother and Auntie. Nothing had been prepared by the staff. Today was their day, presents from us to each of them were opened at their leisure. Frieda ended up organizing gift givers, people to call out names and bring gifts. Everyone received at least one clothing item, one frivolous gift, a stocking with tangerines, nuts, sweets, and something handmade. Ida and Sara both cried as they opened their gifts. Much as Eva, everyone took time to acknowledge them and share with them. I suspected everyone understood who the new maids in training were before arriving here. There was nothing but kindness toward them according to Frieda though, and possibly a little flirting from the footmen.

We served dinner in the dining room, after which we all got busy cleaning up. A few of the staff played instruments and music began shortly after dinner ended in the servants' quarters. Father brought out Schnapps, Champagne, and beer for everyone. We left them to it for the night.

Once again, we went to Aunties for our supper, it was wonderful. Eva had even helped a little, they said. After dinner, we moved into the sitting room together, speaking of all the fun we had waiting on the people who took such loving care of us.

"Franz tells me you are still looking for staff in Innsbruck, Alexsander," Uncle Franz said.

"Yes, indeed we will need at least two but preferably four for the Innsbruck residence. Certainly, we will need someone specifically to maintain the building and grounds. I do not anticipate being there often, but it is hard to say just now. You have someone in mind Uncle?" I asked.

"Indeed, several of our longtime staff were unable to come with us for different reasons. If you are interested, I would be happy to make inquiries," Uncle replied.

"Thank you, I will have a better idea of our needs after next week, of course."

As I said it, I realized I had told no one, not even Fritzy, Scheisse! Uncle Franz did not miss a beat,

"Then you will be returning next week?" Everyone was staring at me, Eva, with tears in her eyes, but not of joy this time.

"Yes, please forgive me. It was not my intention to deliver the news this way. I wanted to wait until tomorrow. Franz and I still need to discuss plans to proceed," I said, almost pleading, but looking at Eva, who rose and left the room, excusing herself.

"You, my son, are typically very astute, obviously, this is your weak area," Father said, raising an eyebrow.

I began to excuse myself and heard my aunt say, "No, sit down, let her be."

Mother excused herself following Eva.

"You have news then?" Fritzy asked.

"Indeed, from your running partner," I said cryptically.

"Excellent, I could use a challenge, when do we leave?" Fritzy was taking this frighteningly well.

"The first of the month at the latest," I said, watching his reaction. Nothing, not a twitch, he was completely nonplussed by the news. A meeting in the writing room was sure to follow.

"I'll start back to training in the morning. I expect you will join me to keep me honest?" Fritzy was cornering me, but I could not quite put my finger on why.

"Absolutely, I need to work off all the wonderful food from the last few weeks!" I said, staring back at him.

CHAPTER 15

Mademoiselle Evangeline Allard would not be accepting me in her sitting room for the near future. The note was brought by Ida just minutes after I had knocked several times, given up, and retired to my rooms. In my effort to keep her from disappointment, I had done far worse. She must feel betrayed, my not keeping her confidence would have been a harsh slap. A thought my always busy mind had not considered. I retired to a sleepless night, parceled out to pacing, sitting, writing, and staring. Sometime just after dawn, Franz knocked. I was already dressed and ready to go.

"Do you want coffee first?" he asked.

"No!" was all I had.

We ran the five miles to Feldkirch in silence. When we got back, I went upstairs, drew a bath, and lay in the tub. The hot water soothed my sore muscles and I found myself able to relax enough to sleep. I drained the tub, drew the bed draperies, and climbed in.

I awoke to Frieda's voice; my eyes drowsily opened a sliver. Phew, she had the curtains barely parted allowing only a soft light to enter the room.

"To what do I owe the pleasure?" I inquired from bed.

"Sit up, Mein Herr!" she said buzzing over to lift pillows, fluff them behind me and disappear around the bed. She quickly reappeared, tray in hand.

"There we are you must replenish after such a very long run. Herr Franz said you ran all the way to Feldkirch, no coffee, no breakfast."

Fastened to her collar was the sapphire cameo broach Herr Bergman had crafted for her St. Stephen's Day gift. A huge smile lit her face as she noticed me admiring it.

"Let me pour you some coffee, you have been asleep all day." As she said it, she saw me looking around and guessed at what I was trying to locate. "It is two in the afternoon. I was going to wake you hours ago, but Herr Franz asked you not be disturbed."

"Thank you, Frieda, sleep alluded me last night. Did you enjoy your holiday yesterday?" I asked, redirecting the conversation. Frieda turned red reaching for the broach at her collar.

"Your gift is too much, Mein Herr."

"No Frieda, it is not nearly enough for the care and service you provide this family." I gave her my most serious look with the reply. "You have both of us quite spoiled, we will miss you very much in the coming weeks." I said it to my food, knowing she too would be disappointed at our departure without her.

Frieda went around to open the curtains just a little further on each side of the bed.

"Mein Herr, did you know a woman is able to turn her hair yellow now, like Herr Franz?"

The way she said it was so baited I almost wanted to shut it down instead of allowing it to play out. Frieda coming to her own conclusions was always best though.

"Blond hair, how amazing, what do women do about their eyebrows and skin color though? I mean, women with a more Mediterranean complexion."

The doubt planted, I sipped coffee and tore off a small bite of roll. Gathering all my clothes, she returned to check on my progress.

"I'll bring more coffee if you like?"

"That will be fine, Frieda, thank you!" I smiled reassuringly at her.

She would spend the entire day figuring out how to color her eyebrows and hide her beautiful olive complexion. I would sorely miss her coffee, no one made coffee quite like it. Although, contemplating it, obviously her whole family does.

The bite of the roll did nothing to spur my appetite. After dressing, I moved into the writing room. More correspondence had arrived. Thumbing through, I grabbed what I wanted to read, made myself comfortable, and went through each one methodically.

Soon I found myself with a book in my hands. It was the Christmas gift from Eva, a children's book, but supposedly all the rage. A British author named Tolkien wrote it. Frieda appeared with more coffee and butter cookies. She set the tray up beside me, retrieved the old one, shaking her head at the food still left, and returned to her duties. Minutes later, it seemed, I was up turning on lights. Only to discover it was almost eight o'clock. No matter, I returned to the book. Again, Frieda made an entrance bringing water, juice, meat, cheese, crackers, and some dried figs. She removed the other tray, inquiring about my needs, then left. The book captivated me. Frieda returned at ten o'clock to turn the bed down and retrieve my clothes. To fulfill my obligations, I removed them, put on a robe, and returned to my chair. She brought a blanket for me and went to smolder the fire and light the heater.

"Please stoke the fire up, I'd prefer not to use the heater tonight," I asked, and I returned to my book. She built up the fire, disappeared momentarily, and returned shortly with a bundle of wood.

"Mein Herr, you must eat something, I will leave the tray," and she was gone. The tray, yes, I gathered up a few items, drank some water, and returned to my book.

Sometime around one in the morning, my eyes started burning horribly, surrender being imminent, I found my way to bed. Sleep found me immediately, dreams of tiny creatures, dragons and rings filled my night. I awoke feeling somewhat refreshed at around half past five. Rising, I attended to a toilette, dressed, and awaited Franz in the vestibule. Our run was leisurely today and half the pace from yesterday.

"Well, I am happy to not engage in a marathon this morning. Are we speaking yet or still brooding?" Franz said in a light manner.

"The book Eva gave me is quite good. I will lend it to you when I finish it," I said.

"I will look forward to it. Will you be joining us for breakfast this morning?" Franz looked at me with a brow raised as he said it.

"Yes, when would you like to make our tentative plans for the trip?" I asked.

"After breakfast, if you've time?"

"Perfect!" I said, entering the front door and returning to my room to bathe and change.

When I returned downstairs, only father and Fritzy were in the dining room. It was a bit early for the ladies.

"Will Uncle Franz be joining us this morning?" I inquired.

"No, I believe they are dining at home this morning," Father said offhandedly. After a light conversation over coffee, sausage, and a roll we headed off to my sitting room.

"What exactly is the plan? From your statement over dinner the other night I gather Henry will be here around the first of the month." Franz went right to it.

I explained, "Yes, Henry is returning around the first, and he will be bringing us a second machine. He will spend time training us on them. We will be able to not only relay messages with better encryption between each other, but with him also. Then, of course, we need to get to Vienna with Karl and Wilhelm."

Franz rose from his seat and paced around the room for a bit.

"What harm would there be if you were to stay here with Eva? I could continue without you, working with Henry, Karl, and Wilhelm. The two of you could continue planning the wedding, perhaps take a few trips to France or Portugal."

"Franz, what?" I asked, he was holding back.

"Sandy, since we arrived here, the feeling of foreboding is gone. As if your being here changes something." He came back to sit across from me again.

"Fritzy, I trust you with my life. If you have a feeling, I know to my core there is something to it. However, I just cannot bring myself to stay here, I am sorry. If avoiding whatever danger your foreboding is means not living my life the way I want; then what life is that? I hear you and I believe you; we'll be cautious, I promise."

He shook his head, and for a moment I thought he was going to say he would not come along, but he did not. Plans were made to leave on the last day of the month, we would return to Innsbruck and retrieve the automobile for the journey to Mayrhofen. Henry's last correspondence would put him there within the day of our arrival. After Franz left, I rang Klaus to plan.

After speaking with Klaus, I sat down at my writing desk. Taking time to organize my thoughts, I drafted a short letter to Eva.

Dearest Evangeline,

Darling, please understand there was no malice in withholding the information of my imminent departure. The holiday brought you so much joy it seemed criminal to ruin it with the news. My plan was to tell you the morning of the 27th, then relay the news to the family. Please, my darling, forgive me. We have such a short time before my departure, allow us to spend it beside each other?

Your betrothed,

Rather than involve the staff, I sealed the envelope, made my way over to her room, and slipped it under her sitting room door. I then sought out father.

"Might I have a word, Father?" I asked, stepping into his private study.

"Of course, Alexsander, please come in, sit down." He motioned to the chairs over by the fireplace. He rose and came over, choosing one opposite me.

"Father, if something should happen to me, I would like Evangeline to be well cared for, prior to the wedding I mean. Obviously, once we are married circumstances will change for her."

Father sat back considering, "Do you have specifics in mind?" he asked.

"I am uncertain as to what I am able to provide her with for stability, what would you suggest, Father?"

He rose, rang for the staff, and returned. A young footman showed up almost instantly inquiring about his needs. Father requested coffee and the young man was off like lightening.

"The obvious choice is to provide her with a monthly stipend, an allowance of sorts. Of course, she is one of the family now regardless. The vows are a formality as far as your mother and I are concerned. How does she feel about it?" He looked at me, but I had no answer. "Approach her, be frank, she is not a foolish young girl. She understands the danger you place yourself in. These are realities that must be faced head on. If something were to happen, what choices might she make?"

The footman reappeared with coffee, Father had him set it down and leave. He poured for us both. We sat in silence, enjoying each other's company without the need to say more.

I retired to my room, anxious to return to the book. It was quite impressive, perhaps it was branded a children's book, but the writing undermined that idea. It was articulate, well planned, and had all the components necessary for an enjoyable read. The book seemed to be written more for adults than many I had read in my life. Hours slipped by Frieda brought tea with biscuits in the afternoon. A letter, in Eva's hand, also lay on the tray. Setting the book down I retrieved a letter opener from the desk.

Dearest Alexsander,

Please attend me in my rooms at 5 this afternoon, a modicum of humility would be wise.

E

It was better than a "no," so I returned to the book, tea and biscuits while hoping for the best. The hour approached, I washed my face, put on a touch of cologne, combed my hair, and put on a jacket. Precisely at five, I tapped on the door.

Evangeline opened the door inviting me in. She was resplendent in a pink, crushed velvet supper dress I had never seen before. The bustier gathered tightly just under her breasts, fitting snugly down to her hips and into a flowing skirt just grazing the floor. Long sleeves and high shoulders accentuated her neck and décolletage, her hair was piled high on her head. It was obvious it had been tailored specifically for her. Truly, she could have been an angel with invisible wings. She asked me in again.

"Excuse me, I...you look lovely, Eva" I said, a little roughly as I tried to pull myself together.

"Please, Alexsander, do have a seat, would you care for something to drink?" She went to the dry bar and poured an apertif.

"I see Father has made you a fan, yes I will imbibe, thank you."

Pouring a second, she brought it over and handed it to me, motioning to the love seat. I chose an end, and she followed me, sitting in the middle, turned slightly toward me.

Sitting forward, the words poured from my mouth.

"Evangeline, please find it in your heart to forgive me. No plot was formed to keep the information from you, I simply wanted to give you the best possible holiday. An error on my part I do not plan to repeat," I said, reaching for her hand, which she willingly placed in mine. We both set our glasses down untouched.

"Finding out that way in front of everyone, no warning. Leaving me behind is quite hard enough without feeling a fool. Oh, Alexsander, I understand why you chose to keep it from me, but please do not repeat these mistakes." She threw her arms around me. I pulled her so close I must have been crushing her.

"My darling Evangeline, I love you so!" I whispered in her ear.

She found my lips with hers, passion took hold, I needed to feel her, every inch of her to kiss her, touch her.

"Oh, Alexsander, oh no, we must not." Eva backed away, breathless, flushed, beautiful. The stabbing pain in my groin was momentarily overwhelming.

"My love, forgive me, I must excuse myself, but I will rejoin you shortly."

My entire body was on fire, especially the lower extremities. I made my way back to my room. In the lavatory, I turned on the coldest water I could stand, stripped down, and stepped into the shower hoping to be relieved by something short of a thousand shards of ice stabbing into my entire body. Forcing myself to stay as long as possible, I finally shut off the faucet and stepped out of the tub, shivering from head to toe. My blood had cooled, for the moment. Toweling off quickly, I redressed, quite grateful for the warmth of everything around me. I addressed my hair and so forth before stepping into the writing room to find Eva seated waiting for me.

"Alexsander, forgive me, I do not wish to torment you so. Perhaps the time has come to accept God's grace and forgiveness. I simply cannot bear to see the pain you are in when it could so easily be relieved."

Crossing over to her I bent over kissing her forehead. Kneeling, I took her hands.

"Eva, darling, you won't compromise for me. We will have our entire lives together. Besides, it is a bit of my own medicine in a way. If I had been truthful from the beginning, we wouldn't even be having these conversations."

"Oh, Alexsander, please, the thought of you leaving without me is too much!" Eva said, a tear falling on her lovely dress.

"Darling, we must speak about something, time is of the essence, or I would not broach the subject under the current circumstances. Please, dearest, try to resist being caught in the emotion of the subject. I need my strong levelheaded businesswoman to answer this question."

Eva nodded a yes at the request, dabbing her eyes with her handkerchief. Bolstering myself I pushed forward.

"Eva, if the worst should happen to me, what would you choose for yourself?"

As I said it, I saw the horror cross her face. I gave her hand a squeeze then repositioned to wrap an arm around her. She looked away, handkerchief to her mouth.

We sat quietly while she waded through the emotion, the possibilities. Finally, she cleared her throat and turned back to me.

"My former life, I could not return to, it is no longer who I am. Perhaps a monastery?"

"Darling, understand you are family, you are my parents' daughter, they adore you. You need never want for anything again, least of all love. Please understand these things as you navigate your decisions." She smiled the most loving smile, kissing me lightly.

"They feel like my family, as if a thief stole me away and sold me, now I am home where I always belonged. Your mother and father are not kind out of obligation. Love comes to me directly from their hearts, I feel it when I am with them." She sat quietly for a moment, piecing together more of her thoughts. "Yes, I would stay with them for as long as they would have me. Auntie and Uncle also, they too treat me as if I were their long-lost daughter."

"Because you are, my dear. Both my mother and father have implied they tried for a daughter many times until Otto died. After that they were so heartbroken, too heartbroken. If anything were to happen, my love, rest assured they will wrap you in the bosom of our family for the rest of their days."

Eva laid her head against my shoulder, grasping my arm. A silence filled with everything unspoken flowed between us.

CHAPTER 16

Supper included the entire family, as if by design. After, we all adjourned to our places, men to the study, women to the sitting room. Uncle Franz and I spent the evening at the chess board while Fritzy and Father played backgammon. The ladies must have had a game of their own going on. A light subtle sound of laughter drifting through occasionally.

The hour grew late, and we all adjourned to accompany the ladies. Fritzy took his mother's arm, beating his father to it. He wrapped her up as if she were on an arctic expedition, not simply crossing the gardens to the guest house. We all chuckled saying our good nights.

Eva invited me in for a nightcap, instead, I asked her to my room. A hint of suspicion crossed her face, then disappeared as she took my arm again. Once in the rooms I asked her into the boudoir, I assured her it was not at all what she thought. Bringing her around to the wardrobe room, I opened the tie cabinet, popped a corner, and opened the false back to show her my safe.

"If you should ever need money, gold, anything along those lines, you come here. There are three different currencies and a substantial amount of gold. Father will be placing your name on several of my accounts, you will be listed as my wife. Documentation is being made available for you, just in case," I said smiling at her. "Now remember this—33-11-66, I'll close it and I want you to open and close it several times, so it will stay in your memory. Clear it to the left three times, now right twice, yes, now left to stop yes and back around. Perfect, do it again, please."

I patiently watched her open and close the safe box several more times. I inventoried the contents with her so that she would know what was immediately available to her should the need arise. She felt confident she would remember it and we moved to her sitting room.

We sat holding hands, but not overly close to each other, each in their own thoughts for a while.

"Alexsander, our appointment on the fifteenth?" she inquired.

"Day after tomorrow, darling, I rescheduled immediately upon finding out. He will push our future appointments to the 30th of each month, well, excluding February of course. Damn Gregorian calendar, the church did us no favors with that mess, forgive me, Father."

Eva giggled; we slowly worked our way closer to each other on the love seat until she finally laid her head upon my chest. Stroking her hair, we fell asleep, perfectly at peace just being able to hold each other. I awoke around two, Eva still laying across me. She was so beautiful; I felt the stir of more than my heart. Very gently, I brought my arm under her head, managing to bring my other arm under her lovely behind, I pulled her into me. She repositioned, sighing. Holding her close, I arose with a little effort from the awkward position and carried her to the bed. I gently placed her on top, moved down to slip off her shoes, then grabbed a blanket and placed it over her. Leaving her clothes on seemed wrong, but under the circumstances I determined it would be better for both of us. Although she needed not know, self-control was becoming a torment for me.

Returning to my own room, I found the bed lonely. I retrieved the book and read for much of the early morning hours, until the time I knew Fritzy would be ready to beat me at a run. Maybe he would be inclined to practice some fencing this morning, I, for one, needed to expend some aggression.

Fritzy, elated with the change of exercise, went off at once to change. Frieda brought coffee for us, and we set to it. Our matches were even, with both of us focused. An hour later we were drenched, in desperate need of bathing and sustenance in that order. We both headed in to get cleaned up. While shaving, a movement caught my eye. I nicked myself with the razor but stood still watching. Weird, nothing, I swished the lather from the razor, pressed the washcloth to my jawline, and walked into the writing room. Fully expecting to see someone sitting and waiting, I looked everywhere. Nothing, I peeked out the door into the hall, nothing. Strange, I returned to shaving, dressed, after the wound had stopped bleeding, and checked all the rooms. No one, nothing stirred, and yet I could not shake the feeling someone was there.

With our departure imminent, everyone appeared for breakfast. Fritzy outdid himself as usual, even though I put away a good share of food. Eva, seated on my left and mother on my right, was brimming with wedding conversation. None of which I had the slightest interest in but put up a good pretense in deference to the happiness they both displayed. We met with the priest mid-morning. When we arrived home, Father was in the study ready for us.

There was quite a stack of papers, including updates for everything should I encounter an untimely death. Evangeline became visibly agitated when we came to those documents, but Father emphasized the necessity of her well-being.

Franz popped in, "Oh, good, you are back, Uncle Otto, you asked to see me?" Franz inquired, coming over to the desk.

"Franz, you will be witnessing these documents here. Do pull up a chair. Also, the documents you wished updated are here. We shall address those next," Father said.

Franz witnessed ours, I witnessed Franz's, it took the better part of two hours to see things complete. Eva excused herself, and I moved to escort her but was rebuffed. When she had gone, Father explained what my inexperience had caused me to miss.

"You have asked the woman you are marrying to sign documents regarding your death. It is an uneasy proposition for her, for any woman really. If you were married and hated each other, circumstances might be different," Father said, chuckling. "Oh, Franz, have you explained everything?" Father inquired. Fritzy gave me a wry grin.

"No, Uncle, it was to be a surprise should I be the lucky ticket winner to hell. I left you everything, Sandy, same as always, may have thrown a little something in for any heirs you might stumble upon though," Fritzy said laughing.

"Franz, I understand your jest, but you know my feelings about your statement. You will refrain in the future!" Father basically slapped him across the face with a leather glove for the hell reference, and Franz took it like the son my father considered him.

"My apologies, Uncle Otto, it was uncouth and unnecessary," Franz said with total sincerity.

I patted him on the back. Nice to hear him looking at me having a future though. After another half hour of small talk about the estates, costs, and the anticipation of what was coming, I excused myself.

Seeking out Frieda, I inquired about a rather elegant menu, the hope being a private dinner with just Eva and me. Frieda, full of assurances, went to assess how to manage to make it happen. I found Mother in the library reading next to a large window. The winter sunlight was pouring through the glass causing her golden hair, now streaked with white, to appear as a halo upon her head. Looking up, she smiled and reached her hand out.

"I hope I am not interrupting!" I said, sitting on the ottoman she had her feet on.

"Oh, my goodness, no, Alexsander. Your father informed me you men had business to attend to this afternoon. After the priest this morning, and the legal affairs this afternoon, I was certain Eva would want to withdraw to her rooms until evening. So, I am just catching up on a little light reading," she said. I peeked over at the title of the book in her other hand.

"Frost, usually not a favorite of yours?" I inquired.

"No, he isn't, I am a little melancholy today with you both leaving us again. He seemed appropriate for my mood." She patted my hand as she said it.

I recited for her:

> *The way a crow*
> *Shook down on me*
> *The dust of snow*
> *From a hemlock tree*
>
> *Has given my heart*
> *A change of mood*
> *And saved some part*
> *Of a day I had rued.*[9]

"Oh, Alexsander, that gave me chills."

I squeezed her hand a bit, "It certainly was not meant to, Mother. What I am actually here for is permission." Smiling a winning smile at her, I continued, "Frieda is attempting to arrange a private supper for Evangeline and me, would you mind terribly? I realize it is my last night home for a while."

"I think it is an absolutely delightful idea, we shan't expect either of you for supper. Now scoot, go make your plans and we shall see you off

---

[9] Robert Frost, A Dust of Snow 1923

tomorrow." She kissed my cheek, and I rose to go track down Frieda.

I was Just crossing into the hall, headed for the kitchens, when Frieda and I almost collided.

"Mein Herr, all arrangements are made, will seven o'clock be acceptable?"

"Perfect, Frieda, you are wonderful!"

I rushed up to write an invitation to supper here in my room, sealed it, walked down the hall, and slipped it under her door. Satisfied with my plan, I returned to my room to relax, read, and wait for her reply.

Engrossed in a battle with a dragon, I barely heard Frieda knock, pop in, deposit tea with biscuits, and leave. A moment later, there was a light knock.

"Come!" I said, thinking it might be Ida or Sara with a reply. Eva appeared and sat in the chair next to me. I immediately set the book down.

"Darling, forgive me, I thought it… well it doesn't matter. Are you feeling better?" I asked. Her eyes were red rimmed, even with the makeup she had deftly applied.

"Yes, thank you, I thought I might accept your invitation in person. Perhaps, spend the evening if you do not mind?" Her voice was soft, accepting.

"Of course, my dear, would you care for tea, Frieda just brought a small pot?"

I poured her a cup without waiting for her answer and rose to ring for Frieda.

"Thank you, Alexsander." She set the cup down, "I would like to apologize for leaving so abruptly today. The details must be attended to, it is just…" she trailed off.

"Dealing with the reality of losing a husband you have yet to marry is no way to spend our last day together. I am the one offering an apology, it should have been addressed right after we arrived." I returned to my chair having tried to reassure her with my words.

Frieda came in, "Mein Herr, oh, excuse me, Mademoiselle," Frieda hesitated.

"Frieda, would you be so kind as to bring an additional cup and perhaps more tea?" I asked. Frieda swung around and took the tray with assurances of a quick return. "She will of course overdo," we both laughed at my assessment.

"Oh, my you are almost done with the book?" Eva remarked, looking at the marker. "I had hoped it might make a good traveling book," she sounded disappointed.

"It is quite engrossing, hard to put down really. Once you stop reading it is fine, while reading, though, it is hard to walk away from, an exceptional gift!" I said, leaning over to kiss her cheek. "Perhaps you would care to read it. I would be happy to leave it for you," I said.

"Please do not rush to finish it on my account," she replied, but I could sense her interest.

"Alexsander, do you think... well, do you think if we wore night clothes we could stay together tonight?"

Her voice was so quiet I had to lean in to hear her words. Would I be able to control myself? Especially in the middle of the night, with sleep shrouding my senses and her there beside me.

"My darling, we may do whatever you wish. I must ask though; will this violate any agreement you have?" She hesitated, but I saw the determination set in her face.

"If we were to fall asleep right now in our seats, how would that be different. The only difference I see is one is sitting up and one is laying down!"

There was a subtle hostility in her voice that betrayed her true sentiments. However, being our age brought the wisdom of understanding, she must be allowed to wrestle with herself in this fight, without a referee or interference from me or anyone else, save the higher power with which she was rationalizing. She stood, then walked to the window.

A knock, Frieda swept into the room with the tray. She placed it on the table between seats.

"Would you like me to pour, Mein Herr?"

"Yes, Frieda, if you please. Frieda, you do understand we shall be dining in a short while?" I asked, the tray had finger sandwiches, biscuits, sliced apples with cinnamon and sliced cheese.

"A snack to hold you both until supper," Frieda said.

Eva made her way over and took a seat opposite me, she accepted the cup of tea that Freida had offered.

"Frieda, really, you must not spoil us so. Why, I will be as big as a house if you continue this!" Eva teased.

"We must keep you healthy for Herr Alexsander," Frieda replied with conviction before excusing herself.

I sighed, "If the kitchen was not preparing a meal specifically for us, I would suggest we dine on this small feast. However, I suspect extra work was required to complete the supper requested."

Eva smiled and came back over to sit beside me.

"Certainly, the staff will be only too happy to snack on all of this," she suggested.

"I hope so, it is a waste, where is Franz when you need him?" I joked.

"Packing, I suspect," Eva said, threading her arm through mine.

"Hhhmmm, yes, packing, how would you feel about helping me?" I asked her.

I stood and offered her my hand. She seemed less than enthusiastic, as you would expect, but put on a smile and indulged me by going with me into the bedroom.

I dug out my favorite suitcase and we got to work. Eva worked on small clothes, while I chose items that may not be present at the locations we would be living at, along with a few pairs of favorite shoes. Toiletries would wait until morning. Eva returned to the window.

"It is a shame, if it were spring, we could go for a nice evening stroll," I said to her while bringing the suitcase around.

"No matter, just being with you is enough."

She said this so wistfully, I could not help but go to the window and wrap my arms around her. We stood staring out at the streetlamps illuminating the roads below. Holding her always made me feel so peaceful, like all was right with the world. As if there were no madman waiting in the wings. I should stay, it was just my ego coercing me into believing we could make a difference.

Standing there with Eva in my arms I began to assess my effectiveness. Suddenly, a question came to me that I could not answer, almost as if it arose from my heart. How do you measure what has yet to be done? The question provoked the same feeling that always showed up whenever I thought of setting aside the work we were trying to do. As if the cue for my scene in the play just had not come yet. I squeezed Eva a little tighter, happy to have these moments together, grateful for the chance to feel her in my arms, smell the sweet scent of her hair as it tickled my nose.

"I love you, my darling, I will miss you so," I whispered in her ear as I nuzzled in a kiss on her neck. She arched her back leaning her head over to give me access.

A raging fire is the closest description for what happened to me next. Sweeping her into my arms, I carried her to the bed, lay her down, and kissed her hard on the mouth. Overcome by the need burning within, I tore at buttons, laces, and zippers. Eva was pushing away my clothing, somehow undoing buttons, our skin touching each other brought a frenzied drive to touch, taste every part of her. Eva rolled me onto my back somehow, I reached up to grab her face and bring her lips to mine. She fought to push my arms down and I allowed her to. Breathing heavily, flushed, and beautiful I realized why she held my arms. The front of her clothes torn, some in tatters, my God, how rough had I been? Something crossed her eyes and she laughed.

"You were no more an animal than I," she said, motioning with her head to look down. My shirt was partially unbuttoned then torn, buttons missing. We both broke out laughing, lightly at first, but as happens when the stress of a situation builds, we were taken by it. Within a minute, the laughter was uncontrollable, both of us crying while the laughter came until we rolled together unable to laugh another moment for the pain in our ribs and jaw.

"Well, that is one way to relieve tension!" I said, sweeping her hair from her face. We lay staring at each other momentarily spent. "My passion quite overtook me, truly, I apologize, darling. I do hope no barriers were breached in the gauntlet" I said, and leaned in to kiss her forehead, laughing just a little."

"No, believe it or not, my underclothes are still intact. Although, I do not know how with the frenzy we both were overtaken by!" Eva said, trying not to smile.

"Will you need to go to confession? Does this set you back?" I propped my head up on my hand looking down at her in earnest.

"No matter, I will go regardless, it is what Saint Mary of Egypt would do. I would be lying if I did not say I feel it would be better if there was something to confess." She stroked my face gently, then pulled her hand away.

"What does it say if you simply touch me, and I lose all control?"

Reluctantly, I left the bed. I removed what was left of my clothing and went to the wardrobe closet to retrieve two sets of nightclothes. One I donned before exiting the room, and the other I tossed on the bed for Eva.

"I do hope repairs are able to be made, my darling. The dress is particularly lovely on you!" I leaned over and kissed her arm. "I will await you in the writing room. The test of temptation may not have been passed gracefully. Nonetheless, we passed it. We are more than capable of staying the night together fully clothed."

I heard her sigh in happiness as I left the room. The thought was wrong, but it came anyway. I wish her sigh were of satisfaction, for both of us. I detoured to the lavatory for reasons that need no explanation.

CHAPTER 17

The day dawned after a mostly sleepless night. Eva had slept well, and I had taken care to cuddle and hold her as much as I could stand. There were two cold showers during the night. After all, there is a fine line between relief and abuse. A line I had been walking for some time now. The plan for confession of that sin was planned for my death bed as that would be around the time it would stop.

The roast pheasant supper presented in Eva's honor went very well. The staff had truly outdone themselves. We finished with a delicious blackberry trifle. I won strong accolades for remembering her favorite fruit. Promises were made for amazing sexual favors once we were wed, but I did not care. Seeing her happy, giddy like a schoolgirl is all I cared about. Her joy became my joy, her sorrow my sorrow, which brings us to this moment. Perhaps she thought I would not hear her in the lavatory. As I shaved, her muffled sobs tore my heart out. I wanted nothing more than to take her in my arms and reassure her that I would not leave her, but I knew I could not. We had agreed the previous night that she would spend the day with Mother after a late morning in bed. I knew Mother and Auntie would keep her busy. However, she needed time to work into her strength before, so there would be no breakdowns later.

I finished, packed my shaving kit, and took it out to the writing room.

Placing it in the suitcase, I returned to the wardrobe room where I donned shoes, shirt coat and tie. As I went to tie it, Eva stepped in front of me and took over.

"I love you, please come back to me, Alexsander." She finished her work on my tie and left without saying another word.

I retrieved my billfold and went out to the bed to hold her, but she was gone. Looking through the other rooms, I realized she must have quietly left through the bedroom door. "Should I follow her?" I asked myself. No, she had a very particular way of dealing with things. Prolonging a painful goodbye would not help either of us. I went to the night table and swept up the book. I had finished reading it the night before after a cold shower.

In the writing room, I scribbled an endearing note to Eva and placed it in the front of the book. A knock came, followed by Frieda.

"Good morning, Mein Herr, I still think you should have let me bring you breakfast. You will starve if you do not eat something, no, I will take your bag down. I am a perfectly strong woman; I hardly need a man to carry things around for me." And she continued this all the way down to the vestibule.

Both sets of parents were awaiting us in the vestibule, where we donned coats, scarves, and hats. Franz looked the worst for wear, which I found interesting. I handed Father my book requesting he deliver it to Eva. I hoped it would give her some small measure of joy to read it while I was away. He assured me Eva would be well cared for and urged me to keep my mind on being safe and so forth. Mother, Auntie and Uncle Franz repeated the same, there were handshakes and kisses as we made our way out the door.

With that chaos, Franz and I set off on our mission. Acknowledging the need to keep up appearances, we had decided upon hiring a chauffeur to drive us out to Schaan for the train.

"I am almost afraid to wish you good morning from the look of you," I said.

Franz laughed, "Just a rough night of sleep, nothing I won't recover from."

"Well, I thought my night was rough, I rather think you took the worst of it!" I joked with him. He laughed a bit but off, just not himself. "Franz, I apologize if all of this with Eva has stirred up any ghosts."

I had said it completely unintentionally. From the look on his face, it would be safe to say the target was struck dead center. The tone set, we proceeded to pass a very quiet trip to Innsbruck.

"Father made arrangements for the staff as discussed, so the house should be in better circumstances than when we left it," Franz said.

"Are you completely familiar with the staff?" I asked, not to be paranoid, however, it was difficult to tell where political loyalties lay oftentimes.

"No, not well enough to vouch for them, so we should remain cautious. My understanding is Madame Renee will have correspondence for us. I thought I might swing by tonight to pick it up. Care to join me?"

Franz winked at me, which quickly turned to shock when I said, "Yes, actually I would love to."

Arriving at Innsbruck station, we caught a ride to the house. The staff were familiar, but not enough to know by name for either of us. They were efficient though; they had rearranged the remnants of the house to make quite a nice sitting room and study. Assuring us all the staff accommodation was intact. Mother had left our rooms alone entirely. The truth of Austria's situation made it very unlikely she would use this home in the foreseeable future, if ever. Being an optimist, she would believe otherwise.

The staff had prepared a lovely luncheon and had all our possessions unpacked and neatly stored before we finished the brief tour of inspection.

We both agreed on a nap before the night's escapades commenced. Knowing we were book poor in this property. I had borrowed several volumes from the manse in Vaduz. I settled into my nicely worn copy of the phantom of the opera and was out before I could turn a page.

The left side of my head was killing me, God it hurt. I was holding my head and running around the room looking for a mirror to see what had happened to me. Shaking, furious shaking, someone had hold of me. "Stop! Stop! My head hurts, what is wrong with my head?" I screamed, no one would listen to me.

Suddenly, Franz was there. I was on the floor, holding my head.

"Sandy, are you awake? Do you hear me? It is me, Fritzy, I am here," he kept saying while pushing my hands away. "Sandy, I don't see anything wrong with your head. Did you strike it on something?"

Dazed, I was trying to think, my head did not hurt at all. Had I been dreaming?

"Fritzy...I.......don't know, it feels fine..........I don't understand. My head had the most intense pain on the left side, but now I feel fine. I do not understand!" I said, looking up at him while he continued looking in my eyes, checking my color, checking my head.

"I awoke about 20 minutes ago. In fact, I was just coming to wake you when I heard you screaming. Sandy, I want an X-Ray, NO! Do not fight me on this!" he said in response to the protestations he could see I was about to proffer. "We are going to the hospital right now!"

Franz got me up. The disorientation persisted while I redressed in my suit. Fritzy helped me with my tie, I could not quite manage it for some reason. I felt disconnected, like stepping into another reality and back again.

Most of the trip to the auto was a blur. On the way to the hospital, I began feeling normal again. More grounded, solidly here in this automobile, speeding down the road. Fritzy took charge as he came through the door, no one dared question him and the physician on duty knew him, so things went fast. Before I knew it, I was being manipulated this way and that, all the while, scandalously scantily clad. A very lovely nurse took me off to a private room to dress, wait, and pace. Quite probably, little time had passed, but it felt as if hours were ticking by.

Eventually, Fritzy stuck his head in and asked me to come with him. After several hallways with multiple turns, we arrived in a kind of office, an examination room, maybe. Another doctor introduced himself.

"There is an anomaly we cannot account for, but there seems to be nothing out of the ordinary. Let me explain," he placed slides on a bright panel. There were quite a few shots of a skull. "See these films?" he pointed to the first three.

"Yes," I said, and he continued.

"You notice how the left side of the skull is missing? It seems foggy, but it is gone. There is no solid line, nothing physical. Now, in these next two, you see how the lines are faint, like the skull is somehow coming back?"

"Yes," I said, and he resumed.

"Then, in these last films, your skull is completely fine!" the doctor concluded. He looked at me as if expecting me to solve his mystery.

"Yes? So, what is wrong with the machine?" I asked.

"Well, that is it, Sandy," Franz interjected, "there is nothing wrong with the machine. We have tried it with other people. The machine is not replicating the anomaly."

"Then I am fine, we are able to go now?" I asked.

"Hold on, Sandy, just hang on, yes we can go, but I think we should run more tests." Franz gave me a pleading look as he said it.

"Franz, we are on a bit of a schedule, what kind of tests and how long?" The last thing I wanted was to give in, but I also knew the hounding would never stop if the tests were not done.

"Just a few hours and then we can go. I will not make you stay to wait out the results, fair?"

"Fair enough, let's get started," I said, pulling my jacket back off and removing my tie.

The next few hours went by in a blur of needles, thumping, bumping, pinching, picking, pulling, stretching, the list just goes on and on. Finally, I was allowed to use the lavatory, of course, a specimen was required. At last, I was cleared to leave. Thanks were given, handshakes, and so forth, and we made our way to the automobile.

"Let's wait until tomorrow on driving, shall we?" Fritzy suggested, heading me off as I came around to the driver's door. "Just until we get the results, okay?"

"Part of me wants to accuse you of doing this so you get to drive," I teased, but kind of meant it and he knew it.

"We'll skip Madame's tonight, I'll stop by in the morning to grab the correspondence before we leave to meet Henry," he said.

"Fritzy, you are my brother, thank you for everything you just did, but you will not now or ever dictate my life. We will be going to Madame's tonight. Now let us find supper, I am starving," I responded in my most matter-of-fact tone.

Fortunately, arriving home supplied a much more pleasant experience. Supper had been prepared in anticipation of our return. A telegram had arrived, and Eva had phoned from Vaduz. Eva came first, I rang the operator to place the call. The operator would ring back when they had her on the line, so I went to wash up for supper. I felt like I still had the hospital clinging all over me. A scar of the war, surely. God knows what Fritzy would be going through. I stripped, took a quick shower, and put on fresh clothes.

The phone rang just as I entered the study to read the telegram.

"Oh, my darling, I miss you already!" Eva's voice was so lovely.

"I miss you, my love, how did the rest of the day go?"

The minutiae of her day were then relayed with proper fervor: they had shopped, enjoyed an afternoon meal, and she had been introduced to a new friend who had arrived. Father had only just given her the book with the message in it a few moments before the operator connected the call. Overall, she had an enjoyable day, despite the morning, of course. We sat on the phone like children for some time. I had to make my apologies and say goodbye. I truly did miss her.

As expected, the telegram was from Henry, brief, as was his manner. He would arrive on time tomorrow morning and make his way out of the house the same as before, thereby preventing any overt show of our acquaintance. Klaus was aware of his arrival; he would be welcomed with open arms and quite probably a full table. Onto supper, Fritzy already graced the table, but he did not seem to be barreling through supper as he normally would. My goodness, he was worried!

"Sandy, there you are, telegram from our mutual friend, is it?" he inquired.

"Indeed, tomorrow morning, I believe," I said, wondering if I should have.

His avoidance of Henry's name reminded me we were in unknown waters. I excused myself quickly, retrieved the telegram, and placed it in the fire, then returned to supper. Of course, anyone who was at the disposition could have easily opened it and resealed it before we even made it home.

"Would you reconsider our jaunt tonight?" He asked before I even had my chair.

"No!" I sat down and looked over our not so meager supper. My stomach growled as I reached for sausages. Once I had begun eating, Fritzy recovered his appetite. Supper passed with little conversation. We moved into the study after supper, expecting privacy.

"Look, Sandy, I know you, you aren't going with me for the reason I'm going. Hell, I can count on one hand the women with whom you have fornicated. Evangeline's hold on you is eternal. So why are you going?" Fritzy eyed me.

"Actually, with Eva's new vows, she is unable to fornicate until we are married." I said it as sarcastically as possible to make the possibility of me seeking solace elsewhere believable.

Fritzy only looked harder at me, reconsidering his assessment.

"You haven't...?" he asked, rather shocked.

"Since she was Madame Evangeline La Chabanais."

"Well, that explains a hell of a lot!" Fritzy said with a sarcastic tone. He went over and poured us both a schnapps. He handed me the glass with a salute, "You, Sandy, are a saint with that woman next to you."

"Trust me, I am no saint, cold showers have become so commonplace they barely work anymore. She wanted so badly to stay the night last night and I had not the heart to deny her. There we were, both in our nightclothes, in my bed, and I had to run off for cold showers every time she backed against me in her sleep. I will not recount the borderline rape that transpired earlier in the evening."

I threw back the schnapps and retrieved another. Confessing to the events of my last night with Eva played into the ruse. "Thankfully, her restraint of my arms had brought me round, otherwise..."

"You should have let me bribe the priest in Brandberg when we had the chance, Sandy."

"Believe me, Fritzy, when I tell you, if the decision could have been made by me, we would be on our honeymoon right now." We both raised our glasses to that.

"Does she mind you being with someone else?" There was a question I never expected from him.

"I don't know, the subject only centered around Renee continuing the spying and retrieving any current information she had gathered. Finding relief with another woman, surprisingly, did not occur to me until today."

With time to think about it, Fritzy would not believe it, but for the moment he accepted my story. Thus, moving to a room with Renee would appear to be for reasons of self-gratification. Frankly, I found the proposition of a real encounter unlikely at best, but desire had me literally by the balls. Never would I have believed myself capable of ripping a woman's clothes off. There could be no measure of the sin I was obviously capable of currently. Better not to go down the sin rabbit hole.

"It is a bit early, but would you care to stroll over to Madame's?" I asked, making my way to the door.

"Allow me to freshen up first, if you do not mind, twenty minutes?"

With that, Franz headed off to do all the necessary things one should do when one would be romping with ladies for physical pleasure. I made my way out to the kitchen, checking on the staff, renewing introductions with those who had been otherwise engaged upon arrival, giving updates on our departure, (which they seemed disappointed to hear) and thanks for their dedication. I assured them we would be back within the month, but left any destinations out of the conversations, and they did not inquire. They seemed very much the staff we were looking for. There were four in all, more than necessary, but we were happy to provide them with continued service. They were all from the same family, unable to leave for Vaduz due to ailing parents. As Uncle Otto had implied, they had been with them for some time, and it was truly unlikely they would have any ties to Nazi's. The worry, however, would be who they knew and spoke with, not necessarily their own character.

Franz, good as his word, appeared twenty minutes later; showered, shaved, and dressed more appropriately.

"Amazing how a little motivation lights a fire of urgency," I said.

He instantly rebuffed, "Says the man who has been trying to quell the fire for weeks!"

"Touché, Fritzy, if you prefer, we could certainly spend the evening fencing."

"Not on your life, I am going to bury my face, never mind, I wouldn't want to get you too worked up before we get there!"

We set off. Bantering the entire walk, nonstop.

CHAPTER 18

Our arrival, although early by house standards, brought almost as vivacious a greeting as Eva would have provided. Madame Renee performed the role well. Once we settled in our private sitting room, the ladies were brought in. Alcohol and Franz's traditional hors d'oeuvres were ordered into the room. Within the first quarter hour, Renee had already made excuses for us to step out. We made a show of it, leaving no room to imagine why we were vacationing. Franz seemed amused by the turn of events but was entirely distracted by his entertainment. Renee and I sat with a schnapps in her private office.

"Please, tell me all about Madame. Is she quite happy? We miss her so; you must tell her how much she is missed."

Renee made a point of acting as if she did not already know. A ruse for someone's benefit, very well.

"I believe she is quite happy under the current circumstances. She very much wanted to return with me. You understand why I did not want to expose her to a location where so many may be, shall we say, familiar with her," I said, sipping schnapps. I motioned for a pen and paper, "You may of course telephone her anytime here. I am certain she would enjoy speaking with you, Renee."

Renee had been in touch with Eva since the day she left, but it sounded good if anyone was listening. I slid the pad back with one word on it, "correspondence." She understood at once.

"You are too kind; I will telephone her tomorrow and we shall catch up. You understand, of course, why we cannot speak at this hour."

Renee motioned back toward the sitting room and went to retrieve a stack of papers from the safe.

The doorknob to the office turned slightly, making a small grating sound. We looked at each other but kept talking as if we had not heard it. So that was why Renee had locked the door when we came in.

"And you, Herr Alexsander, have you come all this way just to provide me with this information, or is there something more intimate we might do for you?"

Renee scribbled on the same pad handing it back while she was speaking, "Not Safe," it read, which I had already surmised when she brought me to the office and locked the door.

"Not at all, Madame, I am happily betrothed, however it is in my interest to protect my future wife's assets. Of course, Herr Franz had an appointment, so I merely accompanied him for the trip," I said, winking at her.

"Well then, we shall have to see if we cannot change your mind. Surely betrothal customs have not changed. The tension must indeed be building beyond tolerance."

She winked when she said it, and I realized that Eva had been talking to her. I distinctly felt her going somewhere with this, so I decided to follow.

"Abstinence is hardly a joyful event, Madame, but I could not be so callous as to betray the faith of the one I love. After all, abstinence is observed equally."

I winked back and she nodded in acknowledgment. Very well I would play the role.

"There are many ways to satisfy a man that do not technically breach the definition of intercourse," Renee purred, yet her body language was static, she sat, almost mechanically, sipping her schnapps, as if reading for someone studying lines for a play.

"Would you have someone available to demonstrate these techniques, Madame?" I asked, as she encouraged me to continue. Almost willing me with the intensity of her gaze to go somewhere... Ah, yes! I understood.

"Perhaps, Mein Herr," she pointed at me, as if to say, "your turn."

"Then may we adjourn to a more comfortable location for these demonstrations?" As I asked, Renee mouthed the words "Bravo" and clapped without sound.

"Of course, your privacy is my very livelihood."

Renee got up, placed the entire pad of paper in a hidden pocket of her outfit, and checked the safe. She took my arm and whispered to me that I should just go along with it. She unlocked the door and proceeded to lead me down a hall. My stomach shifted uncomfortably as I recognized the back route to Eva's boudoir. Renee must have sensed my misgivings as she gently patted my arm with her hand. At the top of the stairs, we took the right to the hallway where Eva's rooms were. Renee stopped and locked the door to the hallway. We passed the doors to Eva's rooms, or rather former rooms, on our way to the very last room at the end. Luckily, we had met no one in either hallways or stairs.

She produced a key, unlocked the room, and entered. I followed behind her, she immediately turned and locked the door, only turning the lights on after a cursory glance around the room. Another office, however, this one was quite different. In this room, maps covered walls, locations pinpointed throughout, creating a wealth of information. Colors linked items to people and locations. It looked very much like the study in Vienna when we were working.

"Eva tells me you prefer Jim; may I call you Jim?" Renee asked, with a quite different voice than the one I was used to.

"Absolutely, and you, do you prefer Renee, or is that a ruse?" I asked while walking the wall, following coordinates, names, and links around the room.

"A ruse? No. A better use of my talents, perhaps. She did not tell you?" I appreciated Renee's attempt to bait me into the ask, but obviously she was going to disclose it anyway, so I simply said "no."

The wall pulled me in. Here, in this section, she had tied Guido Schmidt to Göring. Impressive, Göring used Schmidt like a puppet in every attempt Schuschnigg had made to ally with Switzerland. Switzerland's President, Giuseppe Motta, a staunch opponent of communism and Stalinism, was for an alliance between Austria and Switzerland. After all, he was a leader in the Christian Democratic People's Party of Switzerland. Our Christian Social party were, for all intents and purposes, the same party. Austria-Hungary had been allied with Switzerland for generations. The alliance made sense and was long overdue. It should have come before the war, instead of the war, but ruminations helped no one.

Schmidt was a busy bee at planting rumor and innuendo, which insured Austria stayed isolated from outside help. He had only recently implied to the French, English, and American delegations that we intended to attack the Czech state. There was, in fact, truth to this, except he had intentionally inferred Austria, when his own Third Reich were the true offenders. Hitler had in fact guaranteed Austrian independence in return for Schuschnigg's support in attacking the Czech state to bring them under German control; he turned him down flat, refusing to enter such aggression or alliance with the Nazi party. As thanks, the information fell into the allies' hands that Austria was the aggressor; even as the Chancellor tried to convince the allies of the dangers to Austria from Hitler's Germany. They took no care for the Austria they vilified for an act committed more than 20 years before. An act executed by a monarchy that was subsequently exiled, her people left to suffer a fate they had not chosen.

"Let us just say, I am not every man's preference."

I turned as she said it, the voice was not entirely masculine, however, there was no doubt the name Renee was being used across genders in this case.

"As you see, we have been quite effective these last weeks. Madame Eva took it to heart to learn absolutely everything we possibly could to assist you both in your work. She is quite concerned about your well-being. We will, of course, continue, but as you have guessed by our encounter downstairs, we may have to stop for the time being."

"Renee, the work you have done is extraordinary. You have found things in weeks it took us years to find. We were still piecing much of this together. As to your pursuits, it is none of my business, but if I may say, you certainly could fool anyone."

Renee went to a wall and pointed at two names.

"She is a worker here, relatively new, he is one of the original groups you ran across. Olga, who I believe you know, overheard several conversations between them. It seems, in exchange for his promise to marry her, she has very recently revealed our methods and motives for procuring information from his comrades."

Renee went to the desk in the corner, retrieved two glasses and, surprisingly, filled them with water. He offered me a seat on an old, overused love seat and we sat facing the largest wall. A peaceful silence fell between us as we surveyed the wall together. Sometime later, Renee broke the silence.

"Madame Evangeline saved my life. I will spare you the graphic details, but when I tell you the possibility of me lasting more than another day or two in the circumstances, I was in… well, it would have been a miracle. She was my miracle really. She took me back to Le Chabanais, hid me and nursed me back to health. When my recovery was sufficient, she brought me to her master and convinced her to train me. We pooled resources over the years and when our master allowed it, we left. We made our way together. The war had left Austria devastated financially, which allowed us to procure a house and establish ourselves for much less than we had saved. We were able to make a great start and have profited every year since. There is nothing I would not do for her." Renee sat quietly looking at me, almost as if awaiting my judgment.

"She is a singularly unique person. Please know, Renee, you will always be welcome in our home. As to this..." I swept my hand in indication of the walls, "please do not continue if you are in jeopardy. Understand, Renee, it is not if the Nazi's are coming, it is when the Nazi's are coming. When the time comes, get out, go to Eva, if you do not get out in the initial take over, you will risk never getting out. Which, under the circumstances, may result in something worse than death if you were found out."

The look on Renee's face said all there was to say. We sat chatting for some time. She then left for about a half hour, returning with a tray of light snacks.

"Franz is engaged with his favorites, thankfully our little canary did not appeal to him and is now busy with another. Of course, she is very blond, definitely not his preference."

Renee made me a small plate and poured coffee for each of us.

"When he is done," she continued, "Andre will notify me so you may leave together. Of course, you will be notorious, as everyone believes we are engaging in activities of a different nature." Renee laughed a little and came back to sit on the seat with me.

"Wait, didn't you and Franz, some years back... weren't you in his group?" I looked at Renee, trying to piece it together even as I asked.

"Yes, for many years after Amalia, and yes, he knew. You more than anyone understand the extremely dark place Franz lives in when it comes to women or love," Renee' said.

"Eva told you?"

"That you were in love with her too, yes, and more, she was quite worried about you also. Did Amalia die by his hand? He tortures himself so, we always speculated there was some horrible accident."

I had thought about telling him, had wanted to talk to someone, mostly Franz, about it for years, but he refused.

"No, he had nothing to do with it, but if he had made a different choice, it may have been avoided. Therefore, in his mind he is completely at fault."

"Ah, yes, why does the lord have demons when we torture ourselves so much more effectively than any other could?" Renee asked aloud. The truth in her statement hit home.

"May I use the notepad and pen you have in your pocket? I will be taking it with me if you do not mind?" I asked.

"Not at all, here, let me freshen the coffee and grab a lamp and I will assist you. Oh, and just for the record, Eva did encourage you to relieve yourself, just the messenger!" Renee said, immediately throwing her hands up as she reached for the coffee.

"I appreciate it, but there really is only one woman on this earth I want. We have waited all these years; it will not hurt me to wait a few more months. Being away helps, she is hard to resist when she is close."

A look crossed Renee's face as I said the last few words and I understood. He loves her too!

"Then the two of you were together, a couple?" I asked.

Renee immediately countered, "Not in the way you are presuming, business calls for....an open mind. Have we been together? Yes, do we love each other? Yes. Our love is not your love though, nor can it be. She is not, equipped correctly for a successful relationship with me."

"Thank you for the honesty, Renee. My previous statement stands, if you need to get out, go to Eva. Shall we get to work?"

With a sigh of relief, she said, "please proceed," and the rest of the night, and well into the morning, was spent going through all the notes, names, places, dates, etc. All the while, Franz was losing himself to alcohol and lust. At around three in the morning, Andre brought the semi coherent Franz to the room with Renee and me. He immediately lay on the couch, telling Renee how beautiful she was and asking her where she had been all his life. When he began to snore, we returned to our task. At around five we roused him for coffee, after 2 cups, he was sufficiently capable of the trip home. We thanked Renee and Andre profusely for everything, and after settling Franz's exceptionally large bill, we made our way into the chilly morning air. Franz did a superb job of appearing sober, and we were home in decent time. We both went off to bed for a few hours' sleep before the day would begin again.

Frieda could be frustrating on mornings like this, but equally a treasure. I missed her. The daylight peeking through the draperies told me it must be at least late morning. I rang the staff on my way to the lavatory. Determined to climb back in bed and wait for coffee, I made my way over and pushed the draperies apart. Clouds skimmed through a blue sky, weather was coming, I could feel it. In that case, perhaps, we would skip the return to bed. I needed a glass of water, my clothes brushed, and a toilette.

When I returned to the bedchamber from bathing, a tray with coffee, rolls and boiled eggs had been set up. My clothes were brushed and ready to go. Perhaps I should have accepted the offer for a valet. I dressed while having a cup of coffee and rang the staff again. A full minute could not have passed before the young man named Otto appeared. Luckily, it is an easy name to remember.

"Otto, please take coffee and a full breakfast to Herr Grünne. Prepare his clothes for travel if you would, please. What he wore last night will not be adequate today. Oh, and Otto, tread lightly, he will be rough when he first awakes, shove the food at him immediately." Assurances from Otto intimated he had understood everything, and he set off. I munched on my roll, laughing at the thought of how many Ottos, Franzes, Jakobs, Josefs, Marias, Theresas and so on there were in our country. The monarchist tradition of passing on one's name throughout lineage made for a challenging landscape. Repacking my suitcase, I headed downstairs.

I went out to retrieve the C12 from the garage, she was clean and ready to go. After warming her up, I pulled her round the front of the house and went back in. Otto appeared again, assuring me he needed only to know I required the auto, and he would have seen to it. I reassured him how grateful I was for him to just attend to Herr Grünne. He looked crushed, so I sent him after my bags to be loaded in the auto.

In the study, I ensured no correspondence or notes lay anywhere. The notepad from Renee had been tucked away in my breast pocket upon dressing this morning. No other room would have anything in it except, possibly, Franz's room. There was nothing left to do but wait. A fresh pot of coffee was brought.

"Herr Von Rieser, would you care for Gröstl?" Otto asked.

"No, the coffee is sufficient, Otto, but thank you for inquiring."

I relaxed with my newspaper, sipping coffee, and waiting for Fritzy to recover sufficiently to leave.

A half hour later, Fritzy appeared, bright eyed, dressed, and ready to go.

"You will make a wonderful husband, Sandy! Thank you! Breakfast was a godsend."

Bags were loaded, coats and hats donned, and we were off to Mayrhofen and The Meadows. I found myself wishing Eva were with us.

"The correspondence?" Franz asked as we sped down the road.

"Retrieved from Madame Renee, plus…" I smiled.

"Plus? Are you going to tell me, or shall I spend the entire trip trying to guess?"

The look on Franz's face was priceless. A wrestling match was happening behind his eyes. Was he trying to decide if I had slept with Renee? After all, he would have no idea of the information center they had developed at the house.

"I will say this, Madame Renee showed me things you would not believe."

The impulse to laugh almost overwhelmed me. I resisted though, waiting to see what the retort would be.

"Sandy…" he started and stopped, pausing for what seemed like an eternity. "I am unsure how to phrase this. Sandy, you do realize Madame Renee is a man, physically that is?"

"Indeed, it came as quite a shock, Fritzy, let me tell you. After all the trysts you and she have had, well, in groups of course, I just assumed she was she." I looked over at him with the most innocent expression I could manage.

"You Ass!"

He pulled his hat down over his face, slouched down in the seat, and feinted going to sleep. I could not stop myself from laughing. It transported me to when I was around five years old, seeing him want to throw a temper tantrum, and knowing what would happen if he did, he would do the same thing, except with a lip sticking out.

A full half hour went by before he sat up, pushed his hat back and stared at me.

"Neither of us make sexual judgments about the other. I think we should keep it that way. Both of us always see human beings as human beings, without judgment. The only exception ever being the truly evil ones."

"Fritzy, there is none, all I have ever wanted is for you to be happy. Scheisse, who cares who it is with?! But it was just too tempting to not let you think Renee and I had engaged in more than conversation."

"It wasn't what you think, Sandy."

"I don't think anything Fritzy, which is the point." The quiet crept back in. "Renee and Eva have an entire room set up just to map information. Almost identical to what we do in Vienna. The intelligence they have been able to gather over the last three or four weeks is nothing short of amazing. Renee has managed to connect dots on which we had merely speculated. She is incredibly intelligent; espionage would suit her."

"It isn't safe having a room put together with so many people around!" Fritzy seemed genuinely concerned.

"It is in a location that isn't readily accessible. However, there is a problem. Do you remember the noticeably young blond lady in the sitting room last night?"

"Yes, she was so insistent she be part of our group that Olga almost had to get Renee," Franz said with a questioning look.

"Let me tell you why, Ulrich, the SS trainee, is a frequent customer. She enlightened him about the girls being instructed to procure information. In turn, Ulrich has her spying for him now on the pretense he will marry her for her service."

I turned to Fritzy as the implications hit him.

"She has to stop right now, everything has to go, they will not only kill her, but if they discover her gender, oh God."

"Fritzy, do you truly believe I would even consider leaving her under those circumstances. While you were having an amazing night. I mapped everything and helped her dispose of it all, everything. When I brought you home this morning, there was nothing left for anyone to find. Madame Renee will have instructed all the other girls to stop any coercion. After all, any information obtained now will be tainted and quite likely erroneous," I said.

"The notes will be worthless," Franz stated.

"Yes and no, this just transpired two days ago. There would not have been time to do much. Going forward, yes, it would be too unreliable to depend on any information procured. As for Renee, she will be able to be completely honest. Her former employer insisted on their spying, however, now that Renee is in charge, 'she has finally been able to put a stop to it all.' This is the story she will relay to the girls too."

"Smart, Sandy, it besmirches the former Madame's name with the Nazi's without ramification to Renee. And no, Sandy, I don't doubt you, I just need sleep."

CHAPTER 19

Klaus, as always, provided a warm welcome. After greetings, Franz went straight to bed.

"If there is nothing pressing, Klaus, I will be in the study," I said.

"Nothing that will not keep, would you like coffee?"

"That would be wonderful, thank you!"

One of the boys had taken my luggage up, I believe it was Jakob. I would have to ask Klaus; it should be easy but for some reason I always found it difficult to distinguish them.

There was a neat stack of items to go through for the estate, those would wait, a note written in Klaus's writing. Henry is running a day behind, interesting? A letter from Eva dated from before I left, and one from father. The letter from Eva first.

My darling,

I miss you already and you are still here. We have lost so many years together and I long for them back.

Desperation tears at my soul, it would have me tell some lie, anything for you to remain at my side. Alas, I am as

unwilling to lie to you as I am to surrender my penitence. Therefore, my only

solace is to declare my undying love and

devotion to you. Alexsander, I am eternally grateful for every moment we

have spent together. Every night I will look up. to the sky sending my love to

God, so he may bestow it on you wherever you may be. Please take care, my

love.

Come back to me!

All my love,

Evageline

The heartache in her writing was simply palpable. As much as the words filled my heart, I also knew the pain she must be in with me gone. Perhaps, her letter was a poor first choice, yet it could be my only first choice. Klaus brought in the tray with coffee and cakes.

"Thank you so much, Klaus. Klaus, the message from Henry, did he telephone?"

"No, Mein Herr. The auto that picked him up with the Eigners pulled into the drive last night, the note was then placed in the box by the door. By the time I arrived here at the main house they were gone. Is everything all right?" Klaus asked, looking concerned.

"Yes, quite alright, Henry is delayed a day and will not arrive until tomorrow. Hopefully, this does not create a problem for Greta with supper," I said.

Klaus laughed, "No, Mein Herr, we always have stomachs to fill whether you are here or not. Speaking of supper, it will be ready at six o'clock if that is acceptable."

"Of course, Klaus, whenever Greta says it is time to eat, we will arrive, grateful for her talents and time," I told him with complete honesty.

"Oh, Klaus, before you go, were they able to install the other telephone?"

"Yes, Mein Herr, it is in the vestibule, however, I had them run another line just in case. It is coiled just outside the door. If you will allow me to show you?"

I stepped out of the office and, just to the left, the telephone handset occupied a small table.

"The cord is long enough to go into the study or the library. I hope this is satisfactory?" Klaus asked.

"Outstanding, Klaus, thank you very much," I said, extending my hand for a handshake. He looked extremely pleased with himself, as he should have.

Father's letter was primarily business, accounts, estimates, balances and so forth. At the end, he gave their love with reassurances they would do everything in their power to keep Evangeline in the best spirits possible. For the first time in a very long time, I felt homesick, which hit me hard as this house was the only place I had ever felt at home. Evidently, where Eva is, so is my home.

I pulled out the notepad from Renee. All the notes from her girls were here too, we had copied it all and burned them, leaving nothing around to duplicate. I pulled some large pieces of parchment Father had used for drawings and plans from a shelf. Uncovering the drawing table, I attached them, recovered the necessary tools, and got to work on basic maps. Nothing fancy by any means, but simply enough to track what, where, how many and so forth. It made watching build ups, movements, and patterns easy to spot. I had a good rendition of Tyrol, Upper and Lower Austria, East, and SE Germany. For now, I stayed with towns relating to something in our information and was not worrying about filling anything else in. Removing a few pictures from the wall, I replaced them with three maps. The pictures went to the closet for safe keeping.

Next, I wanted to get names on pieces of paper. Relationships between the names and then locations, work camps, reported repetitive fly overs, troop concentrations and so on. I had finished writing names when Fritzy popped in. He whistled, obviously in a better mood.

"Well, someone is very busy, no nap for you then."

"No, not that I wasn't tempted, but I wanted to start getting to work on this. I would like it to be ready when Henry arrives. He has been delayed a day, he arrives tomorrow, which, as fortune would have it, should be quite enough time," I said.

"Would you like to have supper here in the study, or could you use a break? Klaus woke me a little while ago as supper was almost ready."

"A break, let's have supper and then we can come back in and join forces?" I formed it as a question.

"Looks like a wonderful game of chess to me, let's go!" Franz was heading out as he said it, led by his hunger, if my guess was correct, and it was.

After his second plate, Franz came up for air,

"How long have you been at it?"

"I began just after you headed upstairs. The message from Henry gave me a little extra motivation," I replied.

"Seems to be a virtual horde of information. Certainly not all gleaned from Renee?" Franz immediately followed with "Wait, there was a message from Henry?"

"Yes, he is delayed an additional day. No, not at all the information was from Renee. Our lock box, combined with other intelligence coming from Vienna, some from Henry, even some added information from Munich!" I finished my plate, requesting some coffee before continuing. "Of course, some of it is quite old. The committee of seven, The July Pact propaganda sources, contacts, Vorarlberg's 'ski club' Nazi courier service, RH or Tavs Plot. The latest information we received is tying it all together though. It isn't clear yet, but the cracks in the wallpaper are showing up."

Franz finished off his third round, pushed his plate away, and asked Klaus to bring his coffee to the study.

"Well, let me wade into the fray, Sandy, shall we?"

Klaus brought coffee and dessert at some point. Franz kept trying to coax me to stop and try some. I finally grabbed a few bites, an amazing apple cake.

"I do miss Frieda's coffee, although Greta's is close," I said.

Franz agreed between bites, like an empty hole, I thought to myself. We were tying names together. Almost done with it. Surprises popped up here and there, but one stopped us both dead.

"Sandy, do you see this?"

"Mary mother of God pray for us," it just spilled out of my mouth.

We both stared at each other and then stared at the name Franz had pinned to the wall in the place of the Chancellor's office. Baron Von Froelichsthal, the Chancellors personal secretary was handpicked due to their mutual ties to Stella Matutina. Also, on the Nazi payroll.

"He'll never believe us; he already doesn't believe us when we point out the ones who are obviously Nazis."

"Sandy, Froelichsthal is privy to everything! Vienna is out of the question. The night you dispatched the eavesdropper in the hall, he was there."

"Fritzy, I believe I have discovered the basis of your foreboding," I said, heading for the schnapps.

Pouring a much too generous portion, I walked over to the name on the wall and took a very large swallow.

I am not certain why Franz felt the need to state the obvious, to make the level of betrayal real. To reinforce the danger all of us were in.

Taking another healthy swallow. I walked over, turned a chair around for a full view of the wall, and dropped into it.

"Remind me to send Renee something worthy of our lives at the next opportunity," I said, and finished off the glass.

Franz took my glass, went to the bar, and poured himself one, refilling mine. I got up and turned the other chair round, sitting back down. He handed me my glass and dropped into it.

"The question is, are Karl and Wilhelm compromised?" I asked.

"Although that is not my first question it is a good one," Franz added.

"Help me work out a telegram, we need to try to get them up here, Fritzy."

"What about Henry, will he be alright with additional company?" he asked.

"I think so, if they are not compromised, it will be even better, as they will be able to train in the radio he is bringing," I said.

Phoning father in Vaduz, I gave him the message and had him send it from there. They would not reply but arrive in Innsbruck. Once there, they would go ahead to the manor. One of us would retrieve them. Klaus would contact the staff in Innsbruck in the morning with instructions.

A sense of trepidation filled me as the full weight of possibilities unfurled in my mind. All the information, people, and events the Chancellors secretary' witnessed were being relayed in real time to the Reich. The Chancellor, unknowingly, sitting in the next room from his ultimate betrayer. All the moves in his private chess game lay before the führer to see.

Chancellor Kurt Schuschnigg, the only thing standing before the tempest about to descend on Austria, in checkmate without ever seeing the play.

About the Author

Elizabeth Sunflower lives in the majestic black hills of South Dakota, close to her loving and supportive family. There she finds inspiration that fires her imagination and creativity. Beyond writing, she enjoys amateur photography, history, philosophy, metaphysical studies, and gardening.

Elizabeth Sunflower FB Page

www.elizabeth-sunflower.com

Acknowledgments

"Thanks to everyone who has supported me on this journey. Special thanks to Emerald, my daughter who believed in me. To my sister in spirit Valerie, who never faltered in her support of this project. To Barbara, who helped me find the healing and the strength to regain my path. My little bear, who is not so little anymore. To my ever-patient editor, Paul Blane, may your cup always be full."

*Thanks for reading A Noble Destiny! Please add **review** on the platform of your choice and let me know what you think!*

Coming soon:

BOOK 2

Whispers of Rebellion

The Noble Resistance Continues

Made in the USA
Monee, IL
15 January 2024

51837456R00136